The Deer Mouse
by

Ken Grant

THE PERMANENT PRESS
SAG HARBOR, NY 11963

Grant, Ken
    The Deer Mouse/by Ken Grant
        p.   cm.
    ISBN 1-877946-84-2
    I. Title.
    PS3557.R2667D44   1997
    813'.54--dc20   96-19961
                                                CIP

First edition, June 1997.

THE PERMANENT PRESS
Noyac Road
Sag Harbor, NY 11963

My thanks to Mary Harman

Dedicated to my father,
Allen U. Grant

. . . I decided in my heart to seek and search out the truth concerning all things which are done under heaven: It's a sad business God has given the sons of men to be busy with. I've seen most all the works that are done under the sun. Guess what? It's vanity, a feeding on the wind. For aren't we each and every one of us blind, self-seeking? half a bubble out of plumb—we tend not to comprehend. What I need you cannot fathom, and what you want—Lord!

Still I said to myself: But haven't I accumulated some vast store of wisdom? Indeed, my mind has had no small experience in grasping at what goes on—could it be I'm a teensy bit ahead of any ever come before? So I bent my mind to put this great hoard of knowledge to work, thinking I might recognize madness, and folly, thus find means to avoid both. I perceived this also was but chasing the tail of the wind.

For to cling so dear to a vision how you want life to turn out (while taking note simultaneously how this old world couldn't care less), brings on a vexation which causes much sorrow. And he who dares chase dreams into the face of the age-old storm will most likely lose the trail and end up in the ditch.

Ecclesiastes: Chapter One

But wait now—hold up!—remember: If you're still kicking, you can yet cling to hope, for a living dog has more going than do a dozen dead lions. Though the living must bear the burden knowing death is round the bend, the dead are dead, their fun is over, memory of them will fade. The lives they led, the love they made—those awful moments of heat and rampage—gone. And what they did and what they might have done is vanished forever from under the sun.

Ecclesiastes: Chapter Nine

Wyoming

Spring
1980

Tuesday,
13th May

In the spring, in the evening, while the killdeers that had
just returned flew calling out ahead into the coming dark, a
woman and a man walked out across the muddy yard
toward the sad beginnings of a two-track road whose ruts
led off between the hawthornes bristling tight by the edge of
the meadows and the cottonwoods along the creek bottom
below. It was growing colder: Those earthy odors, soft,
fresh, organic hints of springtime, which had been released
by the warmth of that afternoon's sun, were being locked
away again beneath the freeze winter would use right on
into next month to reclaim the season each night. But there
were buttercups blooming between the snowdrifts in the
bottoms of the draws; green grass already was sprouted next
to the buildings' foundations on the south sides. And there
were only a few cows left, held prisoner still inside the corral fences, those cows all sprawled together on a knob of
high ground where the soil was mostly gravel and stone that
let the water sink away so the mud was not quite as deep.
They lay groaning, gasping, huge with calf; but they
chewed their cuds steadily, rolling their wads and rumbling
belches, content, because someone at last had found time to
feed them.
     The man stopped once to send home the dog, yelled at
it—screamed. But the dog ignored him like he didn't exist,
padded on past, until the woman spoke once softly to send
it slinking back. The man glared after it, hands on hips.
Then he turned, and saw how she'd gone on without him; so
he hurried, stumbling over the freezing ruts that criss-
crossed the yard, intent only upon staying close enough to
speak above the roar of the rising creek.
     "Are you cold?"
     Karen said, "Not like you think."
     There was still light left on the horizon west, though not
enough for him to use to tell a shadow from the real thing,
that light up there drawing his eyes and then making him
blind when he tried to follow her into the tunnel the road
made going away beneath the trees. The birds came back,

flying into the light, calling, "deer, killdeer," as they came and went. But when he swung to stare up for them he could not find them. And when he turned back and saw her waiting, all he was given to use to try to fathom her mood was the white oval of her face floating framed by her dark hair and the upturned collar of her coat.

Frank said, "If I could really see what I'm doing, I guess I'd know this is all wrong."

"It's that bad then," she said. And she smiled (she smiled like a cynic: lips only).

"Now I didn't mean it that way," he told her, "that's not what I meant at all. What I meant was I only hoped—" He stopped himself there because he heard himself whining. And hadn't she warned against it? Many times. "What I meant was," he said carefully, "it's too bad it can't all be clear before, like it is when you look back after."

"You take your chances," she said wearily, like she'd explained it all too often. She sagged back against the harsh old bark of a cottonwood tree, crossed her arms. She heard the rasping of the stiffened cloth of the old army coat; and when she looked down she saw that last light reflected, shining dully off the amniotic fluids smeared there and dried like egg white mixed with mud and the blood where she'd hugged newborn calves against herself while she'd packed them through the corral slop, night, after night, after night. She smelled the acrid stink of the barnyard about her, and she thought how she hadn't taken time to wash the coat for months. She thought: _And I won't, for as long as I can still bend the arms—hah!_ She grinned, very grim; closed her eyes tight when Frank cleared his throat.

"I had to work hard when I was young: raking hay when I was seven, on a tractor in the sun all day long. When I was nine, from then on, I had to stack baled hay by myself, my father made me. Mother had me wear a wet cloth tied over my head underneath my hat because I'd get these awful headaches." Frank looked down at the woman, once, quickly. But she didn't speak, she did not move, she never even bothered to open her eyes; and the voice of the creek was too loud for him to hear her sigh.

Frank said, "Mother used to warn him how if anything

happened because he worked me so hard while I was still so young—"

She pushed with her hands away from the tree; she felt a great, breathless need to be free of him: He stood too close, leaning above her, talking loud into the night so he could be certain she heard him over the rushing of the waters, his breath shoving each word straight into her face, bringing little drops of spittle. She ducked under his arm and walked away with her hands stuck deep inside the pockets of her coat. But she glanced back once; and when she did, Frank's eyes lighted up, for he thought he'd been wrong: Ah, it wasn't me! She just wants us to go on to somewheres else. Frank hurried after her, slipping, sliding—nearly fell flat while crossing the ruts. He wiped the mud from his hands on the seat of his pants, trotted to catch up:

"And I had to—here, wait—had to pick rocks, I hated that: little frost-heaved rocks what popped up every year— best crop we ever raised!" Frank giggled, hurrying along (stepping out ahead so he could glance down at her face to see if she'd found that funny) . . . he said, "The big ones, we'd take a star drill, hammer a hole in them and tamp it full of powder, blow them to bits. They were shaped like great teardrops, big end in the ground, the tips of them showing were rusted from the metal they'd knocked off the haying machinery they were constantly making break down. My father used to take me out to the shop, where in a corner was a pile of mower parts and rake teeth and all sorts of busted junk. We'd just stand there looking, not say a word, before we went that day to work at the rocks."

She stopped, shrugged; and he stared down at her, pleased. But she said without looking, like she was speaking to the night: "Are you trying to get somewhere with this, or are you just talking again to shoot the shit?" So then it was Frank who moved off alone, while she stood and looked after him, and played in her mind with just going home. She saw him glance back once, saw how he pretended to try to hide it—she knew already by the slump of his shoulders the wounded, self-pitying, little-boy look on his face. She grimaced, and gazed longingly back along the way. . . sighed again, and trailed slowly after him.

* * *

"Just before I had to leave," Frank said softly, "my father told me, he said: 'Out here, you learn how to work, and all about a dollar; and how to accept exactly what life allows you.' He said: 'If it's dry, don't matter how hard you work, you're gonna stay poor, years it's dry.' He said: 'But one thing the earth don't do is prepare you for what's not honest. It don't teach you what selfish sonsabitches people can be.'

"It was like this in the evening, except later in the year, because there were nighthawks flying, booming when they dived. He looked at me, my father did, took me by my shoulders and looked me in the eye—my father never being one to think of such things: never thought to teach me how you're supposed to shake hands hard—said: 'Lots of them make quite a case how it's the right thing, sending our boys over there, I've heard lots of them say how it's God's will, a test of some sort. But it's people like them always been on top: Ain't their boys, they don't seem to care how the dollar they're making is at the expense of poor folks' sons.' He said: 'What strikes me most though is how come, if God's so real—real as you get—why's He playing us like pieces in a game?' Then my father did something very strange: He pulled me over and laid his cheek next to mine. And he whispered to me like he wanted no one else to hear: 'Son, if you feel like you don't want to go, I'd understand; and I think I can keep you out of it.'"

Frank stopped then, stared bleakly at the ground. "All I could think was how I wanted to look around, see if anybody else was watching."

It was full dark by then, stars were out. When she turned to start back there were only the thin, twin lines for her to follow, ruts, frozen solid, slicing away through the snow in underneath the trees where the sun had not yet found the strength to look in and take the drifts. There were calves in the open across the creek, huddled together where the sun earlier had warmed them some while their mothers had gone chasing the green grass and were late now coming back. She glimpsed the calves moving, winking, dog-like shadows—a pack of silhouettes—felt sudden terror wrinkle up her spine, saluted by a raise of hair at the nape of her neck. Then a hungry calf bawled, told her what was over there. She shook her head in great disgust, turned again to try to see the ruts and ridges so she wouldn't stumble over them. And Frank, flopping and lurching like some great hatchling bird, held out a gallant hand to help her. She left it empty, went on without him, and he had to flounder along, breathing hard, struggling to catch up again: "I jus' need—hey!. . . slow down . . . would you?"

But Karen had quit listening; she was staring at the ground, absently seeing her way home, ignoring what she believed was only more aimless chatter, while her thoughts ran on to other things: She was, she felt certain now, pregnant again—*Christ!* She moved along, lost in thought, not missing him for the longest time . . . until finally she realized the voice of the waters was the only sound. She blinked . . . focused, turned and saw him waiting—felt the curly presence of his anger reach out, like ice.

"Yes?" she said. "Go on. I hear you."

She heard his brittle, pouting voice: "I was through with it."

"That was all?"—Karen failed to keep her relief from sounding in the words; heard it, and at once pretended some flair of her own anger, for cover—"You dragged me out here just to hear you say that? That was it?"

"Well, no, I—"

"Of course, there's more, I should've known—get on with it then, make your point. I haven't got all night!" She flounced away, shaking off the touch of his awkward hand.

* * *

"I think about it now and it comes back as symbols, see? the warnings having been there, all along, and me just not understanding, until here I am back where it does no good. Like we'd go out through the jungle—straight through the middle of it—everything growing over there having some sort of hook or thorn or tangle, making any little movement a major kind of struggle. We couldn't use the paths: Those were *their* paths—we'd come out of the bush onto a trail all cleared and packed, looking like a stroll; but the paths weren't ours to use. We'd hide at the edge, look and listen, and if we thought it was all right we'd run like monkeys across the footpath back into the jungle so thick you couldn't see the man ahead, hardly ever the point. All the while we'd be thinking: Might be fire. If the brush seemed too cluttered or the leaves were dry: Might be fire.

"Come out on a clearing: little rice, little hut. There might be smoke still coming from the cook pit, maybe some cooked-up rice set down on the ground. Nobody ever around. We'd go in, take the place, room in there for four or five, more rice than that by the fire outside: Cooked rice don't keep. The lieutenant would start us then trying to find something, bunkers or tunnels, stores of stuff. We'd tear the place apart, scared to death all we'd find was a trip wire, too late. Not that I could blame them: When I looked at the mess after we were through, I could see what they must think."

* * *

She'd led him by then out from under the trees, back into the open, east of the big house by the edge of the mead-ows, where now all the natural light of day was gone; but where the glow from the yardlight scattered pale twinklers on the drifts of snow left between the gravel mounds and reflected softly green off the stones set at the heads of the graves. She turned toward them, already reaching— stopped, and thought: *My, but it's hard to quit old habits.* Then she had to smile, because she wasn't fooled: The only old habits she still kept around were a few she could count on, a smattering of good ones, like trusted friends, which gave her a safe place when she needed it. She moved on in, allowing the graves to draw her, knelt, and touched the cold marble face of the military stone. And Frank, following slowly, like he didn't know if he should intrude, stood awkwardly waiting . . . whispered, almost reverently:

"For a few dollars, you could get yourself a bag of the best marijuana, or heroin would make your heart stop." Frank watched her turn—he felt her astonishment as she stared up at him.

"What?" she said. "What are you saying?"

"I said—"

"I heard what you said. You did that?"

"Well . . . I know I don't seem like someone to use the stuff, but—"

"Are you sure?"

"What? . . . yeah. 'Course I'm sure. Whataya think? I'm making up stories?"

"Sometimes."

"Really? Why in the world would I want to do that?"

"Because it makes it sound worse for you."

* * *

"There was brush in tight all around the clearing, see?" The smoke off the fire in front of the hooch was being knocked to pieces when the chopper came around; I could hear them on the radio: 'Nothing in there, nothing a 'tall.' So the lieutenant had the radio tell them to back off some, let us go in without them stirring things up so much. 'Git-your-ass-on-over-there, that's an order,' him no older than me, but he thought he was God. Except that fire burning hadn't started by itself: People were in there, they just didn't want us to see them—I knew for certain this would turn out bad.

"I wanted to cross on the dike, not get wet; and if things came apart I could get down behind it. But he wouldn't allow that: Said it tore the dikes up, made the locals mad. I mean, what did he care—after all we'd done—what the hell did it matter anymore?

"Wasn't deep, maybe up to my waist, but the stuff seemed bottomless, with all we had to carry, rice every-where, muck sucking at my boots. There wasn't a sound, except the chopper way off behind us; until all at once—I'm certain it happened this way, like I'd always imagined it—

the water seemed to raise up like a fountain spout, rainbows and everything, rice sprouts raining down. I yelled it was incoming.

"And our lieutenant said: 'Incoming,' like we needed him to verify it; except he said it, 'Incoming?' like asking, Gotta match?—I knew then that he didn't believe it, so I opened up. Next thing I knew, our lieutenant was down.

"The radio man was screaming, and the chopper came back around, popped over the hill and set down right on top of us, pivoted, looking for something to kill. I was yelling, pointing, trying to get them to see; and finally they let go.

"The hut just vanished.

"She came out of the brush in back of the hooch, running like a crazy woman, long black hair—she looked like a kid. But she grew and grew, until she was frozen out there in the rifle's sights . . . like there wasn't any motion, like she wasn't going anywhere. She folded up, and bounced when she hit the ground. When I finally got over there, she was like a pile of old rags.

"Sure was little.

"But then, the lieutenant looked little, too, like that.

"Anyhow, she was . . . you know . . . adult; I mean, you could see she had . . . breasts, down inside those things she wore.

"Baby in the bushes most likely was hers."

* * *

They moved on in, Frank and the woman, drifting back toward the big house as if drawn to the light. Except now they walked apart, alone, hands clasped behind their backs; their shadows lay out long and thin whenever they paused to gaze around. It was freezing, the air brittle; both figures breathed out long, slow vapors that floated away like smoke. The earth crunched like charcoal beneath their feet as they moved to cross the last of the ruts and came to stand beneath the light, one facing west, the other east. From behind his back—so loud in the stillness it made Frank jump—she said: "So, that's it? You've told me all you wanted to say?"

"I guess so . . . that's about all."

"And are you over the mess you were when you came back home?"

"Yeah, mostly . . . I think so."

"You think so."

"There still are a few things—"

"Still a few things, sure, why aren't I surprised—what is it with you? Do you really believe you have all the problems? Do you honestly feel you got dealt all the big troubles, so much more than anybody should ever have to pack around?—shit! Look: You went off and did that—it was your choice!—all you had to do was say so, your father would've kept you home. But you couldn't do that, had to show up like a man. And we both know all that time over there you were peeing in your pants. Then you had to shoot somebody; leastways, you say you had to shoot somebody, I haven't decided yet what's wrong there—shut up—you shut up. My turn to talk. I'll even give you credit for it, I'll give you the benefit of the doubt: We'll pretend you did kill someone, isn't that what war's about? Let's even say—God forbid—let's say it was a woman. You think that makes a difference? Oh, I suppose you still believe it's men who die, while we women just sometime go floating off to heaven, legs crossed, a halo, shining like little moonbeams—makes me sick. But you got all twisted up over it, doped up, too, thinking that might help, because this was too much—this was too big a deal—so maybe if you tuned out it would all go away. Except each time you woke back up, there it was again. And now you're telling me your troubles, how awfully brave you've been, carrying it all by yourself for so long, when what you really want is to hand the whole thing off, asking: 'Hold me tight, won't you, because I've had a hard ol' time?' You want me to say: 'Poor baby, here, have a tit, because you certainly do deserve it.' That's what you want, isn't it? *Goddamn it, isn't it?* There's something right here you'd better understand.

"I already listened to one man have his troubles, and believe it or not they were worse than your own—I even tried to help, for a long time I tried to help. But when one problem seemed about ironed out, up popped another; until I knew for certain it was never going to end. No matter what I did, no matter how I tried, he would have a hard time—it's just how it was for him, that's the way it'd always been.

"So I've listened to you, I've done that much. And I hope for your sake you can work it out. But I'm telling you—no, I'm warning you: I don't want to hear any more about it, see? I don't want it mentioned again."

"But I need—"

"No, no!"

Summer
One Year Earlier
1979

Monday,
6th August

1.

Late afternoon, Blue was sweated out. The sun had
pulled more water from his body than he figured life could
stand, and the wind had stolen the rest, left him burnt up like
a hunk of meat forgotten in the frying pan. He rocked along,
hypnotized by the slow plod of horse steps, forearm broiling
on the saddle horn; he nodded, dozing—shaking himself
awake—Blue warned himself he would not allow it, sleeping
on the job like that. Not even here, he thought, both sides of
the county road fenced in by barb wire, whole damned herd
couldn't go nowheres but straight on; ever'body up to and
including them cows so wore out, hardly put one foot before
the other . . . 'less those cows got together . . . hatched up a
plan. Blue grinned, drifting: Wait now, you all know the pro-
gram? It's this side, this way, easy, hold on—wait, goddamn
it—'til you get the word . . . ready? . . . an' . . . now!
    He sensed a surge go through the herd; saw the whole
bunch of them all at once swing left and smash against the
fence: splintering of posts—he heard the sing of barbed
wires, felt his horse be swept sideways out from under
him—Blue began to fall, tumbling down toward where the
hard packed road was being ground to dust beneath the
hooves of a wild stampede.
    Blue grabbed heavily for the saddle horn, realized he'd
fallen fast asleep—had nearly tumbled from the saddle
while he dozed and dreamed. He jerked himself upright, sat
up very stiff and straight . . . edged a look around. No one
seemed to've noticed. Everybody else rode suspended in
the same heat, plowing head on into the late day sun, with
hats pulled low against the dust streaming back on a stiff
west wind. Blue breathed again. Shoo, what a fool!
    He shook himself to try to wake up, rubbed his eyes and
lightly slapped his cheeks. He could feel windblown grit
crunching between his teeth, spit—winced—tasted blood;
and when he touched a careful finger to his mouth, he saw
a thin red line on his fingertip from the split skin of his

windburned lips. Could he still hear the sound of broken barbed wire singing from out of his dream? Blue squinted upwards, noticed for the first time that he was riding beneath the power lines that led on in to the ranch buildings, the wind moaning dismally past the high wires overhead. Blue was pleasantly amazed—he could recall nearly nothing of the past three miles, now here he was, almost home, another workday damn near done.

There was a thick haze of clouds piling in the west, tinged a brilliant gold, dazzling in the late sun.   Blue squinted into the dust, thought: Means the weather's gonna change, I can feel it in my bones. He raised a shielding hand to try to shade his eyes against the blinding light so he could better study the sky—grabbed his hat as the wind almost got it, clamped it tighter on his head. Prob'ly means the wind's gonna blow, 'stead of this dumpy li'l breeze. He listened again to the whining the wind made gusting past the wires above him, heard it raise from a low moan to a new tenor pitch. Reminded him of the television, old rerun western, cowboys out fighting the elements, the sound of the wind wailing on the soundtrack. Out here, in the real stuff, Blue recalled hearing the wind yell like that only when there was some man-made something close by: power pole, telephone. Sometimes the clothes line. He slitted his eyes trying again to look into the dirty gale, couldn't take it, had to turn away.

TJ was riding off to the left. Blue watched the boy's shirt whip and billow in the blow. Beyond, by the meadows east of the ranch buildings, he could see the stones set at the heads of the graves, the same graves Blue had to chop the resin weeds off of and place the plastic wreaths of flowers out on every year, last Monday in May, where they were left until July, the day after Tom's anniversary. When Jesse and TJ were little, and now with TJ's own kids, the fireworks Tom grudgingly allowed the children to shoot off the evening of the Fourth, if the summer had been kind and the grass was not tinder dry, lit the stones (the old folks', Mary's; and now Jesse's, too), reflecting whatever color the powder burned: white, red, blue, or green. And the plastic flowers, which were stored on the open porch of the big house during the off-season and could just as well been left on the graves all year for what good the storage did them, looked frowsy and cheap in the fireworks light. Blue noticed TJ glance toward the stones, offhanded-like, but Blue knew different. He knew, truth was, TJ had to look, but wanted no one else to notice, and wonder, hadn't TJ got used to it yet, what with Mary in the ground these fourteen years, Jesse laid in alongside her for eleven? Blue knew.

He'd seen TJ standing awkwardly at Jesse's grave, times when nobody else was supposed to be around, TJ twisting his hat in his hands like he used to do in Jesse's presence, except now TJ had to think all the right things instead of say them; he'd seen TJ sitting with his knees drawn up, head bowed and his back propped against the stone, which read:

MARY BROTHERS
Wife and Mother
God Rest Her Soul

And if God did, Blue thought, it was the first rest she'd got since Old Tom cast eyes on her.

Blue glanced around, was relieved to find Tom not staring at him, like he, Tom, was able to read your thoughts, turn and glare and send you hunting cover without uttering a sound, Tom riding chin up, stiff as a ramrod against the gale, as if the wind itself dare not steal the hat off Tom Brothers's head.

The wind scudded a tumbleweed toward the graves, plastered it for a moment against a stone, tore it loose, and hurried it on. Blue remembered Jesse's funeral: frozen chips of earth spilling out from under the coverlet, the cover itself powdered with new snow. Blue had stood there freezing, clutching the stub of his little finger behind his back inside his other hand because it always seemed to frost up first, trying at the same time to hide (at least attempting to keep folks from passing behind him where they might chance to see) the stitches his woman had so recently put in the seat of his one pair of suit pants: big three-cornered tear from where Blue had got hung up in the barbed wire when

27

he'd sneaked outside and climbed the fence for a breath of fresh air and to unburden his bladder of the load of beer he'd taken on at the reception given down the road at the community hall on the occasion of TJ's marriage, three days before. He remembered looking across that six-foot hole— all hairy with grass roots gathered with lumps of dirt reminding Blue of fresh-dug and unwashed potatoes—staring across that most recently occupied grave, to TJ, and Tom, what was left of the family, awkwardly clumped together on display over there for the mourners to study and judge for themselves just how hard this, the latest of deaths, was for them to take. TJ was all shriveled down inside his clothing, his face a mask as white as the snow except for the green around his mouth and the hollow black sockets bottomed out by his eyes, looking as cold that day as Jesse must have been. And when the service was over (the long, long service, the way Tom had wanted it, so that when it was over everyone could be certain so was the life), with the casket lowered—the flag off, of course, and clenched in Tom's hand; the flowers tossed in and scattered over the coffin along with that one handful of dirt Old Tom had thrown down, Blue had made his way around to where TJ was being crushed in embraces received from stout old matrons, grieving aunts whom TJ had not seen in the three years passed since the last such gathering. Blue had asked him, low aside, "TJ, hey, how you doin'?"

Blue remembered how TJ had stared back as if to say: That's a pretty goddamned stupid question, Blue. But instead, TJ had whispered, "Oh good, jus' fine." Except Blue had already looked TJ over, both from a distance and now face to face, and thought: TJ, you lie, you look like walkin' death. But Blue hadn't said that either, slapped TJ on the back—maybe a little too hard, because TJ had staggered and gasped like he thought he was going to fall in the grave—Blue had grabbed him, given him a big hug to cover up, said, "Well, you're tough, TJ, sure 'nough." Blue remembered how TJ had grinned back at him, real sickly, had gone away then with Karen, headed toward the big house, walking slow beside his new bride to make sure she didn't stumble while she held onto his arm with one hand, held her child-swollen abdomen with the other, the couple walking well out in front of the rest of the company, but still trailing behind the stiff, straight back of Old Tom, who led them all, even the preacher half trotting to keep up with Tom's long, hard strides. The preacher tried to speak, offer condolences, with Tom nodding curtly and not listening while he looked at the horses standing humped in the corral, Tom most likely figuring whether to have Blue feed them or turn them out, he hadn't decided which, because he hadn't yet made up his mind whether he would sell Jesse's horse this week or next.

I had to feed them, Blue remembered. I had to go in to change my clothes, go back out again, after dark, in the freezing cold after I was all warmed up, had to climb up in the loft and drop down the hay bales, carry them one by one across the corral, the wind blowin' a blizzard, spread the hay out so's the horses wouldn't fight. When I could've— fresh from the graveside and still in my suit pants—just opened the gate and not even bothered to shut it nor watch them horses go, because the next day Tom decided the market wasn't good enough to sell no horse, not that week, not that month—not 'til summer the next year. Tom. Shoo!

* * *

Tom rode straight up into the hot, dirty wind. The light that came near eye level now was even more stark than it had been at noon, so Tom could do nothing but stare straight into it, for the sun was so low if he shaded his eyes with either hat or hand he would not have seen anything beyond his own boots and the road crawling past beneath him. The clouds that came riding the hot wind in did less than little to block the sun. Instead they took on the sun's light, magnified its brilliance—not only made no shadows of their own, but allowed no shadow at all: caught the light and bounced it into every corner, behind every rock; until there was no place to rest the eyes except bathed in the blood red color found behind closed lids.

Which Tom could not do, close his eyes, not even to rest them. He must keep on looking his cattle over and decide how to sort them, and figure where to go with the bunches he'd already sorted in his mind a dozen different ways, knowing without looking he must put them on handy water and good feed for the next eighty days to come close to breaking even with the sale of his calves against interest at the bank. And he did not have it, not this dry year, a pasture flush with both water and feed, except maybe the meadows, which he could not consider. He would need those meadows desperately in the middle of winter; besides, he hoped maybe to hay a little more of the scrawny alfalfa before the leaves all fell off and the stems withered to sticks. Tom could not even slump, his back hurt him so. He'd stopped bothering to wipe away the tears full of dust and burning sunlight, just let them course down his cheeks for an inch or so until the hot wind licked them up like an ember passed too close.

He thought, I used to calve them by myself. When the folks both went in almost the same year, I calved all those cows with no help. And not because I'd planned it so, but because when I walked into that barroom in town in February, asked right out if anybody in there was looking for work, told them what at and how much I could pay, they laughed at me. So I came back home and did it alone.

But then I didn't have to tell somebody how I wanted it, and later go see had they done it that way? I was free to choose, however I saw it, that's how it went; and if I changed my mind in the middle there was nobody I had to explain how come to and get them lined out again in some different direction. 'Course, there were times when one more trip through the calving corrals would've killed me. Times like that were worst, because then I lost calves. But I had to sleep, an hour here, half a wink there. And with both the folks gone, I was in the clear.

Except for the bank.

This ranch was all mine, except for what I owed at the bank, except for the debt I'd inherited and the money I had to borrow to pay inheritance on the land left me and more money I had to have to pay interest on both. The bank said in order to protect their investment, I'd best figure some way to save more calves. They advised me to find help.

So I decided I'd raise some sons.

Teach them exactly how I wanted things done. I should've knowed better—*it slipped right by me*: Everything that comes must be handled by my decision, right or wrong; and with no time to consider nor any real sense of what to look for, except history, which never repeats itself twice close enough to be much help, except to make you wary. Watch out now, because once there was another situation that looked a lot like this one, when you took it on yourself to go such and such direction, and you was wrong wrong wrong. All that you did then just allowed you the right to say, in the end: See this? This came about because I stuck in my nose—it's my responsibility . . . now that it's turned into a pile of dung.

Why?

Why? . . . well, because something was gonna happen, one way or 'nother, I figured I'd lend a hand—it's not that I'm not patient, because I am. I just hate to be blind—I'd like to think I have something to say about how it all turns out.

That's what you wanted? The right to say that you started something, which gives you some claim to the results?

That's it.

The results having once been a dead son.

Ooh now, you do know where to stick the knife. Yes, I s'pose I must lay claim to that, a dead son. It's just that somewhere along the road it became my way not to let things pass without my word . . . sometimes . . . a fault. I sure never figured my decision would kill him.

It's over and done; what to do next is the question. Think on it, Tom, you've got a moment. You have another son—not like the first, mind you, but maybe good enough—

I got another son so unlike the first it's inconceivable they both came from the same bank of sperm—like an infidelity! Tom thought: I got one son left, and damned if he ain't near useless. I wished I had another. Maybe just a daughter. I wish that Jesse wasn't—

He put that thought away, quickly, unfinished: Never, not ever, wish for something that could not be; a system he had nurtured—a sanctuary? maybe—upon which he'd thought he could always depend: kicked in automatically to channel off a useless notion, immediate as the workings of a well-oiled machine. But lately, there seemed an odd drag in efficiency. Lately, Tom thought, I've been kind of reluctant to give the impossible up. I got one son left, and I've no idea where to start to make him over—he has no sense of responsibility, no concept of what it takes to make a man.

Tom smiled wryly: There now, there 'tis—I knew if I took a moment I could pin the trouble down. It's what I never took time to teach him, responsibility: Teach him how to make a decision, answer for it, and still have the courage to go on and make more. I'll start that lesson right away, from the bottom up.

But wasn't that what you thought you were teaching the first one? And didn't he pay an awful lot for it, thinking it was a game?

Now I don't know that—I thought . . . I ain't decided yet. Because I don't have all the facts. I wanted to allow him to be free to choose . . . even if I had to nudge him a little to get him on the right track. It may be he did learn something . . . meaningful, before the end. I like to think so, I'd like to think it wasn't a total loss—

And what exactly could he have learned that would have done him any good? That life was a gamble, and he'd just tossed in his cards?

I don't know yet!—how'm I s'posed to know? Give me a chance to think, I'll get back—

* * *

"Tom? . . . Tom?"

"Yes?—what is it? I'm right here."

It was Frank, the new man, asking: "You all right?"

"Well hell yes I'm all right. What makes you wonder?"

"You look sorta bothered."

"Thinkin','s all, about these cows."

Frank said: "It's a problem. Dry like it is, no water, no feed. Only good thing I can see is it's all your own, I mean: Can't nobody else tell you what to do about it." Frank was

only half thinking about what he was saying; he was
remembering instead a story told to him the night before by
a long-haired man, an account about war, the death of some
woman, how the long-haired man had had such a hard time
he'd sworn off violence of every kind.

Tom stopped his horse—reined her in hard—swung to
face this new hired man (who'd been so brash to've said too
much, here on this first day—damn those little pills).

"That's pretty much the way I see it, son," Tom said.
"How high do you think the price for bred heifers will go
this fall?"

* * *

From the top of the last hill, TJ could see them; he'd
already figured them for what they were: three dark lumps
set down in the county road out in front of the herd, the road
down there in shadow now with evening coming on. The
leaders had stopped, stood staring uncertainly, trying to
fathom just what was up ahead; and the rest of the herd was
closing in when the three lumps stood. Two moved off at
once toward the chokecherry bushes clumped outside the
lane fence, the dog snaking along not much taller than it had
been when it was still bellied out in the middle of the road,
the girl pausing once to say something back to the boy who
still held his ground, chin up and spraddle-legged like sun-
down in Dodge, his only weapon an old grass rope he used
to wave his sister on, while he made his stand alone out in
front of three hundred and fifty-seven cows, plus calves,
and two less than the tallybook's sixteen bulls (one had
been lame, Blue had told Tom: "Bull's too sore-footed to
make it home." But Tom had kept pushing him, whipping
the bull along; until finally the winded animal had simply
laid down, and no amount of punishment would get him on
his feet again. Tom had twisted the bull's tail until Blue
thought the bones would pop; then even Tom had given up,
rode on without a word. The other? Tom suspects maybe
his neighbors liked its looks, used fencing pliers to borrow
him for a week or so . . . will return him in the fall together
with a bill for having pastured his best bull for him all sum-

mer long. Only TJ knows the missing bull isn't ever coming home).

The cattle were all bawling back there behind the first,
silent, nervous ones who stood staring at the boy bug-eyed
and anxiously testing the wind. A whoop or two came
floating down from the tired and windblown riders who
pushed the cattle a little harder now on this last leg home—
TJ screamed, "Owen! Goddamn it, get outa the way!" clear
as a bell even against the wind. But Owen stood a little
longer, scratched a line with the toe of his boot in what
gravel was left on the hardpack of the road, and waited
behind it for a long count, arms crossed, lip curled the way
Old Tom's did, before he sidled on over to the bushes where
his sister hid. Owen stopped there for a last look, then he
crossed the wires and hunkered down out of sight.

"Christ sakes!" TJ said to himself; but he spoke plenty
loud enough for all the rest to hear, and he glanced sidelong
at the other men, trying frantically to think of something
more to say. But Tom was talking too earnestly with that
new hired man; and Blue had his own rope down, was using
it to pop the stragglers and snap the heads off the stunted
sunflowers growing alongside the road. Christ sakes, TJ
thought again, because hadn't what his son had done been
way out of line?—yet it appeared not to've caused the
slightest stir of concern. TJ wondered why not?

But, then, TJ wondered why not about lots of things:
Like why had he not been allowed to miss finding the body
of that dead bull?—how come he'd gone that way instead of
somebody else? And then why was he unable to find again
the cow and calf pair he'd lost while he was poking about
the stinking carcass trying to figure exactly what bull this
was so's to have it right when he got around to telling Tom?
When he shoved his way up beside Tom to help count the
herd out through the pasture gate (crossing through the cattle to get there, turning them all back . . . and having to sit,
and wait, while Tom stared a hole through the side of his
head while Blue and that new man had galloped frantically
to head off the herd and get them started back out through
the gate again), how come Tom had to make such a point,

saying in front of everybody, after the last cow had dashed through: "Short a pair and another bull, way I count."

TJ had mumbled, "Way I counted, they was all there. But if we're short anything, we're gonna find them back behind where the new man rode." TJ could not quite come up with the insolence necessary then to carry through and meet the new man's eyes, had to swing the black stud and ride off alone.

Now TJ was way low on cigarettes: had just one left, which he'd worried for miles, rolling it between his fingers, putting it to his mouth, wishing it lit almost more than life itself. But he had only one match, too, which was nearly worse than none: In this wind? TJ stared off toward the big house, wondering how things went inside? Like rolling dice, coming home: Most times you crapped right out. He shook his head and squinted at the graves again: No problems there—(uh-oh, here it came again, that sensation not of dread, none whatsoever, which TJ had felt while he'd stared into the abyss as they'd lowered his brother away, TJ realizing then: *If it ever gets too much*—relief so astonishing, so peacefully enveloping, TJ used it sparingly for fear it might become too easy: either overwhelm him with its seduction or else wear completely out like the heady abuse of a fantasy of sex). TJ planned each move, tried to cover everything . . . but he lost his last match to a sudden gust of wind, rode into the evening with the cigarette clinched cold between his teeth. He would not, he decided, ask if anyone else might have a light.

2.

There'd been a time when Karen had waited by the window, evenings, watching for TJ to come home—maybe not eagerly, not even then, but at least with a quiet sense of security; a time when she still believed in him and the dreams she thought they shared.

She'd felt all she needed was patience, because TJ needed time, a decent interval to get things done; so she'd taught herself to wait for him to come tell her how the day had gone, how their dreams (maybe they were all his; but she'd listened intently, claiming her part in between what she heard and what she'd learned to imagine beyond what he allowed himself to tell her, silently threading her own dreams in between his big plans and the baby . . . paring parts off to fit the smaller space after the second child was born, a girl that time; and having to shave away more when things never seemed to work out: no money left after groceries and kids' shoes, no time ever for what she'd wanted anyhow)—how their dreams were climbing toward the heights dreams must ascend to if they were ever to be fulfilled. She'd watched TJ slowly stop talking to her and take to drink.

She'd cared for the children, nursed the first at her own breast: cradled her son's head there and tenderly touched his soft spot—felt the terror of her duty and the blind innocence of her baby's great need. She watched the baby boy closely to learn the difference between gas and a real smile, taught the baby to frown comically upon tender command. She waited for TJ to come marvel with her at this miracle of life . . . she'd felt the growing bones in the head of her next child and urged them to join quickly: Daughter, grow fast, I need your help. Karen had fed the second child on formula: It wasn't easy chasing all through the big house after a toddling boy with her blouse undone and her breast hanging out as she tried to nurse the baby girl while the men of the ranch came and went as if where she lived and tried to call home was as open to trespass as government land.

She glanced out the window now, just to see how far the cattle had come, trailed by the men who would be expecting a meal set down for them as soon as they came in—she could hear the baby whimpering again (third child, another girl, too old to still be called a baby, way too big to be sleeping in a crib). Karen thought she could stand it though, the child's fussing, for a little longer . . . if only her nagging headache would allow it. Tired of holding that one anyhow, she told herself; and right away she felt the guilt: Because she'd not held that third child enough since its birthday for any cause to feel weary. Maybe I don't love this third one like the others, she thought—maybe I don't love this third one at all? My, but that was hard to live with; better to pretend I love them all the same, and leave this third child alone as I can.

She called for Sarah to please come help her; no answer came echoing back through the big, old house. (Big, old, empty house, stuffed full of memories left behind by that other woman, TJ's mother, long dead. And how to compete with that?—nothing here for Karen, intrusive maid.) Karen remembered then how the two of them, her eldest daughter and her son, had gone out to the lane to wait for the cattle— had told Karen so with a shout and banged the kitchen door on their way out; left Karen to shudder inside the hollow impact of sound, holding her temples while she waited wearily for the baby to cry. Now, the baby—three years old? no, not a baby—now the third child was awake, and wanting up; Karen could hear her whining from that tiny room off down the hallway. She glanced once more hopefully out the window, saw the little blond head of her daughter Sarah come bobbing past the sill. The porch screen slammed, the kitchen door burst open; Karen turned to the clatter of Sarah's shoes on the worn linoleum.

But Sarah said it first: "Caroline's crying"—no question, simply a flat, knowledgeble statement, pointedly anticipating what Karen had planned to say, in a tone Karen hated. Sarah's voice reflected all the numb housewife dreariness Karen herself felt, a tired little voice—that's what Karen hated most, the dull fatigue she heard whenever Sarah spoke, for Karen felt her own guilt strongest when her daughter seemed so weary. But Sarah went obediently on by, disappeared down the hallway toward that tiny room (which was to've served as a temporary nursery, eleven years ago. If Karen was to have babies—there being small doubt of that the day she was married—she was going to have a nursery, had to settle for a temporary one. "Only for the first year," TJ had promised, "just for this first kid," the one unplanned and already kicking Karen's insides like an angry mule. The nursery would be in a new house, TJ said: "One set back in the trees away from this ol' ramshackle place, with a lawn, and a garden, brand-new, Karen, any way you want it." Now a son, a daughter, and the third child, too, had squalled their way into the world to bunk their turn in that closet-sized room where the junk families collect, and save, to neither use again nor ever throw out, had become piled so deep there was only space left for the crib and a thin path to it so that Karen had to move the first row of stacked boxes into the hallway each time all she wanted was to shake the rug). After a moment, the baby quit crying.

Karen opened the oven and stabbed savagely at the roast. Instead, TJ bought me a horse. Now what in God's name was I supposed to do with a horse?

3.

The light in the west was just about gone; the hills stood against it in black silhouette. The cattle were in the corrals now and nearly all paired; what had been bedlam an hour ago was almost sorted out, with cows standing quiet, content with their cuds, while their calves sucked off the pressure of full bags of milk. The only movement in the last light was of a single cow, still walking, calling for her lost calf, and the slow, heavy plod of men leading the horses to the barn.

Inside the barn was black as a cave; that first horse knocked hollow echoes out of the plank floor, until Tom reached the light and tugged it on to give the room some distance and cut some emptiness out of the sounds. The heat of day passing from the air outside was trapped in here, caught by the walls and insulated by the hay stacked in the loft overhead. The long, low room filled quickly with the rank smell of hot horses . . . began slowly to fill with quiet sound: rattle of buckles turned loose, the gradual creak and slide as a saddle came off—the checked breath of the man who caught it and a soft moan of relief from the horse. There was the measured jingle of weary steps wearing spurs, no talk. Dust and hay stems filtered down, marking where someone moved across the loft. Slices from a broken bale tumbled into the mangers; the horses snuffled into it, began at once to feed.

TJ leaned against the saddle, eyes closed, for a long, drifting moment; he was deathly tired. The evening chill, which had got to him outside, was leaving him now, but the closeness of the room was fast becoming stifling. Though he did not yet bother to raise his head, TJ fumbled for the cinch. The stud flinched, rippling muscles, but it was all for show: The horse was drained, too, from prancing and shying, fighting with TJ all day long. TJ was wondering whether he still had the strength to bear the saddle's weight, when he heard the footsteps above him turn toward his stall. He blinked— jerked alert—had just time to yank the saddle free, before a big wad of hay flopped into the manger in front of the stud.

The horse froze, rigid as carved ebony, staring wide-eyed into the darkness before him for what had all at once leaped down and made so much noise. TJ backed off, searching desperately for some way out. But the horse stood with its rump swung, blocking any escape from the narrow stall; all TJ could do was hold the saddle up like some silly shield and wait despairingly for things to come apart.

The hay settled over with a swooning hiss—the horse lunged back from it in a terrible panic, was brought up short by the halter rope. He fought the restraint, twisting in the tiny space, hooves clattering against the slick plank floor; swept TJ aside and jolted him back against the stall's rough wall. The stud screamed and reared, knocking his skull hard against a ceiling joist, stumbled forward, stunned and trembling. TJ coughed and sucked air, touched the dazed and trembling animal; ruffled the hay so the stud would take note. He watched the horse nose hesitantly into the manger, watched him immediately, hungrily, start to eat. TJ heard Blue call softly from the loft: "Damn, TJ, sorry. I didn't think." TJ gently shoved the black horse over for room to squeeze past.

The hinges of the tackroom gate squalled punishingly loud; TJ staggered in, lugging the saddle, slung it on an empty tree. Beside it was another, filthy with dust, steep cantle, deep seat for a bronc rider: Jesse's. And beyond was the small one, neat, with fancy leather beneath still deeper dirt, the skirts curling from lack of oil, human or otherwise, for a fourteen years. Longer than that, TJ thought: Mother didn't ride those last few years before she . . . she never liked to much anyhow. TJ tried to store a mental note how he must clean and oil the saddles when he found a moment, and the strength. He fumbled in his shirt pocket for that last bedraggled cigarette—time now to slip away, see if he could mend. He squinted down the length of the barn to gauge the gauntlet he must run.

Halfway along, the new man was searching for an empty nail upon which to hang his gear; and beyond, Old Tom was squatted by the door, staring out into the night. TJ watched Tom stand, saw his father place a hand to the small of his back to help align old bones, straightening coming painfully slow. Tom thumbed back his hat and wearily rubbed his eyes; and his son, watching, felt a sudden warm glow of comraderie: Why, that old man is tired, too! TJ grinned, and moved down the alley behind the row of horses toward where his father leaned.

"That your boy?" TJ whirled, crouching like to meet an enemy. The new man was speaking, asking as TJ passed by: "That your boy, out in front of the cows when we came down the lane?"

"He weren't hurting nothin'!" TJ hurled back.

"No, 'course not, I never thought so. I only was askin'—"

"Here now!" Tom came striding. "What's the trouble?—nobody said a word about it, did they, TJ? Nobody said nothin' about that boy bein' in the road." Tom pulled up to glare at his son, his hand flashed out—there was an arcing flair of light. Tom held a burning match before TJ's face. "Light your smoke, boy." He watched TJ lean in reflexively.

"Frank here was only tryna be friendly, but I s'pose it's natural you'd not understand." Tom blew gently across the flame. "But now that he's woke you, maybe you're ready to do some work, seein's how you been dozin' in the saddle all day. I want you to load some hay bales in the tractor bucket, feed them cows. I want them taken 'crost the crick, get them behind that better fence, because we both know who never got around to fixing the corrals, don't we—TJ,

40

you lis'nin'? I want that hay scattered good so's all the cows get a taste—"

"But I'm tired!" TJ blurted, coughing on smoke—spoke, before he'd considered it, just like he'd accepted that match and then by matchlight seen the smirk on Tom's face.

"Well now," Tom said gently, while he carefully broke the dead matchstick and tucked the pieces into TJ's shirt pocket, "we're all a bit weary. Put in quite a day, didn't we?" Tom all but patted TJ's head. "But we can't quit yet; tired or not, still work needing done."

TJ stood stunned—the cigarette dangled forgotten, as TJ whispered urgently, for Tom alone to hear: "I thought maybe one of these hired men could go do, you know, the small stuff, while you and me—"

"These men are tired." Tom's voice was stern, much too loud. "Frank here was on the road, while you were still in bed—even Blue was up, wranglin' in the horses, before the thought of waking ever rolled you over" *(—ah, TJ, remember the dawn? How you'd begun to believe it would never come?—how you'd fought with your dreams, all through the night; until first light at last arrived: struggle was over, for another long day. So you gave it up, fell sound asleep for an hour past when you should have been out).* "An' both them'll be there tomorrow, before you, I know it. Now git. And TJ, watch that smoke: One spark in here, you'll burn down the barn."

TJ staggered out into darkness, helped along by his father's hand—stumbled off into the night which was supposed to've enveloped him. He hurled away the cigarette, sent it tumbling end over end out across the corral, where it hit with a tiny eruption of sparks like a small, impotent anger dashed out against dirt.

4.

Sarah stood in the dark hallway, listening behind her for sounds from the baby, while she watched her father move around in his room. She'd not gone to him like she usually did when he came home at night; she watched his face. His jaw muscles worked like he chewed on something—gum,

41

she thought, not because she believed that was it, but to give the motion some identity so she could feel how it went. Muscles leaped, relaxed; Sarah studied him to get it right. But when she tried it herself, her teeth grated, sent a shiver all through her; she stopped it at once, watched TJ unwrap a pack of cigarettes, watched him drink from a bottle he'd taken from the closet.

He looked terribly tired—Sarah could see he was: Hollows of fatigue underneath his eyes, cheeks drawn and pinched, made his face look old. But that was no different: tired in the morning, tired at night—too tired to do anything she'd ever want to do. That's all right, Sarah thought automatically. She felt a vague guilt for not speaking to him, like she was uncomfortable in her heart with what she'd decided. But it was weak, the guilt. She turned to slip away . . . the old hallway floor chose to squeak—TJ called out, "Sarah, hey!" So Sarah skipped in to meet him, laughing, like always, as TJ swept her up.

He gave her a kiss, big wet smack on her cheek; now his eyes sparkled—still weary, half-blacked by fatigue—now his eyes shined. She could smell tobacco smoke, and the odors of horses and cattle and sage; and underneath the raw odor of liquor she could smell him, the scent he carried into the evenings before he bathed. Sarah nestled tight against him and told him of her day.

And when she felt he wasn't listening, she reached up a hand to each side of his face and turned him so she could see the changes pass through his eyes from what she had to say: "And the baby, guess what she did."

TJ's eyes smiled, as if about an old joke. "She's hardly a baby," he said.

"I know, but was she fussy! Mother needed me constantly to watch over her." (Sarah saw his eyes narrow; was he angry about that?) "I didn't want Owen to do what he did, out in front of those cows—I warned him he'd better not. But you know how Owen is: He never listens."

TJ smiled again, thin, tight grin: "Where is Owen? Have you seen him since?"

"Out somewheres, prob'ly at the barn." (Sarah thought:

But maybe TJ had forgotten about it, what Owen did, and here I am, making trouble, bringing it up again.)

TJ told her, "Find him for me. Tell him we need to talk."

"All right, I'll do it, but you aren't mad, are you? He never hurt nothing, did he, doing that?"

TJ smiled bleakly. "Nobody else seemed to think so."

"That's good, you know why? Because I have to play with him. If I go find him, and he's in trouble for it, he's gonna think it's my fault. I don't want him mad at me, because I got nobody else."

"There's Caroline."

"Yeah, well, maybe she's not a baby, but she's sure not old enough to be much fun. She must've had gas or something today, because all she wanted was to be held constantly—she cried each time I put her down." (Sarah saw TJ's jaw begin to work again—he was angry for certain now.) "I talked to her and played with her, and I rocked her forever, 'til I thought my arms'd fall off—"

"Where was Karen during all this?"

"I don't think Mom was feeling so good—another of those headaches, you know."

"Uh-huh."

"But she cooked a good supper, wait 'til you see."

TJ swung her once around lightly, stood her on the floor and bent to kiss her again, this one for the tip of her nose. "Go find Owen," he said, pushing her on her way. But then he called her back, before she was gone: "Would you like to go with me, help feed the cows? I gotta give them hay. After you find Owen, you want to ride along?"

"Oh yes!" Sarah cried, and she dashed off, stopping once in the hall to listen at the nursery door; she stood, barely breathing, praying that Caroline was asleep . . . Sarah could hear her little sister whimpering and moving about. Sarah sighed, and turned grudgingly to enter the dark and crowded room. Then she stopped again, smiled a smile full of mischief—Sarah sneaked away, darting through the kitchen while her mother's back was turned, carefully closed the door: TJ had sent her, after all.

Outside, the stars were shining brightly, even those deep

in the western sky. Phooey! Sarah thought, hugely disappointed because she'd wanted so to see the fading of the light. But then the night sounds caught her and carried her along: Nighthawks called and crickets sang; June bugs went scratching across the ground. Coyotes howled and raccoons chirred along the banks of the spring pond below the house. The tomcats were fighting, their terrible screams coming from the old tumbled-down coal shed at the corner of the yard. Then the dog stirred itself to answer the tomcats' challenge; and their louder yowls at his savage intervention arced like a spark across the night. There was a brief, brutal encounter against the back fence, before the tomcats squeezed through, fuzzed and spitting, left the dog drooling blood and snarling at the hole. Sarah shivered, and padded on.

There was just a sliver of daylight left in the west—the West, whose name alone caused Sarah's heart to leap, for on clear summer mornings clouds floated like feathers over the western horizon to drift in profound silence across the land; and during the same day's late, hot afternoon, great thunderheads built secretly behind the western skyline, peeked over, then rolled on in to throw down their lightning and laugh a thunderous uproar until the setting sun appeared again briefly beneath the tail of the storm while the thunder, still muttering, stumbled east—it made Sarah realize the east is past, dead and gone, but the West is the future, yet to come. She watched the light go out in the horsebarn doorway, heard the heavy door roll closed, wailing along its track. She heard the voices of the men talking low together in a gutteral language, saw their forms rise out of the night as they moved toward her: strange old simian figures, ponderous, weary as time. Sarah hid in the tall grass in the shadow of the bunkhouse, called out in a stage whisper to the littlest form jittering in their midst, who yelled back with great heat:

"Sarah, what! Whataya want?"

"TJ says you're to come see him."

She heard Owen curse childishly—"Oh goddarn it!"— heard someone else chuckle, while Owen accused: "You tattled on me, didn't you, Sarah—what's he want?—you tell him I'm busy . . . aw, horse crap!" Sarah watched him go off alone, downcast and muttering. She nestled in the shadows, feeling the warmth given off by pockets of the day's heat caught in the coarse grass, the men's voices droning, as they stood awhile, planning tomorrow. Finally, Blue turned and went inside the bunkhouse, and Old Tom and the new man moved on out of sight. Sarah crouched listening to that one gaping, gasping, bovine cry, some cow still bawling for a lost calf with a voice awkward at best, hoarse now from bawling all day long. Owen came trudging by again, lugging the milking pails, shoulders slumped. Sarah heard him say: "Gol-damn you, Sarah, I sure hope you're happy!"— saw him stoop for a rock to hurl, watched it fly way wide: Owen wasn't certain where she was hiding.

Then the tractor cranked over, the diesel motor loping to life; and Sarah leaped up and ran with a long-legged thin girl's fleet, fluid motion—outran the second rock and caught the tractor before it had moved. TJ took her hand and hauled her up, wrapped an arm around her and ground the tractor into gear, gave her trust of the steering wheel as they roared off into the night.

* * *

The light blinked on, single, naked, flyspecked bulb, dimly lighting the dust kicked up by the milkcows' scuffling passage across the cowbarn floor. Owen dropped the buckets with a clang and slouched against the wall. He lashed out a kick at the barn cats crowding around him . . . watched with great disgust while one of the milk cows— after spending the whole day in the pasture, and after standing for an hour more in the corral outside—chose to mess now that she was inside the barn.

"Dirty ol' bitch!" Owen savored the words. He glanced to the doorway: No one there—no sound—save the distant, middle-throttle roar of the tractor, coming from where TJ and Sarah were busy at something, Owen did not know what, didn't much care, except to assume jealously whatever it was it was better than what they'd left for him: "Dirty ol' filthy goddamned sonsabitch'n milk cows!"

45

Owen felt better—marvelous words—which seemed to hang in the air by their own wonderous power, floating like bubbles spit out from a mouthful of soap. But the milk cows' calves bawled in answer to his voice, as if to remind him that they still needed to be fed. Owen sighed again, shuffled across to take down the manure fork hung on nails driven in the wall; he prodded the cows with the tines to move them into their stanchions, dropped the blocks to lock them in. He leaned back against a cow, fists shoved deep into his pockets, watched as a grey-mottled-yellow tabby cat ran her back against his leg in obvious delight. She deftly avoided his angry boot, strolled off to sit and wash her face.

He wondered: How come every time I find something I really want to do, TJ finds something I don't.

There was a one-legged milking stool tossed in the corner; the leg hobbles were hooked on the window sill. Owen gathered them gloomily, thought: I bet Frank would make a good dad, not work me so hard while I'm still so young— Frank said he'd teach me to rope!

Owen danced across the dirt floor, swinging the hobbles above his head, let go: saw the heavy iron flash out on its chain and strike the younger cow hard in the ribs. "Whups . . . sorry." He smoothed the roughened hair where the hobble had struck, felt the moisture of slobbers slung there when the cow had thrown her head around to drive away the flies . . . he found a grub lump, high on the cow's back, stood tottering precariously on the one-legged stool peering in through the parted hair: not ready yet, no crusted ring of plasma around the hole the grub must punch through the cow's tough hide to escape. But Owen gave the lump a hard squeeze anyhow before he gave it up.

He hunkered down, reached beneath the cow's heavy bag to tether her legs, hooked a hobble above each hock, and tugged on the chain. Nothing happened, the cow stood spraddled, legs braced wide (those hobbles Owen's only buffer between a milk cow's disposition and the chance of ending splattered like a windshielded bug against the barn wall): "Aw, get your damned feet together, goddamn your spitty ol' hide!" Owen leaned into her—stuck his shoulder into the cow's flank and shoved . . . felt her slowly shift her great bulk to counter against him—he leaped away, caught the cow stumbling in the sudden vacancy, triumphantly tightened the chain.

"Gotcha!" Owen gloated.   The cow whacked him viciously across his eyes with her tail.

He pounded her ribs until his fists were numb . . . paused to catch his breath and rub away the tears: Prob'ly Frank would never've had his own son do none of this stuff, not when he was still so young—prob'ly he'd care for him more, other'n tellin' him what a wonderful thing work was. Owen pictured TJ, there in the bedroom, smelly old cigarette hanging from his mouth. "Now you listen, Owen, listen son, I know how it is, bein' a boy, wanting only to do what you want to do. But you're gonna find it ain't that easy, comes time to make a livin'. If them milk cows ain't milked, they're gonna dry up; 'sides, this is your big chance to learn responsibility. Go on now, I'm dependin' on you. Milk 'em out, every drop." Owen spit through his teeth . . . sighed.

He set the bucket in place beneath the first cow, balancing himself on the one-legged stool. The cow flinched, like she expected another blow. But Owen merely slapped her bag, trying to persuade her to give down her milk; whacked her again, and felt her flaccid teats begin to swell. Owen thought: Stupid ol' cow, if you hadn't decided to be a milk cow all's you'd have to do is let your own calf suck you whenever it wanted, I wouldn't have to fight you like this ever' night.

'Course, a calf as big as yours'd butt you like to lift your hind end clean off the ground. Owen doubled a fist and punched the cow in her bag about as hard as he figured a calf would butt . . . noted with satisfaction how the leg she raised to kick at him was pulled up short by the hobbles chain. He punched her again, thought: I guess maybe you're better off with me anyhow, 'stead of some ol' hardheaded calf.

The grey-mottled-yellow tabby had finished her toilet; she stretched, and ambled over to plop down beside him, meowing pitifully. Owen rolled his eyes to look at her as he slowly began to milk. He could smell the odor of the steam rising out of the bucket, animal hot, rank with weeds. Stinks like hell, Owen thought, ain't worth keeping, 'cept in the mornings—might as well give it all to the cats. "Get lost," he told the tabby.

But the human voice was attention gained, exactly what she had counted on. Owen watched her stand and preen her whole length against the ticklish backside of the cow's hind foot. "Hey, hey!" Owen yelled, "Don't do that!"

The milk bucket went tumbling as Owen reached out while the cow raised her hind foot, as far as the hobbles would allow, shivered off the tickles, then set her foot back down—Owen shoved the tabby aside, barely in time, felt his own hand be pinned to the floor.

"*Yowowow!*" Owen screamed, his flesh squishing as the hoof ground down—he yanked back hard, trying to wrench free, but he was trapped like in a vice between milk cow and dirt. Then Owen felt the pressure ease, just a bit, as the milk cow's brain registered that something snake-like was squirming underhoof back there—he yanked again, flew tumbling back; lay curled like a fetus around his damaged hand. He shook it, blew on it, squinted through tears: saw a hundred tiny blood blisters formed around the great white blotches and the small blue dents. Broke? dunno—sheezus Christ!—hurts.

Owen watched as the tabby cat picked herself up, shook off the dust, and strolled on over to lap at the milk puddled on the floor—he grabbed her up, swung her high above his head like he meant to dash her against the wall. She hung, limp and purring, gazing at him through the lashes of half-closed eyes, her face all muddied by dirty milk. Owen sighed, uncocked his arm and cradled her gently while he stroked her fur. "You owe me your life, you know that? S'pose you'll bring me a dead mouse some day, call us square."

But what was this?—Owen squinted closer: "You pregnant? Again?" He tenderly kneaded the tabby's swollen belly, his forehead wrinkled with study . . . his probing fingers found again the faint string of lumps he'd felt inside her. "Sure enough, you ol' factory—keep them tomcats busy, don't you?" He stroked her once more, set her carefully down; she turned back immediately and began to beg, purring like a tiny motor.

Owen found his stool and set himself gingerly back in place. He washed the pail with a jet of milk, turned the teat, and shot the stream directly into the face of the begging cat, watched her lean into the current with her mouth open wide, lapping greedily while the surplus milk drenched her. Owen squeezed harder, shooting the stream with still greater force, but the tabby stayed with it, snuffling, blowing bubbles from her nose, until Owen took the milk away, left the tabby blinking blearily, soggily sneezing. He swung the stream like a turret gun, raking all the other cats waiting clustered round the cat pan, chased the milk after them across the floor and jammed them out through the cat hole beside the closed barn door . . . Owen stalked a fly, squinting with his sighting eye, following it with laserlike bursts of milk while it droned across the room, until it came too near the naked bulb.

Don't shoot the light!—remember that?—hoo! The hot glass had shattered at the touch of wet milk, the exposed filament had burst into flame, a tiny blue light reaching up all at once in the sudden dark to caress the dry old ceiling joist, while Owen had scrambled desperately; tripped over the milk bucket because in his panic, while not thinking—thank God—to use the milk to douse an electrical fire, he'd remembered at least not to leave the bucket unattended underneath the cow. So he'd swung the bucket out, set it safely away from the cow's hind feet; and then he'd run right over it in the dark—splashed through the mess of mud made by a nearly full pail of milk, trying to kick his tangled feet out of the bail. He still never found the light switch before the filament burned away and the flame died down. . . it left him shaken, heart pounding, in an utterly black room.

Old Tom never did did figure that one, Owen thought: lightbulb all at once missing from its socket in the shop, blamed TJ. But what else was I supposed to do? Anyhow, I could've kilt myself with a busted neck, sliding upside down out along the shop rafters, back in the dark holding a lightbulb in my mouth; then hanging by my legs in here while I tried to screw the broken bulb out while I tried to remember: Did I ever switch it off? or am I gonna elexicute myself soon as I touch the wrong thing? Sliced my finger on the broken glass and about for sure fell off then—bleeding so bad I had to wash things off aiming the milk by guess because blood on that new bulb would've been a dead giveaway. I had to finish milking in the dark because I wasn't about to turn the damn thing on wet and have it all to do again.

Owen peered at the tiny white scar on the inside of his forefinger, sighed: I do so much, and nobody even knows to 'preciate it.

He tucked himself away then into the cow's flank, told himself he was committed this time: threw himself into milking like a madman, splashing the bottom of the pail into a frenzy of foam . . . gritting his teeth against the pain in his hand . . . too much, too fast . . . soon he was sitting idle again, his milking muscles all played out. Owen stared into the shallow pool of milk he'd collected: Not much in there tonight, cocklebur, a fly. He sank both with a long burst of milk, watched as the burr bobbed back up. Not like in the mornings, after the cows had lain in the corral all night, belly hair full of dried dung crumbs that fell in—maybe that's what made morning's milk taste better?

Owen thought: Frank now, he's all right; talks to me like I was . . . bigger. Owen remembered how Old Tom had picked him up piggyback there in the horsebarn; and Frank had said: "Hey, toss that little man over here." Frank had staggered: "Whew! I figured I'd seen you before. But that was a little guy, out in front of those cows. That was you? Really?"

Owen grinned: Yup, really.

Beautiful, big palomino stud—Frank had boosted Owen up onto the horse's bare back, asked, "You got your own?"

"Naw, not yet. Pretty soon, maybe—I keep askin'. But gettin' a horse seems to come awful slow."

"Well, a man needs a horse." Frank had winked: "Good company, don't talk much."

Owen had sighed, "TJ—my dad—says he can't 'ford me one. And Mom thinks they're dangerous, like I might get hurt."

Frank said, "If your mom feels it's risky, no sense shaking her up—you got to break it to her gentle, see? She's gotta take to the idea a little at a time. But a fellow needs a horse. When you get yourself one, if I'm still around, I'll help you teach it some things."

Owen wondered: What did Frank mean, if he's still around? I'll have to ask him—oh damn! How could I've forgot that? Old Tom had invited Frank in to supper while the men were on their way to the house, right before that sneak Sarah had come along to ruin things. Owen stared down at his work; enormous reason to hurry now, and way too much left to do. He flexed his fingers, trying desperately to work out the soreness—*"Milk them clear out"*—there had to be a better plan.

Owen smiled like a sunrise.

He twirled on his stool, and hurried away to release the hungry calves from their pen, herded them across the room and shoved them up against the flanks of the startled cows. Owen had to show the two calves where the milk came from, for they'd been weaned to the bucket since the day they were born. But they caught on quick: Five minutes' time, both calves stood with tongues lolled out, heads drooping, too full to even bother butting at the cows any more. The cats were clustered round their pan, lapping up what little milk Owen had managed to collect in the bottom of one bucket; the milking was done. Owen hurried the calves back to their pen, knowing by the look of their swollen bellies they'd had more than their share tonight, thought: If anybody says anything, well, I spilt tonight's milk, when that damned cow kicked me—I got a bruised hand to prove it. And yes sir, TJ, those cows are sure enough milked out.

Owen turned the cows loose, shouting them out of the barn. He switched off the light and raced away—clang of empty buckets—Owen was thinking, I wonder if Frank ever was married?—I bet I'd have me a horse by now, if he'd knowed Mom, back then.

But I wonder though, if I'd still be me? if Mom had knowed him, 'stead of TJ, back then?

* * *

They came back across the graveled yard, huge load of hay gripped in the grapple forks, strange shifting shadows flickering before them as the headlights strained to see around the bulk of the bales. They roared up to the corral gate, where Sarah leaped down and sprinted to open it, shouted and threw clods at the cattle that crowded close, while her father edged the tractor in, raising the bucket higher and peering down in front for fear he might run over a calf.

They idled along slowly then, pushing the cattle before them, leading them actually, like with a carrot on a string, the cows packed in around the tractor nearly blocking the way, those cattle just off short pasture and anxious to get at the hay. TJ steered with his knees and clutched Sarah with one hand while he ran the levers lifting the bucket higher, then higher still, as he sent the tractor down across the dry creekbed and up the other bank.

On the other side was another gate leading into a smaller corral, whose fences held in an ancient grove of boxelder trees, squat and prissy, but with knotted trunks and great, swollen butts from which suckers sprouted for the cattle to browse down—hollow, every one of them, rotten at the core, with roots formed inside their empty hearts to trail down and feed off each tree's own slow decay. TJ waved for Sarah to leave the gate open, while he raised the bucket to its utmost. He waited impatiently for his daughter to clamber back on, while the cattle crowded around and balled up in the gate.

With Sarah safely crooked in an arm again, TJ eased ahead, whooping at the cattle, tapping at their heels with the tractor's front wheels. He was forced to clutch—cursed—tried again, felt a stiff new resistance against his forward motion. The tractor bucked, rear wheels spinning in the dirt . . . there came some great tearing sound, rending of wood. TJ glimpsed the fall of a massive limb, trailing a flutter of leaves—heard Sarah cry out, "Oh!" and felt her vanish from his grasp, the cattle scattering away from her in an awkward, lunging stampede. He saw Sarah dart beneath the heavy load of hay—saw her flicker through the lights and fall to her knees beside the huge limb the raised bucket had collided with and torn down.

TJ cursed again, this time at his daughter, while he craned his neck, staring up into the night, trying to see if maybe the rest of the tree might be following, thought: Sarah, what the hell? I can't even let the hay down, you're right underneath it. Can't go forward, and I sure can't back up. TJ set the brakes and clambered down, moving cows out of the way by whacking their butts—felt them leap from under his hand and stampede away again from where they'd come crowding back to stare at Sarah, who lay bellied out on the ground half buried in the debris dropped by the broken tree. TJ shouted: "Chris'sake, Sarah, what you doin'? I got no time for—"

She was in amongst the shattered branches, half veiled by shocked and wilting leaves—laid out flat, not answering, her head twisted at an awkward angle, a dreadful grimace showing on her face. TJ rushed up to her, thinking in a panic she must have become pinned somehow, broken her neck! But Sarah was fine, entirely unharmed. She lay with her hand reached as far as she could up inside the limb's hollow center, arm buried to the shoulder, the strain of her efforts reflected on her face.

"Sarah!" TJ said gruffly, impatient now (impatience supposed to be a parent's best weapon). Sarah paid him no mind—"Youch!" she cried, yanked back her hand. Then she squirmed on the ground to reach further still, until her arm was hilted by her neck.

"Sarah!" TJ yelled, "This ain't no time—"

"Got him!" Sarah shouted, and she scrambled up, triumphantly dangling a deer mouse by its tail before TJ's astonished eyes. "Would you look at that!" she whispered reverently.

"Aw, Sarah," TJ said, slapping at the bobbing mouse, "for Christ sake, put that thing down!"

But Sarah swung away, protecting her prize, glaring sidelong at TJ now while she swung the mouse before her own face to examine it close up. She watched it claw air, saw it double back to look between its hind legs to see what on earth had hold of its tail. TJ warned: "That mouse's gonna bite you, Sarah, if you don't put it down. 'S gonna turn an' chew your finger, make you sick."

"Already bit me," Sarah said absently. She carefully pinched the tail of the mouse from one hand to the other so she could let him see: bits of blood welling from the two tiny wounds in her fingertip.

"Aw Sarah," TJ said, wiping at the blood with his sleeve.

"Shh!" Sarah warned. "You be quiet, TJ. You'll only scare him worse—he's already frightened almost to death!" She held the mouse clawing right above her face, swung him slowly so the headlights could play on him, while his splayed feet worked rigidly like he was trying to walk on air. Sarah inspected him closely, exclaimed at last: "I knew it, I just knew it, TJ, look here." She lifted the mouse higher and hung it again before TJ's eyes.

TJ peered in at the tiny swinging form, trying to focus . . . grew dizzy, said, "Sarah, goddamn it! Let the thing go—I can't take time for this, work to do . . . what exactly am I looking for anyhow?"

"He's hurt!" Sarah told him. "You hurt him when you barged in here, knocked down half the tree!" Then even TJ glimpsed it: smear of mouse blood, a tiny tear in the skin behind a foreleg. TJ was thinking: Now wait a minute, this here ain't my fault.

"Sarah, it's jus' a ol' deer mouse, that's all he is. He don't matter a bit, so you—"

"He does too matter!" Sarah eyes flashed. "And I'm gonna take him home and doctor him well." She clamped her jaw, stuck out her chin.

TJ, who already knew by her look it would do no good, still thought it his duty to warn her: "You'll not get that thing by your mother. You won't get it past the kitchen door."

"I guess I will," Sarah said fiercely.

Sarah directed TJ how to find the nest she'd felt up inside the limb's cavity, TJ muttering all the while, cautioning her because he'd learned long ago how pessimism was best, the slow burn of resignation easier to bear than the sharp anguish of dashed hopes: "You know, little girl, it's prob'ly gonna die. Wild things don't take to being caged."

But it made no difference. Sarah crouched, clutching the tail of her mouse between forefinger and thumb, while she held in her other hand that featherweight nest made of cow hair and thistledown, felt her own heat build beneath it until she could almost believe the nest itself was as vital and alive as the hot little creature who hung struggling so on the end of its own unintentional leash. She waited patiently while TJ cursed the cows, cursed the night, cursed the bales as he lugged them off and spread them around so all the cows could get a bite. Sarah waited for TJ to finish so she could go care for this magical creature she'd been blessed by the night to find, until her fingers were aching; she was already thinking how she had to risk everything to chance backed by common sense, which told her an injured mouse might choose the safety of its own home over the perilous freedom beckoning from out of the night. Sarah carefully lowered the deer mouse down until it hung clawing at the threshold of its house. She let it scratch and scramble, allowing it to just touch the nest material with its rigidly splayed fingers . . . let it build desire . . . then she let go: Watched the deer mouse vanish down the tunnel to its nest, and felt the nest come alive with tiny heartbeats of trembling motion. Sarah carefully pinched the entrance shut and crouched waiting by the tractor tire while TJ finished his work. She could feel her own heart beating quick and strong in her fingertip where the mouse had bitten her.

5.

Karen saw them coming through the steamed glass of the kitchen window, their images fractured like seen through thin ice.

She heard the porch door slam, heard a voice apologize for letting it go, that voice not known, but—thank God and Owen—someone she'd at least halfway been expecting. For when Owen had come grouching back through the kitchen on his way outside again after his talk with TJ, he'd told her why—"Why? Because I gotta go milk, 's why—

whataya usually do with these here milkin' pails? 'Sides, I got no time for dumb questions 'cause Frank is gonna be in to eat with us, so you'd better get a move on, too." Then Owen was gone, banging out, leaving her to ask of the slammed door, "Frank, who?"

She'd thought maybe TJ could tell her; but she couldn't bring herself to ask him when he passed back through the kitchen again, TJ following Owen out without a word, man and wife as silent with each other as if they'd been bickering. Except they'd not been fighting—they had nothing left to fight about; there'd been nothing at all for a long time now, which was why she'd instinctively decided how she wasn't going to hear him when he'd first come in. She'd stood by the window, her back to the door, peering out into the early darkness, pretending she was still searching for signs of the herd supposed to be on its way down the lane (like seven hundred head of lost cows and calves could sneak past the house right through the yard and never gain her attention). What a sight I must be, she'd told herself, craning my neck like some old heifer, trying to see what both of us know is already gone by.

But Karen had begun it, too late to back out. She stared out the window, anxiously listening for TJ's next step, thought: What if he comes to me? What if he reaches to touch me? My, how I don't want that! So she'd searched for reflections in the warped window glass, saw herself and TJ standing by the door . . . she watched as his image passed on by, heard the sounds of him moving quietly off down the hallway—she called after him, "TJ? That you?" and she closed her eyes and gritted her teeth against the plaintive, falsely questioning tone in her voice.

Karen timed their entrance, was cooking when she heard the door open. She turned to the scuffle of boots on the floor, saw Tom, weathered and brown, who grinned at her awkwardly, clearing his throat. (Like a man would, she thought, who's committed me to a favor, taking it for granted before he's even asked. Tom, you're gonna squirm some, getting through this one.) The other man was tall as Tom, clean-cut and muscular (Hmm, Karen thought), with soft, dark eyes, not unlike a deer's, who looked right at her then glanced shyly down. He had thick, dark hair, tumbled and curling, Karen could see, now that the hat he'd worn was whipped off. Old Tom mumbled something, turned to indicate the stranger—noticed the new man had removed his hat and fumbled for his own. There came over Tom's face a look of deep disgust; he left his hat on as he introduced them, and Frank stepped forward, hand out, to take Karen's own.

Tom cleared his throat again, muttered: "Took the liberty of askin' Frank here to supper with us, 's all right?"

"What?—yes!" Karen said. "Of course." She turned away. "That's fine. I'll put on another plate."

"Now you're sure," Frank said. "I don't want to—"

"Of course, there's plenty. No bother at all."

"Well then," Tom said, "come on in, Frank. We'll find us a chair, rest our bones. I feel like it's been a long day, how 'bout you?"

"A chair sounds good," Frank said, and they both laughed, moving off, an awkward dance, with Tom not wanting to lead, not wanting just to turn his back and go; and with his company not knowing where they were headed, both them trying somehow to walk side by side, until they reached the door into the next room through which they could not pass abreast. Frank faltered there, not so much out of deference—though that worked to get Tom on ahead—but to allow instead the chance to send a flirting smile shimmering back across the room, left Karen all in limbo, twisting at her ring.

She blinked at the empty doorway . . . reached to smooth back a damp lock of hair. "Well!" she said softly. She turned, very gracefully, half a pirouette, moved to the cupboard to take down another plate, searched, until she found one whose edge was not chipped, traded the fork with the bent tine for a better one at the table. She stopped for a moment, took stock . . . nodded, then walked off down the hallway toward the bedroom she shared with TJ; she'd decided she would change her blouse.

* * *

So she called all them—"Come and get it!" she announced just as TJ came back in from outside, while Sarah made sly noises, messing with something out on the porch, TJ grinning at his wife so sheepishly, so exactly like Tom, Karen felt moved to ask him, "What's wrong with you?" She glimpsed Sarah ducking by behind TJ, lugging a big empty bucket.

"Sarah?—hey, you, Sarah! What's that you've got?"

Sarah called back, "Be right there. Got to look in on the baby first. It's been a while, right, since anybody has?"

Karen knew something was up; she just didn't have time then to find out what.

Because Owen burst in, breathless from running, slid to a stop by the sink, leaving skid marks of corral grease all across Karen's floor, Owen still able to shout his mother down when she screamed: "Owen!—no! Look what you've done!"

Owen yelled, "Are they . . . here? Have they come . . . in here?" He wheeled about, ready to race on.

"No sir!" Karen collared him and thrust him back outside. "Don't you come in until you've cleaned those boots!"

"Who th' hell is 'they?'" asked TJ.

"How should I know, TJ, don't bother me now!" Karen was frantic, searching beneath the sink for something to use to clean up the mess; while everyone in the house came from all different directions to crowd into the kitchen, where TJ stood shocked, staring at the new hired man whom TJ had figured would be paid for the day and already be long gone, Frank trying his best to talk politely with Tom and still field all Owen's interruptions, Owen dancing between them, in stocking feet. All the while TJ saw that Frank seemed most interested in Karen crawling around scrubbing at the floor; and when he looked, TJ noticed immediately what generous cleavage Karen's new blouse revealed, particularly in that position. He swung to stare at the new man again, measuring this Frank from a brand-new perspective, which caused him to be gruff when Sarah nudged him.

"Later, Sarah," TJ said, "I'll talk with her about it after a while."

"Talk with me about what?" Karen asked, rising, flushed and pretty; "Sarah, what was that I saw you just bring in?"

"Nothin'," Sarah muttered. "Weren't nothing important."

Karen showed them where to sit, all except Tom of course—leaving TJ stunned again because he'd always sat there, beside his wife, and now he was supposed to be here, while the new man took his chair. Karen said: "You all go ahead, don't wait for me. TJ, would you help me put this on the table please?"

TJ blinked like he'd been clipped on the chin: What was going on?—he'd never had to do none of this stuff before? TJ asked, honestly enough: "What for?"

"To help me, TJ." Karen rolled her eyes.

Then Frank jumped up, saying to her: "No, here, let me. Least I can do is help."

"Why, thank you, Frank," Karen said sweetly, shooting TJ a look like a knife. "But I can't have you doing this, you're company, after all."

"Oh, let him," TJ said. "He's not so much company as he is temporary hired hand."

"TJ!"

"No, wait." Frank took a dish from her. "I was hoping we could talk about that, the hired man part." Frank turned to Tom: "I'm sure needing a job, for more than just a day or so—I was thinking this might be more permanent, I could stay on a while?"

Tom said: "Didn't I say so?—pass me the spuds—I must've already figured so far on ahead, planning the work we'd get done with the help of a good man, I forgot to let you know."

TJ blurted: "Hey—what you gonna do that for? We don't need more help, we already got Blue."

Tom said, "If I hire Frank, I'll have two good men: Frank one, Blue three-quarters, and you filling in what's left—we'll need the extra hands, come calving time."

"How come? We've always managed fine."

"I've decided to keep all the bred heifers, so we'll have half again as many more cows to calve out in the spring."

"We'll buy hay?" TJ was triumphant. "I'd like to know where the money's comin' from to pay both for him and the extra feed!"

Tom said, "I'd rather borrow money on a few tons a good hay instead a givin' them purty little cows away for nothin', let a man like Frank go down the road. So unless you think you can keep outa the bottle, we're gonna need the help."

Karen gasped, a strangled sound, swung away to face the stove. "Tom!" she said. "What did you say that for?" TJ, staring at her, thought he could see her shoulders shaking (it seemed she was laughing, trying none too hard to hold it in). He put down the fork with its one bent tine, left the house, carefully closed the door.

Tom said, "So, Frank, you was in the army. Where at?"

Tuesday,
7th August

1.

Daylight came slowly, through a high, thin overcast; the morning seemed sluggish, limbering up. TJ became aware of the change like from very far away, drifting back from where he'd been trying his best to sleep, only to realize his eyes were wide open, and even focused, simply waiting for his mind to grasp what he'd been staring at—for how long? All night he supposed, having no memory of, nor feel for, having slept.

There was the memory of thought, though, or perhaps he'd dreamed that he was thinking: Some conscious effort all night to wrestle the unconscious up close enough to the surface so it could take on a dream's shape revealing a reality more genuine than his own waking hours, so bloated was his daily life with chasing dreams anyway, most not even his own. Despair came—my! and so early—thundering close upon the heels of his realization he was awake again, the dreams gone, scurrying back down their burrows, leaving behind a litter of impressions like broken links in a chain of nonsense. TJ tried to move, felt his arms ache, part fatigue built up and never relieved, part tension from wrestling in the void all night. His eyes burned with sleepless sand—he rubbed at them, it made no difference; the cracked ceiling still hovered close above him, while he cowered inside his desperate need for rest. TJ wondered how long he could keep it up?—he wondered what would happen when he no longer could?

He remembered the cold sweat, which had soaked him in the night—had actually puddled in the hollow of his throat: When he'd clawed there his fingers had come up dripping like he'd dipped them in a spoonful of water. *So, then, you do recall your dreams. Bits at least, the nightmare part: very ill, beastly high temperature, sick and frightened little boy. Your own dead mother had come in the night in answer to your cries, touched you gently and laid a cold cloth across your forehead. She'd left you then, though you'd begged her to stay . . . so finally, and, like always, with the last of all you had, you'd managed to slide the cloth down off your face where it seemed about to smother you, left it draped like icy horror across your throat. That was what you'd been trying to rake away when you discovered the pool of sweat.*

TJ lay shivering, cold and clammy, shriveled in the dawn—he tried once again to burrow beneath the blankets, hide in sleep, could not . . . sat up. It was later than he'd thought, lighter: the flair of the match did not blind him like he'd figured it would. He could see his wife's form: She lay sprawled, nearly naked, like a shipwreck victim tossed on the beach, her nightclothes torn, a small, dark bruise at her throat. TJ cautiously touched his own lips, but they were not so sore as he'd believed they'd be, not nearly so mashed as he felt inside.

He'd come back like a sneak thief from out of the night, stealing into his own house (at least into his only home: like a teenage son coming in way late), bent like a picklock, feeling at the latch. With boots in hand he'd crept into the kitchen, where there still was a light lit, silverware, two plates, one upside down over the other so maybe his supper was still warm. He'd moved on down the hallway, hugging the wall where he knew the floor would squeak . . . stood for a slow moment before the ribbon of light laid like a trip wire across the floor, the gleam of it showing past the edge of the door behind which his brother had once slept . . . heard the new man move in there, groan of bare springs beneath an old mattress—the light blinked out, left TJ to grope darkly on.

For he'd been sulking at the graves outside and was bent on revenge. He tried to walk into the room as if it was fully lighted—collided with the nightstand and made a helluva noise. TJ caught the tottering lamp just before it fell, switched it on and sat down hard on the edge of the bed.

"Whaa—?" she said, waking, "Who? TJ? That you?" Karen giggled sleepily, rolled away—he could see she was beginning to drift again, wondered what to do? But Karen rolled up to peer at him.

"TJ, what are you doing? Where you been?"

"Why'd you laugh?" TJ said.

"Just now? Because I made a little rhyme: 'What, who, that you?' You're too sensitive, TJ. What time is it? Where have you been?" Karen shaded her eyes to peer against the light; but his hat was pulled low, eyes all in shadow—she couldn't even tell if he was looking back at her. Like a child, Karen thought, who is waiting for me to take his hand, drag him back into the world he'd run from, too full of pout to reenter on his own. Karen tried her best not to sound indifferent: "Are you all right?"

And when he finally spoke it was a whisper so low she reached out as if to ask him, "TJ, what?" But he yanked away, stood and glared. Now she could see his eyes, feel his hurt aimed like a bullet—like the willful passing of a virus so the sick could draw warped comfort knowing at least that another felt bad, too: "How come you laughed? in front of that new man, like I'm a family joke."

Karen sighed. "TJ, I wasn't laughing at you—I just was so surprised Tom would say such a thing, I was embarrassed for us all. I couldn't think what else to do." Karen was sincere: "It wasn't fair. We should not have laughed at you, not then."

"When should you have laughed? After I was gone?"

Karen rolled away—such a bad game, so full of traps. She closed her eyes and sighed again. "We shouldn't laugh at you, TJ, not ever. Tom should not have said that, it was mean of him." She thought: Tom should know by now, as long as he's been around, that some people must be pampered, like small children. "Come to bed," she urged half-heartedly. Karen only wanted to get back to sleep.

She heard TJ move—sigh of bedsprings as he sat back down to tug off his boots. She heard him grumbling, complaining about needless things so he could continue to whine without causing another scene: "I wish you'd fix the ceiling, patch them damned cracks—I can't sleep at night for fear the whole thing's gonna fall in."

Karen thought dreamily: Yes TJ, I know, you're scared of most everything. And if you'd bring home some real money instead of the piddly grocery allowance Tom allows you at the end of each month, I'd do lots different. But I suppose if you were half the man you dream of being, all kinds of change would come—

All at once Karen was awake, and filled with dread. She lay anxiously listening—had she spoken aloud? The room was deathly still—Karen knew from it that she had spoken out; now TJ was sitting there, astonished—struck dumb. She steeled herself for the lash of his raging words.

Instead he was on her—hurled himself right on top of her, savage fingers clawing at her gown. Karen tried to fend him off, but TJ slapped her down. He scooped her up—she was amazed at his strength!—hurled her across the bed, her nightclothes torn, buttons clicking on the floor. "So, you want a man!"—words viscious as spit, on whisky breath; icy hands stealing under the rag she now wore, while he sucked with his mouth at the skin of her neck . . . Karen lay stunned, shocked stiff with repulsion, until she felt his cold fingers groping for her chest.

"TJ! Don't!"

"No?" he snarled. "You're the one showin' off what you got, hangin' out all over—what you wore tonight. Or was that for somebody else?"

Karen drew back and fisted him in the mouth. She did

not wait to see what she'd done, rolled away, curled into a ball—no blankets—but with her knees drawn up, arms over her head, while TJ staggered off, spitting blood.

* * *

TJ sat hunched, chilled by the morning, looking down at his sleeping wife. Her arm was thrown back now, torn gown gaping, her breathing calm and relaxed, seen by the dim light on the slow rise and fall of bare breasts. TJ gazed at her reverently, wanting her above all else, but she seemed an infinity away now, lost forever. He spit in his palm, snuffed out his cigarette, crawled from the blankets, shivering more as the air got to him. Through the window he saw the colors of sunrise coming onto the hills . . . something moving? TJ peered out through the glass, saw a tiny figure working across the hillside, walking unevenly, hunting—springing forward—and bending to strip grass seed, winnowing it into a sack. TJ remembered then how he'd promised he would speak to her mother about that damned mouse. He glanced at Karen, shook his head, probably now's not the time. He gathered his clothes and tiptoed from the room.

2.

Blue lunged against the barn door. It yielded grudgingly, rumble of old rollers, thin squeal from want of grease. He leaned into it, gritting his teeth against the ache of sore muscles, inched the door open until it yawned wide enough to allow a horse to pass. Blue slumped against the jamb, very bowlegged, tenderly felt the sore spots where his woman had bandaged the insides of his thighs. He prayed fervently: Lord, don't let her have stuck tape to them raw places, amen; thought, Mus' be gettin' old: ridin' didn't used to hurt so much.

He limped along through the gloom of the barn, pausing to unhook the shutters and let them swing wide to allow the odd sunlight to come flooding in. Blue cocked an ear: was someone yelling? He leaned gingerly to peer out through an opened window, squinting into the strange morning light, saw two figures, one tall, one not so, at each other, here so early. He heard TJ scream, "I ain't a gonna do it. I won't ever, you hear me!"

Tom said back, "Never expected you to. I'll see that horse cut better'n you'd ever know how."

Blue shook his head, looked to the sky.

There was a thick haze building, an ugly sheet of cloud cover, dimming the morning like dirty yellow smoke. Blue chided himself for dozing through last night's weather on the television. Now, he would either have to limp back to the bunkhouse or else risk a soaking without a raincoat. He moved outside to catch his horse, listening absently to the two men squabble, thought, And what about lunch? Tom never said nothin' 'bout lunch. Must be he's planning to be back by noon—ha! Nightfall, I betcha, 'fore we come back home. Blue bridled his horse, bent to gather the reins, groaning as his belt buckle bit him somewhere under the fold of his belly. He guessed missing one lunch wouldn't hurt him, much. He led his horse inside, turned to the sound of running boots.

TJ blew by in a rage. "Goddamn it, Blue—!" But Tom strode through the door behind him, and TJ swung to glare, then hurried on. Blue watched the young man catch the stud with the certainty anger brings; TJ was leading the saddled black horse out even before Blue had finished with his own.

Blue called after him, "You check that cinch again, TJ. You know how that ornery—you know how your horse likes to swell in the morning."

But TJ was gone. Blue heard the clatter of hooves as TJ left the yard, thought, prob'ly ought to cut him, horse like that. No good the way it is: all them hormones. But Tom should know it ain't his decision, he ought to know to allow that much.

Blue turned from shoveling tobacco into his lip, mumbled, "Morning," to the new man, and watched while Frank led the palomino by: saw the swing of the heavy penis, full scrotum on the fancy horse. Blue wondered if Tom would say anything about that one? He led his own mare outside, eased himself down in the shade to wait for Tom to come tell him what to do.

Because it wouldn't help, would it now, to come in between them, like landing between a hammer and nail. Better to have this job, that woman to cook, and warm the bed. 'Cause I knowed long time ago no way I was gonna go back to spittin' in some bunkhouse stove wishin' somebody else'd put wood in it or at least go outside an' pack some in, listenin' to a horny bunch a perpetual losers go on 'bout what they'd do if and when they found the inclination, or the money. Better off knowin' ain't nothing gonna come of all your big dreams—better t' be sittin' with your boots off, socks up next to the fire already built when you come inside; that homely but big-busted woman there askin': 'You want more coffee, Blue? with a touch a the cure in it this time?' Common law or not, she ain't gonna trail along just to somewheres else—you think she's gonna clean out some other rat's nest of a bunkhouse? No, she done made that clear. Mind my own business, keep my nose out, 'specially when there ain't nothin' gonna come of it 'cept get it bloodied.

* * *

Tom had waked up that morning in a terrible fury, a nightmare of apprehension, the age-old rage—his jaws ached from suppressing it; the remnants caused him to lay stiff as a corpse, waiting for the anger to fade—be gone—like a fit finally dwindling away. Tom knew it was merely withdrawing from the surface: *I see it so clear, how it should have been, I resent how it's turned out so wrong.*

He'd dressed in the dark, an hour before dawn, went to putter in the kitchen, boiled an egg, made tea from the same water. But he'd paid no attention to the time; the egg was sadly underdone. He poured the tea down the sink after a taste, glanced up as his granddaughter came out fully dressed. Tom never bothered to hear the kitchen door open or close, could not have told anyone whether Sarah had gone out or not. He was listening to a cow still bawling hoarsely in the corral. Short that cow's calf, two bulls, and another pair. Tom blamed TJ for most of it.

He moved outside, stood by the dinner bell with hat in hand, poised like a man at the edge of a morning stretch. But Tom never bothered: It was no more necessary to stretch his way into the morning than it was to hope or pray. He waited, while the grey faded and the sun came up to touch the hills, until Blue finally came yawning out from the bunkhouse. Tom heard the kitchen door creak behind him, turned, and told Frank to round up Blue, push all the cows except that one bawling back into the woodlot, shut the gate. Tom stayed behind, the process of waiting not so hard now: Something, at least, was getting done. He listened absently to the one cow calling, her cry not emotional—no longer even expressing concern—merely a dull, monotonous, animal pronouncement of some dim sense of loss and a complaint about a tight bag. Tom waited until TJ came stumbling out. Then he told his son what he'd decided for the black stud.

And when he'd finished, Tom moved on to the barn, not following TJ—Tom never followed anyone—he'd sent TJ fleeing ahead trying to get out of his way. He saddled his mare, stepped aboard while she was still inside, ducked through the barn door, and rode on through the corral gate his son had left swinging in his rush to escape. Tom picked up the lone cow TJ never knew he'd let out, shoved her off the sparse alfalfa and turned her up the road between the hawthornes amd the cottonwoods alongside the dry creek. Tom never bothered to look back to see if the other men followed. He pushed the cow hard beneath an overcast sky which had turned now to the color of pus, the night chill changing to an oppressive heat, a gluelike humidity that made you want to scream. Tom glanced for the time, found the sun a punishing blaze, huge behind cloud cover near seven o'clock.

He kicked the mare and drove the cow at a brutal lope across two miles of burnt meadows and out through the pasture gate, never bothered to wait for the other men, left them to decide for themselves where to turn off to work. He booted his mare viciously all the way up the first hill, passing by the winded cow halfway along . . . the mare stood trembling, mouth open and sides heaving, when she finally made the top. Tom turned in the saddle and stared north.

He could see distant hills, twenty miles away, foggy through the hazy heat, high sandstone ridges where the river bent around to pass through the gap. He could see sunlight winking like from off a beer can tossed in the right-of-way ditch: reflection of a metal roof on some oil field supply shed at the outskirts of town. Tom blew his nose between his fingers (the day's first act of cleansing):

Damned ugly shacks spring up overnight like cow turd mushrooms, on that beautiful bottomland—alfalfa fields been there all my life, go by next time they's buildings everywhere. Blade the hay off those riverbank meadows— unlimited water—'til they ain't nothing left but blow sand again; blacktop the whole place just to hold it down in the wind. Then a hundred shanties drop out of the sky, because it's level, ready without work, all that lovely hay ground.

Tom spit: Town's changed so's you don't know it— don't know nobody in it—they can all go to hell. He squinted toward the town again; and while he watched he saw the reflection dim beneath cloud shadow, wink out. Tom began to curse in a slow, low, ugly monotone: He cursed the town, cursed the world, he swore sullenly at the way of his life. And when he'd finished, he found it not near enough. So he stuck the mare hard in the ribs with his spurs—heard her grunt with surprise, and felt her lunge beneath him ahead along the slope:

All I wanted was something I could be sure of, that was all I ever did need—I tried awful hard, gave it everything I got. But still it never come. Don't own my land, don't own my cows, all's I do is go to town whenever the bank calls me in so's I can find out what they think I should've done, when they already know I know the past is past and can't be done again, like they're my daddy making sure I learned a lesson after I done wrong. I gave my boy!—didn't mean a thing. Because what kind of collateral is a dead son?

Tom felt the wind come suddenly from out of nowhere, smelled the scent of fresh rain blowing in from over the hill. He heard the slow, brooding grumble of far-off thunder, the cow behind him bawling once wheezily as if in reply. He drew a shuddering breath, as from a child after crying, swung the mare down the grade. A scattering of raindrops came pelting up the slope like it was hunting him; he felt a ragged shower sweep over, pass on. Tom thought, you're a little late, rain—I could've used you a month ago, not gonna make much difference now.

Just a place of my own, nobody to tell me what to do. I never meant no harm, only meant to get by. Tom looked to the earth, and he knew from what he saw that his pastures were badly overgrazed, quite possibly damaged forever.

Well, what'd you expect—ain't my fault a cow's worth no more now than she was twenty years ago, everything else is ten times as high, though the Lord knows how many more people there must be would gladly eat the beef. Got to run more cows just to break even; and this old earth can't afford it.

Tom shook his head.

Used to be different. Man comes around—used to be you knew him—car dealer from town, maybe the banker hisself. Lots easier then to sit back and listen while he explained: Wanted a little chunk of the mountaintop for summertime, he'd like to build a cabin somewheres so he could get away. Lots easier then to say, well, I know how you feel, 'cause if I wanted you around, I'd move to town myself.

But now? Now, a helicopter comes over, some sorta man up there driving for some other sorta man way off yonder—wall map in his office, pin stuck right on top my head. I don't know him, no desire to; yet here he comes, scares hell outa my cows, sets down right in the middle of my alfalfa field. Whips out the map an' tells me: 'Show me where's this land.' Because there's a chance there might be something under it, and they want to know so's they can lay claim.

'Well, goddamn,' I says, 'I believe that land is mine!'

And this old boy he takes a look around like he can see something I can't, says, offhand-like: 'We pay real good for right-of-way, maybe you could use the cash. Anyhow, all you got is surface right; we can take what's underneath.'

Here I've been running cows on it and hunters off it my whole life; along comes this sombitch, says when I dig a posthole I'm trespassing. And the banker advises me I should let them look! Maybe they'll find something, help out with the debt . . . tells me it's better than waiting for the price of cows to come up.

Tom ducked his head, like dodging a blow: Price of cows ain't gonna come up—

Ahead, all at once, out of ragged brush a nice mule deer buck came crashing up from its bed—wide rack of horns all polished of velvet, nice clean stride to take him bouncing up the hill. It turned at the very top, stood poised and handsome. Tom waved a lazy hand. Yeah, you look real fine.

But it wasn't a huge deer. Tom thought, You don't see huge deer, not anymore, like you never see the big cats. I remember the last time I saw a lion track, it was . . . lordy! Has it been that long? There, in the canyon, where the mountain lion had smashed the thin ice at the edge of a seep, mud still swirling in the fresh pug marks, minutes old. Tracks like bloody shadows against the snow where the lion had stalked out of the red mud and climbed up across the drift heading for the top, the path as clear as the cries of the magpies telling all the world a man was here.

I stayed hunched in the bottom beside this very horse who was still young then, high-strung and skittish of the lion scent. I thought of borrowing the dogs—just the dogs, and not the men whose dogs they were, who'd whoop it up along the trail, thinking it a game instead of the earth's own religion; who'd shoot the lion to bloody rags at trail's end, cut off the tail and wave it around. I sat there thinking how hot I was to do it . . . never did. The sun would get the snow, earth the blood—why hurry it—tomorrow it would still turn out the same. How long's it been? a god-awful long time. I quit because they were becoming scarce as old friends.

You've got no old friends.

'S zackly what I mean. All I got are these cussed disputes I carry on in my head. And I lose both sides of them too, in the end—

Tom was in the bottom, he couldn't recall coming down.

Had the mare done it, all on her own, his old friend, with her muzzle turning white and her eyes grown misty? He'd better think twice before he kicked her around again. There was Frank, not thirty feet away, staring at him from across the wash. Tom had the feeling there was a question hanging, which he'd not heard, thought: Got to quit this, that man over there's gonna think I've grown rickity. Tom looked around, saw a lame bull—same one left behind yesterday—still bedded in the same brush, hugely obvious but trying to hide. And Blue was coming down, driving a lonely calf off the hill.

Frank spoke carefully, like he was repeating for the deaf: "Tom, I don't think this bull's gonna make it over the top, if that's what you had in mind. I come to ask, maybe we should just take him home?"

Tom squinted, looked to Frank, swung to regard the bull. There was a flash of lightning, thunder crashed, deafening in the muggy stillness. Frank's horse shied, and Blue ducked and hugged his saddle horn, stayed low as he came on in. "Christ!" Blue announced as he pulled up beside them.

Tom turned to study a very black sky, imminent threat of rain, shook his head. There came another rumble, muted, but not far. Tom decided, "All right, we gather the bull, this here scrub calf, take them back—you think the bull can make it? We'll pick up the cow, see if we got a pair." Tom said, "Blue—" there came another deep boom of thunder, west, but closer, the sound rolling easily over them, crashing off the hillside and bouncing on. "No, Frank, you mind riding up the hill to bring down the cow? It'll be faster'n the trench Blue would have to dig all that way to stay out of the lightning."

Blue laughed, like it was a silly thing; still, he made no move to intervene when Frank swung his horse to go. Tom clutched, asked after the new man, "You all right with that, son? I mean, I'll go, if the stuff bothers you, too." Tom stopped himself there, wondering: What the hell am I doing? He looked to Frank who grinned lopsidedly. "Now that you mention it—"

Then a heavy shower caught them, sweeping in from

nowhere on a sudden, hard wind. The men ducked their heads, grabbed for their hats. Blue held up a hand to shield his face, yelled to the new man above the sound of pelting rain, "You're gonna get wet, hee." He gestured to the empty tie-down straps at the back of Frank's saddle where a rain-coat should have been. Chuckling still, Blue reached for his own—moaned, cursed—stared at Tom. "I knew it, I jus' knew I was forgettin' somethin'. Look here. I done went off an' left my slicker home—your fault, Tom, you was in such a godamn hurry to go."

"My fault?" Tom said. "Well, here, Blue, you can bor-row mine." Tom swung his mare so Blue could see, no coat either at the back of Tom's saddle. "Never figured it would rain again," Tom explained.

Blue sighed, spoke past water running in torrents off his hat brim, "Tom, you was wrong."

Tom nodded. "First time. Don't know how to handle it. Guess I'll go kill myself." He tapped the mare, rode off into the lightning to bring down the cow.

3.

TJ reined the black stud to stare down at the bull, dead for days, in this awful heat, the body drum-tight with bloat, which had swelled it over almost flat on its back, all four legs and its gas-filled member pointing to the sky. There were flies on the sand, flies on the thin grass, flies so thick on the bushes the branches swayed with their weight. They swarmed across the thin, blue skin where the belly hair had begun to slip and massed in the eye sockets where the vul-tures had been at work. The air was filled with the sound of their swarming, and their maggots spilled by the handfuls to the stained sand underneath.

Then another of the great birds labored up off the ground. The stud reared and backpedaled, plunged out of the brush, and with one great lunge leaped halfway up the gulley's bank. Now TJ could see plainly Tom's brand on the moldering hip. He fought the horse, trying to calm him, but the shadows came racing back down the hillside, and the stud tried to outrun them back across the draw. That's when TJ first noticed the cow and calf standing on the rim above him, the pair jittery, blowing snot from their noses wanting to be rid of the awful stench, their ears flicking forward and back again to make sure death did not sneak around from in front of them to take them from behind.

Well, what'd I expect? TJ thought. There was never the chance offered anyhow to let me skip by until tomorrow, say, when maybe I'd be stronger. Would these vultures care, one way or the other, whether I let them finish breakfast or go in and scare them off, them being raised on the final virtues of patience, knowing full well lunch wasn't about to walk away? I'm not even curious how it happened: Ol' bull, ambling along, glanced up and saw the honey end of some cow mooning down from the bank like the image of Lotsalust, dropped dead from heat. What I wonder is how come he had to land upside down instead of just falling over flat?

TJ sighed and climbed down off the nervous stud, tied the horse well back in the brush. He crouched and smoked a cigarette, lit another from the butt and filled himself with smoke. Carefully, he ground out the coal, moved on in, his eyes squinched against the terrible odor. The flies raised away in a storm, from off the thin grass, from off the soil and the bushes—the smell was horrendous. TJ cupped his hands to try to breathe. He clutched at a horn, tried to twist the head on its rigored neck, but the body lay rigid as an old dead log. TJ gagged, like on sulphur fumes, was retching before he could get scrambled away.

He spit and spit, hunkered down—suddenly slapped his arm with an open palm, caught a fly and crushed it, immediately was sorry. TJ pushed a hole in the sand with his fingertip, tumbled the fly's body in and covered it, but did not pray. He took a great gulp of good air, plunged back in, threw himself flat on his belly and dug furiously at the crusted green mess of sand beneath what would soon drip dry to be a white skull, burrowing with his hand down under a hard horn tip to tug at that rigid left ear (so's to have it all in one basket, decisive and complete, when he finally got around to telling Tom). There was nothing there but an empty hole where the ear tag should have been. TJ spidered away like a man fleeing noxious smoke, tried in vain not to be sick again. He wiped at the ground, flung back a handful of sand, stumbled off thinking:

'S just what I thought—ain't that what I figured, how it would all come up empty when I got to the end? But I've abandoned the middle ground, at least I've done that, where men think, and then do, and think they do good, feeling a certain satisfaction recollecting what they've done, while the best I can do is only break even, because that's what's expected and less ain't enough. Well, by God, I looked! I did that much. What more could he ask for, what more could a father want—?

The stud's head snapped up as TJ came thrashing through the brush; the horse blew through his nose and backed away. TJ stopped, squinted . . . sniffed carefully along his shirtsleeve for the telltale scent of death. "Whoa now," he whispered, "whoa—hey, goddamn you, whoa!"—dived for the reins as the horse wheeled to run. The leather went whistling through TJ's hands, leaving thin, twin bands of neatly polished skin, until the branch tore loose and a knotful of splintered wood jammed there, bloodying both his palms. The horse went grunting round in a circle, bucking at the empty flop of the saddle, trying to be rid of it and that strange bouncing object that trailed after him everywhere, crying out in a choked voice: "Whoa, whoa—hey!—come on, whoa . . ."

* * *

They came out at last on the high ground above the brush, TJ limping, leading the stud, still trying to tuck his shirttail back in below where the buttons were missing from the last three holes. The cow and calf were gone. TJ cursed himself and bent to search the ground for signs of their leaving, the thin grass crackling as the stud minced through it, the horse shying from grasshoppers, yanking TJ around. A few big Mormon crickets went scratching away, their bodies ponderous, too huge for hopping; one struggled, pinned by the juices from its own crushed abdomen in a faint cow track left scored in the hard clay. TJ winced, shuddered, mounted and pushed on. Half a mile along, he found the cow standing on the hillside, her calf beside her, staring down at him. The cow snorted once, then took out in a long, loping gallop, heading straight away from where TJ wanted her to go. TJ cursed again and kicked his horse after them, trying to head them off.

But he failed to beat them to where the trail crossed the bottom, skidded in late, felt the cow go shouldering past. The stud threw a fit, got tangled in the brush—TJ spent precious moments trying to get them lined out. By then the cow and calf had vanished again. TJ kicked the stud into a jittery run following the trail of hanging dust.

It was ominously quiet, stale, heavy air; a strange expectancy seemed huddled down—the crunch of gravel, snap of twigs—those sounds seemed cut off before they were fully carried out. Nothing moved, save a few sparrow birds flushed out from underhoof to flutter for an instant before diving back down and fusing with the sage; no wind—there seemed to be no air at all, like a vacuum had settled in, stifling even the breeze TJ should have felt while they hurtled along. The stud heaved raggedly and stumbled often; and TJ, too, felt he must struggle to breathe. He heard cattle plunge through the trees ahead—muted crash, scuffle of hooves across downed timber. He spurred the stud, pushed him hard, but the cattle had disappeared, their trail lost in the pine needles matting the ground.

So he missed it when the day grew darker as the sky curdled and shut out the sun. TJ was on hands and knees trying to trace out the maze of old cattle trails. He never saw the storm come in, never noticed how black the day had become until he took a guess at the cow's intentions, pushed back out into the open and topped the ridge, where all at once the clouds appeared like a huge dusky bruise spread out before him, trailing away beyond the western horizon. TJ saw the cow and calf working their way down the long slope, already nearly to the flats far below.

Behind him a sudden wind touched the balsam leaves, rattling them like something was following. TJ whirled and saw a rider way off down the valley, and then another, com-

ing on. He turned to stare at the storm again, watched the
first rain draw a curtain across the flats—saw lightning
reach down, stand, wink out. He shivered, peered around
again, saw the red coat of his father's sorrel mare huddled
with two others. TJ faltered . . . wavered . . . made up his
mind at last. He put the black horse over the edge, sent him
sliding down the slope following the cow straight into the
storm.

4.

Jackahearts, Karen thought. And I need a king. She
laid down the cards, turned three more: no help, red trey.
Karen listened absently to the pound of rain on the roof . . .
sighed, and shuffled the discard: Cheating at solitaire, look
how low I've sunk.
There came a rolling blast of thunder to envelope the
old house and pry its way in, rattling the loose windows and
banging in through the walls. Karen started, shivered,
found herself standing, moved to a window to peer out.
Raining hard, commencing to hail, the graveled yard ran
deep in dirty rivulets clogged with marble-sized pellets
while lots more splashed down. Karen wondered about the
men, began to worry. She thought of Owen, the night
before, talking on and on about some great palomino stallion, until Karen finally had to warn him to hush up and eat,
while that new man had grinned at her and winked. Karen
willed her mind around to think of TJ, somewhere out there
in the storm.

* * *

Summer of nineteen hundred and sixty-eight, teenaged
girl in a growed-up body, nothing to do in a sleepy cow
town. Saddled with idle time, sure, she led him on—all she
was doing was trying to have some fun, stave off the boredom, deal with the humdrum, leave him something to think
about on his long drive home. She got caught in a web, all

76

her own making, an insidiously addicting web that year after year snared a young woman or two—but she'd made no commitments, not once had she lied to him (vague designs on playing him out until something better came along)—so what had she done that had been so damned wrong?

It amazed her though—was shocking still—how suddenly she'd been tripped up, how hard she'd hit the ground.

She'd must have believed there was something romantic flowing like deep water beneath the sluggish surface of the dusty town, where downtown stores were passed slowly, begrudgingly, from ancient, bald, and wrinkled owner to middle-aged, balding, wrinkling son, the county's ranches going, if not to the bank by note of foreclosure, then on down the bloodline to a favorite one. She must have dreamed there was some brute, tough, wholly unbluffed and uniquely western chivalry hidden behind the poker faces folks wore to tolerate the foreign rabble, oil-field trash, just beginning to trickle in and soon to flood their town—took their money, oh hell yes, in exchange for whatever an Okie's heart might desire; so even the landless natives who otherwise had no chance at the pie in terms of mineral rights, salt domes, sour gas and crude, could do nearly as well yet still persist in pretending the boom did not exist beyond the gutters of old First Street with its shoddy bars and cheap hotels. She guessed she believed—it was hard to remember what life was like before that nine months began—it would run like the plot from a paperback western, some hometown champion arising out of the dirt and old horse dung to take to the saddle when the right time came along. She'd been stunned to discover—this part remains vivid—that local heroes were cheap: Wouldn't put out a quarter to purchase the armor from the vending machines in the truckstop john.

How, exactly, could she have been so damned dumb?

Those days oozed on, beginning with the hot dawn, the cottonwood cotton collecting in sleek, fuzzy blankets in the gutters with no wind to lift it save the solitary wash from a passing pickup truck loaded with block salt, fence posts, or a saddled horse, along the empty street once a half hour. At

the corner gas station little boys stole the matches absently
left behind in the chromed gums of the cigarette machine,
used them to ignite the perimeters of the cotton sheets and
squatted on the curb to watch the burning of it spread in
long, thin lines like prairie fire. They screamed to each
other how the ants caught in it, which would have been
Indians not long ago, now were Viet Cong, the napalm
dropped by snapping a match across the striker and flicking
it down; until a passerby, some old matron headed downtown, held up her skirts while she stomped out the flames,
took righteous pleasure in lecturing the little boys about
leaky gas tanks when there wasn't a car parked on the street
for blocks. On into those stifling hot and windy afternoons,
the little boys blowing back by, red-faced and puffing, on
bicycles now, ack-acking each other in a reasonable facsim-
ile of fighter planes' sounds as they shot each other down,
weaving back and forth across the centerline on Main
Street, the little boys wearing swimming trunks.

She watched them pass by with the rim of her eye, gazing vacantly into the mesmerizing reflection of the sun
coming off the melting asphalt, saw them, like she might
have seen house sparrows, unable to say afterwards if or
how many sparrows she'd seen, for, to her, they were
merely brown children who happened to exist during this
her seventeenth summer before the start of her senior year.
Still finally she followed them, as if caught in their draft,
tugged along by heat and boredom, drifting along later
climbing the sloping street leading away from the river
toward the city park and the swimming pool in company
with a girlfriend or two, the trip begun with the regal dig-
nity befitting new members of the reigning class at the
town's high school, which collapsed into giggles when they
took off the cover-ups they'd worn out of the house over
swimsuits purchased no more for swimming than they'd
been for constraint. Bought, instead, to show how little
girls do indeed grow up, strutting their stuff, mocking each
other, laughing both in pure joy and shame at what each had
or had not to wiggle or stick out.

Dressed like that, they took to the alleys, striding
unawares on long, clean limbs out into the same frozen bub-

ble that contained the old widow who glared at them over her backyard fence: "You young ladies should go home and put on something decent. Out here in your underwear, for heaven's sake!" She was huffy with anger, or envy (or fear?), having watched her own youth die half a century before while her heart kept on beating, the memory of her own summertime still so clear it seemed like yesterday, so little had happened since. They ran away snickering, yelling back insults, as oblivious to old anger as they were to the web being spun around them.

So the banks of thunderheads that built late each afternoon were as monotonous as the sunrise each morning of the week, as anticipated by now as the ring of the telephone had become across the last eight months, along about suppertime, while the television ran war coverage on the evening news. It was all he could do after so many near misses, coming closer, he hoped, to glory each time, to call, and arrange it so he could try again: install her in his pickup truck, speed away into the hot night, the radio on, her buttons undone while her heart revved up, edging closer and closer by the whisper of moonlight off bare skin—until she thought to check her watch: late! She pushed him off, pulled herself upright, wiped the steam from the inside of the windshield with her own shirt so he could see to speed her home—she dressed, while he drove—she dashed inside, half an hour past midnight, told her grim-faced mother some alternate version of the same old song, either the picture show had run late or else his truck had stalled again. She thought, Don't worry, mother, I'm still intact—it won't be with him, I can promise you that.

* * *

She lay spinning in a lawn chair in her own backyard, while the last of the sunlight poured down hot on her bare legs and black clouds spit lightning at the edge of town. Thunder rolled softly way off in the distance like the sound of guns behind the correspondent on the evening news— until the crackling white light and the crash of thunder became like two hands clapping. Her mother called nervously from behind the closed screen:

"Don't you think you'd better come in?—oh, there's the telephone. And it's probably that boy again. Don't you think you ought not to go out with him anymore? You know how easy it is to get serious, too soon."

So she'd fled inside, treading the razor's edge of some fiery kind of tension just ahead of the first hard spatters of cooling rain. Through the window she watched the cotton washing down the gutters while the voice from the television worked through the day's casualties. She told him (while her mother quietly set the supper table, taking a long time about it, listening in): "No, TJ, not tonight." She smiled, both at the frustrated silence from the other end of the line and the relief suddenly blossoming on her mother's face. "Because I already made plans to go to the drive-in with my friends."

The drive-in? His voice brightened. Well, maybe he'd see her there?

"Maybe so," she told him; and she had to bite her lip to hold back her laughter when she heard his hope come bubbling back. "Yeah, okay! See you then." She saw her mother freeze, like from a sudden chill, turn slowly, and frown. "See you, TJ."

As she hung up the phone, her mother asked, "See him where, when? Karen, didn't we just decide to tell him not to come around?"

* * *

When she opened the door of the pickup truck, by the dim gleam from the cab light she saw a surge of empty bottles come spilling off the seat and floorboards, rattle into darkness, clank on the ground. She saw Jesse slumped behind the steering wheel; she was hit by the smell of stale beer. Karen raked more trash out of the way, climbed on in and slammed the door.

He woke then, stirred . . . must have seen her, because he asked blearily, "Who hell're you?"

Karen told him, "I heard they gave you orders, whatever they do; they're sending you over there."

Jesse struggled upright, peering at her across a bottle,

with his hat scrunched sideways so part of his shaved head showed by the flickering light of the movie screen. He fumbled at his shirt pocket, clumsily fingered a huge pinch of tobacco into his lip, lifted the bottle as if to drink from it, spit in it instead, said: "Who say so?—sen' me noplace I don' wanna go? An' who th' hell're you, in my truck, I never as't you to?"

Jesse seemed to notice then as if for the first time that his hand held a bottle. He blinked . . . lifted it, drank deeply. His face grew puzzled—eyes flared wide—he turned and blew the mouthful of used tobacco spit point-blank against the closed window, threw the bottle at the floor. Karen felt its contents splash her leg, thick, slick fluid oozing into her shoe. She shuddered, while Jesse pawed through the trash on the seat until he found one unopened. He rinsed his mouth, swallowed the wash, drank long.

Karen said, "So I thought maybe you might want to talk about it, before you have to go—"

Jesse lurched suddenly for the dashboard, groping there with a clumsy hand; the cab light came on, horns behind them began to honk. He peered at her, leered: "Thought for minute you mus' be social worker, but you only li'l high school girl." He sniggered again, the sound fading . . . his head sagged . . . until his chin rested on his chest. Karen cleared her throat, watched him bob back up; he lashed out at the dash again. The cab light blinked out and the car horns quieted behind them. He snorted, slobbered, wiped his mouth with a sloppy hand: "Wha' say name was?"

So Karen told him, in her best shy voice, said, "You're taking this well, you must be brave. Isn't there something I can do? Anything I can give you? Some sort of farewell, until you come back home?" Karen was thinking he might treasure a kiss.

"Karen," Jesse muttered, "Karen . . . ha!—you th' one li'l brother sparkin'? You TJ's girl?" Jesse giggled—"Hee hee"—his hat tumbling as his head flopped and rolled.

"What's so funny?"

"You funny, you an' TJ."

"Why? What's funny about us?"

"Jus' com'cal, 's all. TJ's odd fellow—you mus' not know him ver' well, else you'd un'stan'.."

81

"What do you have against TJ?"

"Nothin'. Don' have nothin'. Don' hardly ever think of'm."

"Is that it then? That's what's so amusing?"

"Guess so." Jesse yawned. "Things seem never go well f' TJ, don' work out. He jus' always chooses wrong direction, steps inna shit, gits han'-me-downs." Jesse stirred. "Anyhow, wha' makes you think I come back? Wha' makes you think I live to?"

Karen shivered prettily: "Don't say that!"

"Don' matter." Jesse sneered. "I ain' lef' nothin' here." He turned on her, staring at her chest: "So, wha' you wanna do f' me, Karen? Wha' you su'gest?"

* * *

Crickets were grinding in the stalks of seeding clover, lightning danced in the clouds far off east. The dusty smell of crushed sage came floating in through the open window, with the lights of town spread like two legs wrapped around the river below where they wrestled on the pickup seat—

"Jesse, no!" She pushed him off, dropped her jeans on her shirt on the floor. She lay back down, expecting another brutal kiss, mouth slack, eyes closed; with Jesse back on top of her, forcing her wide, moving against her—her eyes flew open—she tried to close—"O-oh!"

". . . Okay," she whispered, "But hurry. I got to get home."

* * *

Not unlike a cow, Karen thought, I'm so damned fertile—I should have had twins, what with TJ, afterwards. She watched the electricity dance outside the window, wondered again about the men. Karen thought suddenly, Where is Owen, where can he be? She turned, and went through the house almost running, scolding herself for being so mindless—she glimpsed furious lightning through a window, blindingly bright on the hill across the creek. Karen tensed . . . quaking with the old house inside a thunderous blast. Shivering, she hurried on down the dark hallway to the baby's room. Sarah was there, sitting on the floor, slowly rocking back and forth, holding her baby sister. Karen sighed, somewhat relieved, "Have you seen Owen? Is he inside, too?"

"Don't know." Sarah rocked. "He was out on the porch earlier, watching the storm."

"Baby all right?"

"She was bad scared, but it helped some when I picked her up. Do you want to hold her? My arms are 'bout numb."

"I have to find Owen."

"Wait!—don't go. I was scared, too. This is a bad storm, isn't it—that lightning, jeez!"

"Don't say 'jeez.'"

"I won't—I'm sorry. I was mostly scared it would hit the house. TJ says sometimes it comes down the chimney, on in to the stove. Could that happen here?"

"Oh, TJ says lots of things—" Karen stopped herself; she wasn't being fair. "Well, I guess it could . . . ." She stopped again when she saw the fear in Sarah's eyes, thought: Say something right, Karen, for heaven's sake. "It's all chance, Sarah. There are lots of things outside for lightning to strike instead of this old house. Almost any-thing out there is more likely—"

"Like if you're on a horse?" Sarah said. "What about TJ? On a horse, stuck up in the air. Will TJ be all right?"

Karen smiled wearily. "And Tom? Blue? And what about Frank? You know how the men are—they always come through fine." Karen turned away, hurried off to look for Owen.

He was on the porch, staring out into the storm. He turned to the sound of the opening door, and Karen saw how soaked he was, clothes dripping, face wet; wild, happy eyes. Karen was stunned. Why, he looks exactly like . . . not much doubt who his father was.

Through the screen, Karen could see a thin line of light growing in the west, the hail tapering off to soft, splashy pellets, rain fading to a drizzle. Most of the thunder came from behind the house now, east in the distance, with just a few strokes of lightning scattering nearby. One popped, very close, the thunder striking mother and son like a blast of wind.

"That," Owen spoke reverently, "was one hell of a storm."

"Owen!" Karen cried, "What's the matter with you? You can't use curse words, I won't allow it! Don't you ever let me catch you saying such a thing again!"

"Okay, all right! Do you think Frank and Blue and Old Tom made it through alive?"

"And TJ? Yes, the men know how to take care of themselves. But . . . then you haven't seen them?"

"No. What a storm! Musta rained a foot, prob'ly's gonna flood! You think so? Think it'll flood? That'd be something!"

Karen smiled down at him, pushed open the screen and peered out, then stepped into the light rain, Owen following, the screen door banging because no one thought to catch it. Karen turned to scold him, frowning her displeasure. But Owen was shouting: "Hey, there they come! And they got cows—I'm gonna go help!"

"Owen, no!" Karen said. "Not in the mud. Anyhow, you'll just be in the way, scare the cattle, like you did yesterday."

"I never scared no cows yesterday. All's I'm gonna do is open the gate, for Christ sake." He turned and raced off, and his mother sighed. "Owen, please don't use His name in that way."

She stood for a moment on the step, watching the riders, then she walked out toward them . . . saw three. Karen could not find the black horse TJ rode. She moved further along, with growing concern, could see the cattle more clearly now: two cows, no, a cow and calf pair, and a lame bull hobbling slowly along behind. There was Tom. And Blue and Frank. But no TJ. Karen drifted along the fence, stood waiting at the corner, goosebumps on her arms from the chill after the rain. She hugged herself, watching as the little wet cavalcade came on in.

Here was Blue, riding into the muddy yard, soaked and

miserable, but smiling still, offering an outrageous bow from the saddle. Frank touched his hat, then quit the tired cattle and turned his horse to join Blue at the fence. "Whee," Blue said, wringing water from his sleeve.

Karen smiled, trying her best to be calm: "Have you seen TJ?" She saw Blue cock an ear, as if unsure he'd heard her right.

"TJ? He ain't been in yet?"

"No, I don't think so." Karen felt another chill, a prickle of alarm. "I haven't seen him since he left with you this morning."

"He's not been with us," Frank told her. "We haven't seen him since he went out alone—"

"Now wait." Blue turned, stared hard at Frank. "I'm sure those was his tracks we seen on our way in—I bet he's in the barn, right this minute, laughing at us drowned out here in the rain."

Frank frowned, "I don't recall—" noted the warning in Blue's eyes. "Oh . . . sure, the tracks."

"Uh-huh." Blue smiled. "I bet he's yonder. We'll send him to see you, Karen, soon as he gets through givin' us a hard time."

"I just want to know everything's all right," Karen said. "That was some storm, wasn't it."

"Wet one, sure," Blue said. "Worst goddamned lightning I think I ever seen."

"Don't say—" Karen rolled her eyes. "Owen has the gate open for you."

"That's some boy," Frank said. "Always on top of what's to happen next. You must be real proud, son like that." Frank said to Blue, "We better git, 'fore Tom does it all, realizes he don't need us around." Frank touched his hat again, swung to go.

Karen, gazing after him, thought, Thank you, Frank, for noticing.

5.

All his life, TJ had dreaded lightning—that chance for a blinding white death like the flip of a coin. When he was young, and thunder gave a slow roll out of the summer afternoon—a sound that froze him, put ice in his heart—he'd hunker down, stare at the sky, noting for the first time the great black cloud suddenly rearing up over the western horizon. It made him realize how empty hope was, he'd been hoping since the last storm lightning might never come again.

He'd try then to remember where they'd gone, father, brother, especially Mom. The first two were out working, who knew where they went—no sense whatsoever in looking for them. But she wasn't in the garden, nor was she at her flower beds, so maybe she was inside, where she should be, because it was supposed to be the safest place, in a lightning storm. Anyhow sooner or later the storm would drive him in, too, but he didn't want to be alone in there, under those cracked ceilings the thunder might shake down. He had a serious sinking feeling she'd told him earlier that she was off for somewhere, he'd been only half listening, involved as he was in the level of imagination a little boy must sustain who played all alone. Now it was too late to run and look for her, no idea where to look anyhow—hey, maybe if he rang the dinner bell! No, he guessed he'd better not.

What TJ wanted was to gather everyone and tuck them away inside the big house where he could see for certain they were still alive and well, not because he believed he could protect them in there, for he'd heard the story how lightning had come down a chimney, blew some stove to smithereens. He could no more protect them than he could find means to call them home, for they might all come running to the tolling of the dinner bell, but then they'd laugh at him and his childish fears or else curse the interruption.

So he crouched and watched the storm come on, mesmerized, like a rabbit watching a snake, that dog sitting beside him wanting petted, it was all the dog ever seemed to need. The clouds drifted in, almost serenely, those soft, far-off rumbles amiable now in the quiet afternoon, the fresh smell of rain coming ahead on an easy breeze like an emissary of good faith. TJ knew better. He knew the breeze was an ally sent before the storm, whose mission was to lull him into dropping his guard. The breeze freshened and hissed in the trees, as if ashamed and angry at having been found out. The trees tossed in torment, bowed by the gale that picked up bits of things to hurl; sand and hard splatters of rain stung TJ's face—

Then the clouds spit fire; thunder screamed with glee, for hadn't that boy been so neatly deceived, who knew already how devious these storms could be. (For hadn't he seen himself the corpses of horses, killed by lightning not outright and proper but because one of them was on the wrong side of the fence, and the other two were lending comfort, hanging their necks across the wires when lightning struck a post way off somewhere else. "Musta been what happened here," Blue had said, "'cause they's all been branded beneath the chin, popped their eyes right outa their heads.") Now he'd let this one sneak up and pounce on him: lightning flickering down all around followed so closely by the thunder—one thousand boom!—the deafening blast came while the blistering white light still stood shivering in the graveled yard, so near he felt the heat of it; and the charge conducted through the wet air was like when his older brother had once touched him with an electric cattle prod.

The screen door banged, he was crouched behind it, no memory at all of having come in. The dog was choking, struggling on a stranglehold, ready to curl around and nip the hand that held his collar twisted so, in there where the broom had taught the dog long ago he was not allowed to be. Then God or Whoever let fly another of His arrows to hit precisely what He intended for there followed God's own merry thunder of applause—the dog was free—at least no longer shackled by a hand to the boy; though still very much a prisoner who could do no more than whine and scratch the door and pound a wet tail on the floor beside where the boy huddled crying, waiting for someone to come home.

Finally. . . she came.

The dog was out, screen door banging (as if in her absence the dog had learned to let itself in and back out again). She scolded it briefly in the pouring rain, sent it slinking off toward the barn, the porch floor a mess of muddy paw prints mixed with the footsteps made by a little boy. She tried the kitchen door, expecting it stuck (wet weather, and a crumbling foundation); turned the knob and lunged against it, found it not even latched, merely bumped up against the jamb—sent her hurtling on into the room where she discovered him crouched in the entrance to the hallway.

He asked her immediately, voice quavering through chattering teeth, like she'd done something awfully wrong, "Mom, where you been?"

"TJ," she said, "how'd you get so wet? Come over here, I'll build a fire, we'll get you warmed up." Ka-rack! went the lightning, right outside the door; thunder rattled the walls, making both them jump. He was staring at the ceiling when the lights blinked out. "I don't think so," he told her, "a' you'd ought to get away from that stove, too."

"Damn!" she said (her strongest word, until years after), as she brushed past him on down the hallway to that tiny room where she kept things stored. When she returned, bringing back the strong smell of kerosene, she draped him in a blanket, set the oil lamp on the table, working quickly to wipe clean the globe, as he watched, fascinated, the oily smoking of the wick's naked flame, a solid stream of carbon drifting off in soft, snaking tendrils. He caught one, held the smoke like a feather, stared at the black smudge it made across his skin. Sorcery: For while outside the calm splendor of summertime was shattered—survival out there was a matter of chance alone never minding how he was young and good and terrified of dying—inside, smoke lay solid in the palm of his hand.

"Mother," he asked her, her face by lantern light all hard planes and shadows, "how can this be?"

"Hush," she told him, "no reason to cry. That's just the way things are."

* * *

TJ was halfway down the hillside when the real wind caught him, bringing rain like gravel flung against his face—he was halfway to the bottom when the heart of the storm came flailing out of the west like a barrelful of boom whose staves caved in straight over his head. The stud whirled on the steep slope like he meant to take the barn in one good leap, while thunder roared like sheets of tin in the wind and the rain poured down like God's own toe had hooked out the plug.

TJ was down in the mud now, trying to hold the stud; he couldn't recall having been thrown, so he figured he must have stepped off to get his slicker on. "Whoa!" he yelled. "Christ sakes! Ain't you seen lightning before?" But the stud kept whirling, TJ chasing after him, fumbling with the wet leather tie-downs behind the saddle with fingers shaking even more fiercely than the black horse was. Across the stud's back TJ could see lightning—one, two, three bolts at a time; and way down below, bleary through rain like a bad watercolor, he could just make out the dark shape of the cow, leading her calf on.

So he fought his way into the raincoat, the slicker popping like firecrackers in the hard, wet wind. TJ struggled back on, pointed the stud more or less downhill—jabbed with his spurs and grabbed for his hat, just managed to catch the brim of it. He stuffed it inside his coat and rode bareheaded down the slope, one hand up trying to shield his eyes during those rare moments when he dared to let loose of the saddle horn, the stud leaping bushes, plummeting ten yards at a time, landing slithering, sliding, plowing full tilt down the greasy slope, front legs stuck out like poles trying to check the skid, hind legs splayed like the runners of a sled, TJ not so much riding, but more along for the ride, like some chap in earring and leathers might try to pray a big hog across an oil-slicked piece of highway. They were still together, one on the other, when they hit the bottom, with mud clinging to both stirrups and stuffed down TJ's boot from when the stud lost his footing and plunged sideways on his knees for the last fifty feet to the flats.

Like a tabletop, TJ thought with wonder, staring off across the plain: swales and shallow swells—nothing higher than a yucca spike towering its full twenty inches above the stunted grass and antelope browse. No place out there where TJ's bare head would not stick up like a monument to idiocy, even if he walked. TJ was alone, the stud having no more sense than a tractor would about which way to go. Then lightning struck the nearest knoll, and the thunder that followed nearly knocked them both flat. TJ was down again, dragging on the reins. This time, he told himself, he was searching for sign.

There was a faint trace of a trail, melting quickly in the downpour, cow tracks made in mud, trudging off into the rain. He turned to follow, dragging the frightened stud behind him, slipping, sliding, in old smooth-soled boots, thinking: I couldn't catch a dead cow going at this rate. So he climbed back on, sent the stud trotting alongside the worn cow path, now a channel of filthy water like a flooded irrigation ditch, TJ leaning way down, not to study the ground better, but to be closer to it. He was thinking of that dead bull, had there been any burn marks? How long now since the last lightning storm? But down in that gulley— was no place safe? Got him to contemplating the root cellar dug back underneath the ranch house: dark, dry, walled with rock—if he could be there now he swore to God he might never come back out. He kicked the stud into a fidgeting gallop, the horse loping sideways against the wind and rain.

They crossed three ridges abristle with lightning, forded two shallow swales running water hock deep, before they found the old cow standing placidly chewing her cud, her calf huddled beside her downwind. TJ swooped in, howling like a banshee: "Heeeyaw! Whooey!"—yanked the stud to a splashy stop; both stood staring, waiting on a response. The cow traded cheeks with the wad of her cud, calmly closed her eyes again against the pouring rain.

Then the most recent of lightning bolts—still smelling of the forge—sheared out of the sky and crashed to earth beside them. TJ was down for a third time, tingling from the shock of it, crawling stunned on hands and knees beneath the plunging stud (no excusing him his fear this time: he could feel a warm wetness at the crotch of his jeans). Down underneath this four-footed lightning rod where if the lightning don't get me this horse'll tromp me in the mud. He grabbed for a stirrup, crawled hand over hand until he'd found his feet again—there was a deafening crash—crisp lightning glimmered at the edge of TJ's vision like the crinkling lights at the onset of a migraine. "Jesus!" TJ screamed—he couldn't help it—thought: So what's gonna happen if I do catch the calf?

He tied off his rope to the saddle horn, built a wet loop, but never climbed back on: TJ wasn't much at roping anyhow, and he'd not ever tried it from the back of the stud. He managed to force the horse to follow him back to where the cow still stood watching now each time the horse and the crazy man on foot chased her calf round her like she was a maypole. TJ let fly, missed the calf by a yard, saw the rain stiffened rope slap up against the cow's wet hide. He watched the old cow blow snot and go rolling out of the bottom, her calf swinging to follow, running head and shoulders through the stiff, standing loop.

The noose tightened down like a bucking cinch, way back around the big calf's flanks; the rope came snaking up out of the filthy water flooding deep enough now to fill TJ's boots. He heard Blue's voice as if Blue stood right next to him: "Check that cinch, TJ—" saw his horse stagger sideways as the calf rammed the slack, the saddle holding for an instant before it came rolling off the horse's back. The stud went berserk, barreled up the gulley bucking at that strange, leachlike thing that had suddenly appeared clinging to his belly, snapped TJ face first into the filthy water, brought him plowing along behind at the end of the reins. TJ was thinking, That musta been the saddle blanket, yup, that must've been it, that soggy thing that had lodged for a moment against TJ's face before he was dragged on over it, left it floating off down the wash—I can't even let go—sledding along, throwing out spray, the calf thrashing on the rope right behind him, ready to drag right over him should he lose his hold. TJ had given up yelling, because last time he'd screamed, "Whoa!" he'd been force-fed enough water to fill both lungs with a little extra to shoot out his nose.

So maybe it was his waterlogged body together with the weight of the drowning calf plus the obvious effects when a horse tries to run wearing a saddle between its legs galloping up a gulley running water a foot deep that made the stud wear down, slow to a walk, wade on for a hundred yards, then finally stop. The horse stood leaning into the creaking rope that led from the horn of the inverted saddle back between his hind legs past TJ to the calf who'd managed to stand and was bucking feebly, facing the opposite direction. TJ rolled up, disgorged a gallon of filthy water to mix with the rest of the stuff coursing down the bottom waist-deep to now a sitting man.

It began to hail then.

6.

Blue was reminded—didn't yet know why—of a wasp he'd once seen involved in some dark work, a long time back on a hot summer day. Blue had been resting, shovel laid aside, at the head of a ditch in the shade of a cotton-wood tree, with nettles growing thick along the creek banks and a cow parsnip rooted in the damp soil, its fan leaves hung out over the water, its umbels of flowers drawing the sugar flies.

There'd been a solitary wasp hunting methodically along the stalks—hovering—and swooping in amongst the flowers and leaves, swinging out again carrying the body and fluttering wings of a captured fly. Blue had watched the wasp lug its load up to land with a bump on the sunny side of a cottonwood leaf, hunter and prey screened like a shadowbox for Blue underneath. Calmly, the larger shadow had slipped home its stinger; in a moment, the little bug had ceased to fight. Bits of mica fluttered away; something rattled like a grain of sand over the leaf's edge: The fly's wings were cropped, the body beheaded; the leaf bobbed once, and hunter and victim were gone. When Blue pulled the leaf down there was a jointed leg glued by bug juice to the leaf's slick face; the sugar flies were out again, swinging in droves. Blue was left in the grip of a lonely melancholy: How easy it was for life to end.

"Well," Tom said, striding out of the barn, "he sure as hell ain't here."

Frank grinned. "You check the mangers? Maybe he crawled in one to take a nap. Or maybe that witless horse of his throwed him so high he decided to hang around up there 'til the rain was done." Frank laughed aloud; laughed again indulgently when Tom growled:

"He's late, as usual. Rain's done, and he still ain't come down."

When Blue looked at Frank, and then back to Tom, he knew TJ didn't stand a chance. For even if TJ had some-how made it through the awful storm, Tom would clip his wings while Frank stung him from behind.

* * *

Of course it had to be Frank who found the first sign where TJ's horse had gone over the rim, leading Tom to remark, "Frank, I didn't know you was a tracker, too."

Blue felt forced then to straighten things out: "Ain't so much that. Frank's jus' got a good nose for horse shit." Sour grapes? Maybe so—Blue just couldn't stand the smug look on Frank's face. Blue led the way on over the edge, with Frank riding hard behind him; but Blue wouldn't sur-render the lead.

Half a mile out onto the flats they discovered the saddle blanket, soaked and leaking, lodged up against the sage. Blue volunteered Frank, since he was the tracker, to search down the draw, maybe he could find more hoof prints.

Tom said: "Whataya figure, Blue? That this here blan-ket floated upstream?"

But Blue was content, because the new man had already swung to start down that way; Frank had to turn and retrace his steps, in front of Blue and Tom, his face red.

They found tracks of a horse, and those of a calf; and underneath both were the boot prints of a walking man who plainly led the way, skidding in the greasy clay, the trail heading south. They found queer, snake-like signs slapped in the mud. Frank jumped on the theory it was marks from a rope, which made Blue cranky for being so slow. They began to discover clumps of foam slobbered out of a winded calf, so they knew the trail they followed was made after even the drizzle had stopped. When they topped the next rise, TJ was down below.

* * *

He never quit walking, never bothered to look around. When the tired stud tried to turn to nicker to the horses coming up behind, TJ trudged on monotonously, tugging at the reins, not quite plodding in place; until Old Tom pulled up in front of him, threw the blanket on the ground. TJ stared down at it . . . snuffled his nose, turned to unsaddle his horse.

Blue had hung back, meaning to keep out of the way, while father and son had their reunion. But Frank rode right up, ringside for the show. So Blue nudged his own horse ahead to join them—he didn't think it right, but he knew Tom alone was more than TJ could handle. If this new man thought to add anything, Blue meant to whop the lips off his face with a coiled rope.

Tom was saying: "Lost your cow, so you decided to wean the calf—drag him to death—that what you had in mind? You lost your blanket, couldn't ride, goin' completely the wrong way, stop me if I'm wrong, home's back behind; 's fair then to speculate you're lost your own self, on the very land where you growed up—you even lost your hat! 'sa only thing 'sides the cow we never found to tote along—"

Blue watched TJ reach a hand inside his mud-caked slicker, saw him tug out the squashed hat and raise it high. Tommy, Jr., jammed the crushed hat sideways on his head, said: "They's a dead bull back yonder in a gulley you missed, too—weren't my fault. He was like that when I found him. He didn't have no eartag, but maybe you can tell what one he was by the expression on his face."

Then Tom had nothing more to say. But Blue saw, as Tom spurred the sorrel mare away, how white the old man's face was, lips thin, jaw clenched and trembling. Still Blue waited, for he was certain the most important part was yet to come. He could feel Frank just itching to speak, could almost see it all turning inside Frank's brain, the building of the impudence it took to butt in. Blue inched his mare fore-ward, tightened his grip on the rope.

But Tom's boy took care of that, too—made Blue proud. TJ swung and stared at Frank, never even blinked, and though he should have appeared ludicrous—soaking wet, caked with mud, hat on sideways like from a three-day drunk—there was nothing funny about those cold, grey eyes. He shut Frank up without saying a word, swung him around and sent him trailing Tom. For a moment, TJ gazed after him, then he pursed his lips and looked to the ground.

"Something you want to add, Blue? Something that old fart mighta missed?"

Blue said gently, "I'll let the calf loose for you, son."

TJ had the stud saddled again by the time Blue returned, the cinch sucked up so tight it made the tired horse groan. He took the coiled rope Blue offered and stepped into the saddle, the stud standing, head hanging, too tired to even shy. As the men swung to go, the calf jerked to attention, began to tag along behind like he thought he was still caught. But he lagged farther and farther back . . . until at last he stood staring as the men rode on without him, spittle stringing from his mouth like the gossamer threads of a spi-der's web sparkling in the late sunshine.

Blue was saying, "Now don't start thinking on it, TJ, don't dwell on it, son. I'll come back tomorrow, gather that cow an' calf—they'll be back together by then—bring'm both in. So don't you give it 'nother thought—"

TJ raised his arm like to ward Blue off, fluttered a hand so Blue would shut up.

Still, Blue had to add: "You know, TJ, you was the only one had sense enough to've took along a slicker."

* * *

She made love to him in the night, Karen sensing his torment, felt his pain. She'd heard the story anyway, while she'd leaned in the doorway of the barn, interrupting Blue from time to time to remind her son: "Don't curse the cows, Owen," or: "Don't you dare use his name that way," Owen, slowly milking, muttering: "Three times, in two days! Last night, this morning, and here tonight again. I'll be milkin' for the rest of my life, for Christ—" She rolled to TJ in the dark, curled against him, felt his terrible tension as he fought to find a handle on the day all used up and gone. She climbed on top, over the strong smell of whiskey, settled in.

And TJ felt her go, her hands on his shoulders pinning him down, while she rode him to a standstill, bucking him out. She shuddered, rolled off . . . slept nestled tight behind him, her breasts pressed against his back like the warm muzzles of a double-barreled gun. TJ wondered, had he given her pleasure? Or had she taken it—ripped it from him—another part of all he'd lost? So, then . . . were days like that, living, breathing entities, out to get him given half a chance—adversaries, enemies?—Christ!—days, too? TJ tried all night to think it through . . . crawled cold and aching into the dawn, drenched with sweat and wrinkled like a drowned man.

Wednesday,
8th August

1.

Day breaks cool, and fresh and clean—there'd even been dew in the night from the rain, crystal droplets clinging to the cheat grass shimmering like quicksilver in the first light.

But the dew will rise with the sun. Wind will come again to belly through the thin grass; midmorning gusts will kick up dust along the county road, the puddles' silt floors already cracked and curling. Water beetles will fry on the hoods of the vehicles, the smooth reflection of sun off paint all they can find that faintly resembles water.

While inside the storm still rages: that conflict forever summoning the soul of everyman out to buck the day. Time never slows, but sluggish humanity, at each day's end, must stop, to rest, and puzzle things through, their only tool slow thought walled up inside a skull. Resigned to creeping along in the dust left by the heels of a fleeing world, they dream: If only I could have it so I made the world turn, instead of at best being pliant, at worst subservient, to the interminable grindings of a wheel.

If only—

What? exactly, would you have the world do? Stand still, for you? So you at your own pace could catch your breath, perhaps pull even: walk burdened neither by yesterday's failures nor tomorrow's doubts straight into the present—step not only into the Moment but into Time itself, where all moments are suspended—where else could they have gone?—each wing stroke pumping a northbound goose home across the spring sky. Where is your childhood? Where are mother's hours? Unless here, in the Moments, recorded heartbeat for heartbeat, set down faithfully like the minutes of a meeting, assembled meticulously like commerce accounts, so you can view them and know for certain what was, is, and forever will be, useful and worth doing, business in the black; and what is, will be and always has been, red ink, a waste of precious time. You'd like it so easy?—

No, life's knocked you down! You want revenge, for all those holes left in your heart by exploded dreams. You vow: I'm willing to take the world on not only at its own game, but on its own turf and terms. You shudder, having sworn such an oath, for you know instinctively that you're not up to the fight. Because you're blind; you cannot see what's coming up next moment, let alone next week—

See? Down below, a snake is crawling out of shadow, easing into the sunlight stiff as an old man's morning joints, waiting for the heat of the moment to dictate its fate. That snake has its part to play, same as you; and, same as him, you don't know what your role will be. You must wait, and see, and abide by the differences when all's said and done.

2.

Sarah turned in her bed, carefully hooded her head so all she could see was the window, grey with first light, and the wall immediately to each side. She thought: Make believe I'm outside, doesn't matter where, where there are cows, or horses, or people I know. And along comes a storm. (Sarah could hear her heartbeat in her ear laid on the pillow; could not think around the sensation or the sound. She rolled to her back, wriggled around until the wrinkles in her blankets were smoothed again.) Bad storm, with thunder and lightning and buckets of rain. And lightning hits a cow (no), a horse? (worse; but still not bad enough)—or Blue or Old Tom (oh, this wasn't working—all she wanted was to imagine a scene so she could explore her fear, with its keen edge of death that she'd felt so intensely during yesterday's storm. But now it seemed wrong, making victims of other folks, like she was casting spells). Or me. Better, me. TJ said it wouldn't hurt: "Lightning—bang—you're dead." Out of everything out there, I'm just one little kid, still it chooses to hit me. That must be what fate is.

There came a faint scratching sound from the bucket set so out of place in the corner of the bedroom. Sarah climbed quietly from her bed, tiptoed across the cold floor, and peeked cautiously over the edge. Flash of brown! The nest inside skidded sideways like from a sudden gust of wind. Sarah smiled, and reached in to give it a nudge. It leaped away from under her hand, shivered . . . grew still. Sarah noticed how the water was spilled again; she carefully noted that there still were no empty seed husks to clutter the bucket's floor. It worried her, knowing her mouse was not eating. She stood for a long minute, pondering how on earth she could stop her mouse from starving itself to death. And then, for a blink, she saw the soft, pink nose, gazed into those big, dark, depthless eyes, as the deer mouse peered up at her from the mouth of its nest. Then the deer mouse was gone again, the nest bucking away in another sudden retreat.

Sarah grinned, and clicked her tongue like she was calling chickens whle she sprinkled down more grass seed. She hoped the mouse might learn to recognize the sound meant breakfast; if, she thought grimly, it ever decides to eat. She sopped up the spilled water with one of yesterday's socks, padded back to her bed, and lay staring up at the dip of springs in the bunk above where her brother sprawled sleeping.

I wonder how come that new guy Frank takes to Owen so? He's only just another little kid. But then, TJ likes me, more so maybe than he does Owen—leastways he's not always after me to go do the chores. Sarah poked at the dip in the bed above her, watched while it changed position as her brother stirred in his sleep.

So there's Owen and Frank . . . and TJ likes me . . . who is there for Caroline?

Sarah sighed. That's my job, I guess. But it sure gets tiresome taking care of her all the time. Caroline would be a whole lot more fun if she wasn't so darned much bother.

Sarah thought, It seems to me we're given jobs, doesn't matter who we are or whether we want to or not—or even if the job fits—along it comes like it's all planned out. We got no choice because there it is, every day, needing done, until just thinking about it makes us want to lay down and die.

Sarah sighed: I guess that must mean there's a God. Because only God would know how much we can stand, and He plans it so's our time is filled up with just a little more than that.

But then, if it's all so planned out, and we have no choice, what happens if somebody really does get tired enough to choose not to bother? What happens if we're so fed up with our job we decide we just *can't*?

I wonder what God would do then?

Maybe the reason why things change sometimes is because God sees and knows for certain whether a person's faking or not. I wonder if maybe things sometimes end because God knows just from looking even if nobody else can tell that the poor thing is so worn out from doing what it has to do it really wants it all to stop, no matter how?

So He sends down a lightning bolt to take care of the problem. Maybe God makes changes like that—bingo— not exactly how I'd've done it if I were in control; but at least so's it's different when it's over and done.

I suppose that'd be fair, at least to have that much for an option.

Sarah reached up and snapped one of the springs on the bunk above, heard Owen stir; saw a bare foot come sliding out over the edge. She stretched to tickle it, watched it twitch and wiggle, until Owen, still sleeping, kicked his foot back out of sight.

So maybe if I want something changed, all's I have to do is mean it, and God will send down some way for it to happen. Maybe if I'm really tired enough for a change to be approved, God will see to it and get it done.

Sarah sat up and composed herself: crossed her legs and smoothed back her tousled hair, clasped her hands and closed her eyes. She prayed passionately: I'm sick and tired of taking care of Caroline, fix it, God, please, amen.

When she opened her eyes to stare around the room, everything looked mighty strange to her—it all seemed different, so vividly clear, like she was seeing her room for the very first time. It took her a moment to realize she was only looking too hard for signs of change . . . because nothing had happened . . . it was all still the same old stuff in its old familiar places, except it was later now, lighter outside. So Sarah shut her eyes and listened: Perhaps there would be a thunderous Voice, dark and deep, ordering the situation to shape up or else! All she heard were those too-familiar sounds coming from that room down the hallway: Caroline was awake.

Sarah sighed and climbed out of bed, wriggling her knees so her bunched nightgown would fall to cover her legs, and thought, I wonder how long it takes? I suppose He's awfully busy. She shook her head, picked up the water dish, and went off down the hall. Caroline, she knew, would be staring out through the crib's railing, waiting for Sarah to come lift her down.

Please, God, Sarah begged silently, do get a move on.

* * *

TJ heard the snicking of bare feet come padding past a second time, saw the little gowned figure with the tousled hair tiptoe by his bedroom door, Sarah tottering now under a heavy load. TJ sat up, glared down at his sleeping wife. Gathering his resolve, he shook Karen awake.

"Wha'ya want?" Disgusted voice. "Go 'way—sleeping!"

"Why ain't you up takin' care of the baby?" TJ spoke very loud. "Why you make Sarah to do all the work?"

"You do it then, TJ." Karen rolled over and covered her head. "Anyhow," she said, her voice muffled from beneath blankets, "Sarah doesn't mind. Gives her something, you know . . . important to do."

TJ called, "Sarah!"

"Oh, for goodness sake!" Karen hissed, rolling up. "TJ, you'll wake the house!"

"I couldn't wake this house if I had to," TJ said; called again, "Hey Sarah!" In a bit, his daughter appeared in the door-way, leaning to brace herself against the weight of the big child she hauled. "Come over here, Sarah." TJ held out his hand.

Sarah wavered toward him, bent back like she lugged a huge and heavy doll. She hooked an arm beneath her load, reached out to take hold of one of TJ's fingers, gazed up at him warily. "Now Sarah," TJ said, "tell the truth—"

"You like Caroline, don't you?" Karen smiled when Sarah nodded.

"Damn it, Karen!" TJ exploded, "that's not what I meant to ask!"

"It's all you needed to ask." Karen lay back. "I just said it for you, saved you the time."

TJ spoke, through gritted teeth: "What you done was change it around so's you don't feel guilty—that's all you're concerned with, loading things so's you don't look bad. You be quiet now, Karen, let me talk." He turned to Sarah, while Karen made a face at his back, but rolled up again to watch; TJ said, "Now Sarah, tell us exactly how you feel—"

"She already told you, didn't you, Sarah. You're making her nervous now, TJ, that's mean."

"Be quiet, Karen," TJ told his wife grimly. "Sarah, say how you feel about having to take care of Caroline all the time."

"Wait a minute!" Karen said hotly. "Sarah doesn't have

101

to take care of Caroline all the time! It's not 'all the time'—
who's trying to load things now?"

"Shut up, Karen," TJ said. "Sarah, tell us just exactly
how you feel."

Both TJ and Karen leaned forward, heard Sarah speak in
tiny voice: "I don't know how to feel, 'bout that."

"Sure you do," TJ urged. "Jus' go ahead. You don't
have to be scared of Karen, 'cause I'm here."

"Scared? Of me?" Karen stared openmouthed at TJ.
"Whatever have I done to make Sarah scared of me? TJ,
what *are* you trying to do?"

"Damn it, Karen," TJ said through clenched teeth, "I
done told you to shut up! Now go ahead, li'l girl, say how
you feel."

"Something's gonna happen here," Sarah said.
"Something bad's agonna."

"Ain't nothin' gonna happen," TJ urged. "Just say—"

"I know something bad's gonna come," Sarah whim-
pered; "because if I tell you it's all right, then you're gonna
be mad; and if I tell you it's not, then Mom's gonna be—
what am I s'posed to do?"

"You're not being honest," TJ chided, smiling benevo-
lently. "That's not how you feel. All's you're doing is
thinking—you're tryna say the right things, what you
believe we both want to hear. That's where the mix-up is.
You go ahead now, tell us what you really feel, an' don't be
afraid who thinks what."

"But that is how I feel," Sarah said. "I feel like I don't
know what to tell you!"

"See?" TJ turned on Karen. "See what you done? You
got the poor kid so's she don't even know how she feels!"

"I didn't do that," Karen said blandly. "She was fine,
until you started in." Karen moved her pillow up the wall,
leaned back against it. "You did it yourself, TJ, by asking
her a question she couldn't answer without making you
angry."

TJ glared at his wife with such heat Karen shrank back,
her arm half raised as if to shield herself. But TJ lunged out
of bed, took the baby from Sarah—grabbed it away from
her—while Sarah stumbled backwards trying to get out of

his path, said: "Sarah, you get dressed—here." He shoved the baby back into her arms, "Take Caroline, get both you dressed—where's Owen? Well, tell him it's time he got up. And all of you find yourselves some breakfast." TJ was hopping around, one leg in his pants. "Then meet me out-side, quick as you can—yes, Caroline, too—bring her along. I'll take care of her today. I'm gonna teach you kids how to know what you really feel, so's you can say should anybody ever ask."

"Hoo!" Karen rolled her eyes, then drew back again from TJ's dark glare.

"And tell Owen be prepared to learn how to work." TJ was searching for more clothes, his voice muffled, from down where he was peering underneath the bed: "But eat first, be sure to do that." He popped back up, triumphantly clutching a rumpled shirt, dust motes clinging to its sleeves. "I ain't hungry."

TJ hopped from the room, tugging on his boots; and Karen nodded to Sarah, whispered to her daughter: "Oh, go ahead, get ready and go with him. Let him think he's doing something. We both could use a day off."

Saturday,
11th August

1.

Hot already, at nine in the morning; worse, inside, where the still, stale air, having had no chance to be rid of yesterday's heat, somehow managed to collect more, the musty smell of the Book and Its hymnals filling the room until it seemed there was nothing gained worth the effort it took to breathe. Then there were all those flowers, sent by the good folk who hadn't yet made up their minds late yes-terday whether they would attend today or not. The smell of dead flowers permeated the room, those flowers wilting like they'd been stuck in an oven.

The men chose to stand outside, gathered in a loose knot

underneath the cottonwood tree that grew up through a circle left for it in the hot concrete, where the faint flutter of
leaves at least sounded cool, there being no breeze at all at
ground level; where even the cars passed slowly, solemnly,
like with hats off, past the hearse and the black limousine
and the signs set out since early morning on pavement melting, mirroring up heat like from off a lake's slick surface.
The men drifted aimlessly, jackets removed, clip ties hanging, ducking their heads self-consciously slow away from
the bullets of sunlight glancing off the windows of passing
cars, today forced by occasion to squint into that sudden hot
light that any other time they'd have been quick to avoid.

Inside, in the low room behind the sanctuary, well-
dressed, sweating women took down the folding chairs and
the stacks of tables, straightened the legs and set everything
up, not fast, but efficiently, and with little talk—except
about how godawful hot it was, which left little else to say
. . . only to wonder in low voices why they had to drive all
the way out to Tom Brothers's place, turn, and come back,
just so they could at last put these chairs and tables to use
before having to put them all away again, when a hole in the
ground on a city plot would do the job just as well. They
shrugged, let it go, finished their task, went out and found
their husbands and led them to their seats.

2.

Though the voices spoke in hushed tones from all
around him, murmuring like water, TJ could not force himself to look into their faces—he knew they'd recognized
him, TJ Brothers, they knew what he'd done; and they were
busy addressing that now. He found his way alone to his
place, sat staring at his hands, hunched silent for study by
this jury of his peers beneath the roof of the vast room
whose doors had just been closed, the room sealed like a
tomb. The voices soft, and secret, not at all thunderous like
judgment should have been; but he couldn't help hearing
them, this after he thought he'd sealed himself up, too, body
and soul, day before yesterday; or was it three days ago?—
yes, Wednesday, just before noon. He noticed how the

voices seemed to recede each time he moved, so he leaned back, and nodded, as the voices dwindled out. But then TJ had been hearing voices for three days now anyhow; it was a relief to have faces to go along with what was being said—

* * *

He'd shot the snake; by God he'd done that; a sweet shot, too, what with the snake reared up, its unblinking eyes like inlays of amber held a foot above the ground—swaying—its whole being shivering with furious attention; swiveling instantly like a living machine—blurred hook of scaled body, hard, flat, turret head—to meet the barking of the dog who seemed to think it all a game, the snake pivoting back again to face the baby's screams while TJ stumbled, desperately trying to find some angle that put both baby and dog out of line. A marvelous shot, really, what with the snake's shattered head as positive proof trailing thin twin trails of blood from its forked tongue across the light belly scales as the snake rolled and twisted through its last dance; too good a shot to've been a pity, for that was what it was: a pity TJ hadn't got it done sooner, the baby was already bit.

* * *

Quiet now. The voices had not begun again after that last organ piece had drained off mournfully. TJ sneaked a peek, saw the man in the collar had appeared up there during the interval since the last time he'd chanced to look; that man sensing things, sending out feelers, trying to fathom if now was the time to begin this the most sensitive of human endeavors. (Because inside a birth, inside a marriage, there was still room for error, for inside both there was still room for hope: hope bet on the future, which might just cover any blunders made by God's left hand today. But inside this? Well, the dead are dead: not much margin for hope left. Nothing to save the living from their terrible grief, not in this world; and this man was liaison to the next.) Must he recapture them? Draw them out of the solitude of their terrible anguish they'd withdrawn into three days before. Grief had such a head start—must he take away even the security of their numbness, make them feel loss again so sharply they'd be left with no choice but to turn to him, on this unbearably hot morning:

"From the fifteenth chapter of First Corinthians I say: 'Behold! I show you a mystery: We shall not sleep, but we shall be changed, in an instant, in the twinkling of an eye!'"

So then it seemed someone had yanked the rug on poor TJ, poked him with a sharp stick, let out his air; whether from the last three days, two nights, without sleep—during which time the ceiling had indeed learned to strike back: TJ now wore the blackened eyes of an incurable insomniac—or whether from the terrible tension caused by holding in grief; grief? or guilt, the like of which even TJ had never known. . . .

Or perhaps it was something else, something entirely different, which not even TJ had yet figured out. Give him time, allow him the moment necessary for his mind to blink, and retrack, after he'd recovered from this the latest of seventy-odd hours of recurrent shocks. Give him a chance to realize he had no place to turn now but to total despair. For hadn't he heard the minister begin, clear his throat, and begin again, while he leaned in, not daring to breathe, waiting, like he'd waited for three days and nights, not considering—not once allowing himself to think of—the consequences should the man up there fail him. TJ was poised at the brink of what he'd allowed himself to assume would be the dawn of a new life; and now damned if he, who had the nerve to call himself reverend, hadn't begun picking his way through the Book like the Bible was a Band-Aid instead of God's own knife used to cut the heart out of a situation and reveal it so judgment could have some bounds.

Not that TJ wanted it limited, no finite damnation. All he wanted was to have it defined so he could get on with living it, knowing however merciless it turned out to be, that was how it was supposed to go. It was to've been the kind of judgment TJ had prayed for throughout the long nights while he lay huddled alone on a throw rug beside the empty

crib, never daring to look himself inside The Book for fear
he might miss it (the Message), at best misconstrue it—
somehow or other muck it up. Then there he'd be, off on
the wrong trail again. "Got to be in there!" he'd prayed, a
litany—too bad It must pass through human hands—

*So, there it is, that's what had gone wrong; it's what TJ
had feared most would happen, those human hands fumbling along, knowing nothing at all of one TJ Brothers
beyond a secretary's reminder written on the calendar:
'Funeral, 10:00, Brothers child.' Those hands shuffling
what the mind behind them had long taken for granted were
appropriate passages pulled from the Book, blanket coverage for this circumstance. Would it not have been better
now, during this mad moment of great need, to've opened
The Book your own self like cutting cards—doesn't the gut
have its influence on chance, upon fate? Haven't you ever
opened the Bible blindly and found right there before you
exactly the quotation best fitted to what you required most
right then in your pitiable life, which could not been delivered better had God Himself thundered His Word straight
into your ear, your heart, soul—something—pinpointing
precisely first crack the printed rejoinder, the answer you
sought? Well now . . . I haven't either, not within the Book
anyhow, because too long ago, I admit, I lost the faith to try.
But once, while sitting on a riverbank pondering what life
was and where mine might be heading, I saw a carp come
floating by, belly up—*

TJ felt like he'd been dropped on his head, felt his san-
ity crack, good judgment leaking out. He realized right off
that this man, certainly a devout sort who likely was a kind
fellow and really did care about what he believed was his
duty, was in fact spineless, made yellow by compassion. He
would have neither the wisdom nor the courage to tell the
truth today, even if he knew it; and he did not. TJ shut his
eyes against the pain borne from the murder of his hope—
not some small sliver of hope he'd carried along, but hope
strong enough to've borne him, allowed him to hold onto
life simply because he'd not yet had to respond, not only to
what other folks were saying, or were wanting to say, or
were at least thinking: Your fault, TJ, you're to blame. He'd

not yet had to answer to himself, having channeled all blame off into an overflowing reservoir, simply waiting for this moment to arrive when the reverend who was privy to the Word would finally emerge from his study, take the pulpit, and tell him exactly what God had had to say about where TJ had gone wrong. TJ shut his eyes and let his head sink down. The man up there had failed him, hoo lordy.

* * *

He laid her gently on the pickup seat, saw the great, ugly bruise on her belly below where her shirt rode up—saw it spreading like a plague away from the purple knot swollen apple-sized topped by two tiny holes punched through her skin, which leaked a thin fluid; not blood, but with flecks of blood floating in it, the plasma already drying white around the edges, her skin already feverish like from an infection setting in. She was moaning softly with each breath, saying, "Mommy, Mommy" over and over again while TJ stared down at her and felt the panic tunnel into him.

He heard Sarah yell, whirled, and saw her dragging the rifle by its barrel bumping the stock along the ground: "TJ?—hey, TJ? What should I do with the gun?" "Christ sakes, Sarah!" he screamed, "Forget the damned gun!" He saw her all in one motion drop it and begin to run. TJ moved out to meet her, pivoted, and raced back again because he'd left the baby alone. He found a stick and absently began whacking his palm with it; Sarah was crying, hiccupping, pulling on his sleeve: "IdiditIdidit-Ididit." TJ thought she meant about leaving the gun.

But when he'd grabbed her up and tossed her into the cab, saying, "Hold Caroline!" and climbed in himself, over the top of them both, banging his head hard on the empty gunrack, he heard Sarah say to her little sister: "I'msorrysorrysorry—so sorry!"

TJ was pretty sure then Sarah hadn't meant the gun— "Git in!" he yelled to both Owen and the dog. The motor loped to life, TJ dropped the clutch, sent the pickup careening round and bucked it across the ditch, heard Owen call: "Wha's going on? Where we headed? Hey, wha'd you shoot at anyhow?"

He told Sarah, "Hold her tight," heard Sarah say:

"I did this, TJ, it's all my fault. I asked Him to fix it, but that crazy God missed."

"What you talkin' about, Sarah?" TJ said back. "If it's anybody's fault, it's mine."

* * *

So the one voice droning could only be a summation of all the other sounds prodding at TJ from every side now, all the sighs and moans and shufflings of feet gathered together and reissued from the one mouth speaking collectively up front trying its best to offer sympathy and give support, on this godawful hot morning while TJ knew everyone seated behind him was just too sweat-soaked to give a damn, let alone try to sort this one out. He felt a great pity: Too bad you all had to get mixed up in this, just from being part of the community, coming from the same town; this which is my fault and none of your affair. He was embarrassed for them, wanted to stand up and say so, somehow make it right, so they didn't have to hang around and endure any more. They could clear out, get on with their lives, he wouldn't hold it against them, he'd even hold the door. He wanted to tell that preacher, poor addled man, who was so alive with forgiveness but didn't know the half of it: Hey, look, I know you tried. But stop it, okay?—I'm gonna live with this for the rest of my short life anyway, so just let it lay. Not that I don't appreciate the gesture, yours, and from these good folks; I'm sure you meant well. But why don't you go on home, leave me to deal with it.

TJ had even begun to rise, for they'd not come unbidden, all these fine people; they'd not volunteered, looking forward to it like a Saturday in town, hadn't chosen of their own free will to take time off from working just to be here. No, he, TJ, had obliged them attend—had given them no choice. TJ stopped himself, just in time:

I suppose they wouldn't feel right if they didn't get to finish it. I s'pose it's too late now; because everybody has to believe in something and this here is just part of whatever they feel is fitting; they never had much to work with anyhow, beyond the fact there was a body needed buried, this here's how it's always been done.

TJ folded his hands, looked up at the preacher, and smiled: He had a path, at least for the moment. After that? Well, he'd have to wait until things settled down some, take care of himself then.

* * *

The Preacher: And what has a man for all his labor? More and more misery in his heart. For all his days hold sorrow, all his work brings more pain—it gets so a man can't sleep at night, wondering when trouble will come again.

* * *

Old Tom, with the skeptic's eyes, halfway through his morning's work, had hurried in to the clanging of the dinner bell. He glared, disbelieving, while TJ stumbled through trying to tell him what had happened, as if by staring hard enough, he could pull forth something by which he could abide.

"What-the-hell-you-mean, snakebite? TJ, what you done?"

"It's swelled bad—my god!" Karen cried. "We got to do something. Owen, bring the kit!"

"Kit?" Owen said. "What kit? I don' know nothin' 'bout—"

"Snakebite kit, Owen, it's—never mind. I'll get it myself."

"An' bring a scarf!" TJ yelled. "No, better, a belt."

Tom: "What the hell for?"

"Why, for a tourniquet."

"And jus' where you gonna put a tourniquet, TJ, 'tween her belly an' her heart?"

"Yeah—well . . . no. I guess that wouldn't work. I didn't think—"

"Well, think, goddamn it, for once. Go put gas in the car, git outa the way. No, bring me a razor blade, so's I can open this—wait, goddamn it! Can'tcha see? Karen's got one in her hand."

"She's so quiet, she's so still—is she—?"

"No, Karen, look, she's breathing, she's alive. Now hold her—TJ, hold her! whilst I—"

"I don't think she's gonna move."

"Don't think, TJ, I tol' you not to think."

"No, now that's not quite true. Actually you said—"

"One word more, TJ, I'm gonna smack you. Hold her . . . hold her—there. Put a suction on it, here, I got it—damn it, TJ, let go! Git the—TJ!—git the door! You put gas in the car? I tol' you—oh hell, TJ, jus' stay outa the way."

* * *

"So what we do now?"

"We wait, TJ, what the hell else is there—"

"You think she's gonna make it? Whataya think? Is she gonna make it? or—"

"How should I know? Hush up, here comes Karen."

"They was down in the ditch, see, the baby an' Sarah, playin' in the mud. An' all a sudden there it was, on the bank beside them. I thought it was grasshoppers—"

"I don't want to hear, TJ, not now, not ever. I never thought it was a good idea when you insisted on taking them with you this morning, but you said you'd watch, so I trusted you—"

"I was tryna shoot it—I did shoot it—kilt it, too, but—"

"Shut up, TJ."

"No, not yet, because you still think it's my fault, so I got to tell you: They was down in th' ditch, where the wire grass hangs over, see, and the damned dog all at once went nuts—"

"Stop it, TJ!"

"No way I coulda stopped it! Couldn't nobody've stopped it. Why you always gotta think it's my fault?"

"Well, TJ, 'course it's your fault. Who else was around? You want Sarah to take the blame?"

"Oh, quit it! Both of you. Stop it, now!"

"But wait, let's look at this. Maybe it wasn't—here, listen to me—"

"It was swelled awful bad, Tom. It leaked on my dress, and I got vomit all over me—it's bad, Tom, I know it is. You can tell me."

"Yes, Karen, it's bad—"

"Listen. I jus' thought about it, right now, I thought it through. And I believe maybe it wasn't my fault, maybe not. See, because, I can't un'erstand—"

"Doctor's comin'," Tom said.

"And it's not good news—oh no, look at him—look at his face! Tom, it's not gonna be—"

"Karen!" Tom said, "Karen, here, I got you. We'll see—hush now, hush—we'll see."

"Ah, hey, come back here you two, listen to me. I don't —here, come on, please, you gotta listen to—"

* * *

But when TJ smiled, he knew he'd done wrong, for something stirred deep within him; he felt it like a scream come creeping up his throat behind the cover of his grin, the ache of exhaustion and the tension from waiting all gathered together in one great knot of pain deep down in there alongside his heart. Well, he'd known from the beginning he would not get off scot-free, so TJ just grinned, did nothing to stop it . . . felt grief begin, (which the preacher noted, and believed to be a good sign).

But it was Karen who saw him first, her own hand rising as if of its own volition, not to grab him nor slap him or otherwise try to shut him up—not to clamp across his mouth, but to touch fingers to her own lips, while she stared at her husband, watching TJ leer back, spittle at the corners of his mouth, while it came bursting up his throat, tumbling like vomit in behind his clenched teeth. Karen heard someone moving behind her, long, hard bootsteps coming striding along the length of the pew, past Owen, past Sarah (Sarah's own face set like marble, no tears, teeth clenched, too, while she waited on the preacher to get around to her). Karen felt Old Tom brush by, saw him reach out for TJ . . . too late. TJ had begun to pant, which unlocked his teeth, let him scream:

"—Me!—ah—listentome, listentome—listen . . . to . . . me—"

Tom clamped a hand across TJ's mouth, wrestled his son to the floor.

* * *

And so I returned. And I saw all the suffering that is in the world. I saw the ones who were oppressed—I saw tears on the faces of their children . . . there was no one there to comfort them, tell them to hold on. And on the other side were those who had power, with some yet among them who did what they thought was best; still there was no one there to praise for what they had done . . . there was no one there to comfort them if what they did was wrong. So I cheered for the dead, simply because they were through with it: No longer their duty to contend with this sad song— I thought, better off still are those not born, who never see the madness that is under the sun.

Ecclesiastes

* * *

The harvest is past . . . the summer is ended . . . and we still are not saved.

Jeremiah 8

Autumn

Tuesday,
16th October

1.

Harvest moon, shipping time. Dawn with a heavy sky, high, dismal overcast—cold enough to show a man's breath; and fog clung to the mountain east, as if the trees breathed, too. A skiff of snow had fallen in the night, but the ground underneath remained hard and dry, the cattle's hooves knocking up dust.

The cows were wrangled out of the canyons, their calves sorted off and sent onto the scales whose balance Tom watched with a face set like stone: His calves were fifty pounds lighter than those the year before. And did wooly little calves and lean, long-haired mothers mean a hard winter coming? There was not near enough hay. The calves were driven huddling through the corrals; they turned aside at the dry creek bottom to crowd the fence for one last glimpse of momma through the wires. Then the men yelled them past, shoved them onto the trucks and sent them to market. Tom watched them sell through the ring today: The market was way down.

He came home in the evening, just at dark, wheeling slowly off the county road down his own lane, saw the dim shapes of deer feeding on the meadow's thin, frost-withered alfalfa, this the final night before hunting season began tomorrow at dawn. He saw the graves, vague in the poor light, all except the last one, the small one, still without a memorial, whose new mound of black dirt had managed somehow even today to collect a little heat. It stood bleak and naked like a tiny black ship in the midst of a great white sea (the graveside, where everyone but TJ had gathered, taking turns standing watch over Karen: Tom first, with a hand at her elbow, and then Blue's woman held her hand for a while; and Frank, too, who held her closest, the longest, reaching from time to time to brush the tears from her cheeks; until Blue had cut in with the brusque hand of a dance floor competition, snatching TJ's wife out of Frank's covetous arms; while TJ had passed on it all, wrapped in an

117

old quilt on the couch in the house, sleeping, sedated, his own self like the dead).

Tom braked his pickup in the gravel before the big house, killed the motor and sat for a while in the stillness of evening, staring out through the cold night to that hay stacked in the pen, part of such a small buttress against the winter ahead. He wondered if the winter would indeed be bad? He wondered how much more hay he would have to buy to get through to spring? He wondered if the deer would get in his hay stacks? Tomorrow, before first light, he must get someone out to nail up no-hunting signs on fence posts along the lane. Tom climbed stiffly down and limped toward the house, holding a hand to his bad back, which was giving him fits, sending spasms of pain up into his chest.

* * *

Frank had seen deer, too, early that same morning, while he was out checking fences around the pasture behind the barn, onto whose short grass the cows had been turned, maybe enough to hold them until pregnancy testing was done tomorrow. He'd jumped several does and one nice buck out of beds in the brush on the steep hillside. Frank had swung an imagined rifle to shoot the buck down, brought word of it home to the supper table.

But everyone could see that Tom was low—from the poor sale of his calves, from his visit to the bank. Though Tom seemed to rouse some at the mention of a big deer, promising Owen and Frank they'd look him up first chance they got, Tom went early to bed; while Owen, who Karen supposed was neck deep in homework, was instead in whispered conference with the hired man, Frank. Sarah was in her room, door closed tight; and TJ, as usual, was gone. Tom lay in darkness, fully clothed, trying to ease the pain with a pillow beneath the small of his back, while he forced himself to think on where the money was to come from for the hay he had to have and should have bought months ago before the prices skyrocketed at the end of a year of drought.

But it had been his decision to wait, until at least after the sale of his calves, so maybe he could use some of his own money to avoid going still further in hock at the bank. And now? . . . well, now, the calf money had come out a bit short: hadn't quite managed to straddle last year's interest on the note. So today Tom had had to borrow more just to pay for what it had cost him to use the bank's money the year before; and more still was needed to welfare his cows through to spring—"Christ!"—Tom winced with pain. If he had any sense, he'd get out of this business . . . except he didn't know how to do anything else to make a living.

* * *

Karen and Frank were finally left alone. After Owen had been sent to bed, they were unchaperoned for the very first time, the house still throughout. Frank said, "So . . . ah, Karen. How are things for you?"

"Oh, not so bad, most days."

"Well, I guess you got to carry on, least that's what they say to do." Frank heard Karen sigh, watched the way she moved while she put away the dishes. He shifted in his chair, cleared his throat. "You know, Owen wants a horse, real bad." Frank watched Karen turn, saw the beginnings of a frown, held up his hand. "Wait, jus' wait. I know it ain't none of my business, I'm not tryna butt in. But I also know you're not doin' so good your own self since . . . that bad stuff happened back there. You were hurt, and it takes a while to heal; and that's what you've been concerned with, and not the boy." Frank saw Karen stare with astonishment: "I don't mean you ain't a good mother, that's not what I'm sayin'. But maybe if Owen got something he really wants, it might help you both: give him something to look forward to, and allow you the time to see things through. Understand what I mean?"

"No, Frank, I don't," Karen said grimly. "I don't understand at all. Why are you doing this? What right do you have? And what's wrong with Owen? He seems fine to me."

"Whoa now," Frank said. "I didn't mean to upset you.

I just thought I should bring it up. You're not seein' the changes in him because you're concentrating on yourself. And that's fine—like I said, you had a rough go, need time to sort out what to do next. But meanwhile Owen's been left on his own, doin' his chores, goin' to school—"

"It's what he's supposed to be doing: chores, school. What's wrong with that?"

"Ain't nothin' wrong with it, 'cept it's all he has. And what's it to look forward to? Work all the time—he'll get enough of work when he's growed. He needs something else." Frank winked. "It might make all the difference in his grades at school. Nothing like incentive to—"

"What do you know about his grades at school? How did you find out his school work isn't quite . . . up to par?" Karen moved to the table and sat down.

"Owen told me. Or at least he hinted he didn't think much of schoolin', which I took to mean he wasn't wastin' any time at it. So—none of my business—but I thought maybe a colt—"

"That's very sweet of you, Frank. I appreciate your concern. But even if I believed it was a good idea, there's no money to buy him a horse. And I'm not going to make any empty promises that there ever will be. I don't see how things will change to allow it, not today, not in a hundred years—"

"Won't cost you a dime, here's my plan: You got that mare—"

"Oh, I can't sell her! That would hurt TJ so—"

"You got that mare, and I got a stud horse. Together, you an' me, we'll make us a colt. By summertime, when the mare foals, things'll look different. Owen will have the promise of something great ahead, and time to grow; and you'll have the while to work things out without havin' to worry about him. I'll help train the colt so's it'll come up broke to the saddle before it knows any difference. And you can use the promise of it between now and then to get Owen buckled down to school. It won't cost anything. What do you think?"

Karen cocked her head. "I can't help but think maybe

you and Owen already have this pretty much figured out."

"Oh no ma'am . . . well, not exactly. I did mention to him, long time ago, how if he ever got a horse I'd help him work with it. But he's most likely forgot it by now."

"You don't know Owen, if you think that. Owen would never forget something so important."

"Maybe you're right—you're a woman, after all, as anyone with eyes can see. I'm sure you know what a fellow wants, 'specially when one is your own son. Which means you realize already he'd like a horse. You know it'd give him a boost."

"Yes . . . it might—oh, I don't know. What if he got hurt? I'd never forgive myself if something happened to him, I couldn't stand another . . . accident. Do you think it would be safe?"

"Safe as a rockin' chair."

"Uh-huh. And how many rocking chairs have you seen tromp a little boy in the dirt? He'd like it, though, wouldn't he? His very own horse."

"He'd purely love it. But now . . . how's this gonna work? I don't want you stickin' your pretty neck out if ol' TJ's—"

"You leave TJ to me. He hasn't had much to say lately, and it is my mare, after all—I never thought that horse would be of any use. Let's go ahead with it, like you've planned. TJ will come around, I'll see to it."

"All right then, I'll get the mare in, first chance." Frank smiled. "Owen's gonna be real pleased."

"He will be, won't he . . . why, Frank this is the first time since forever I've felt like there's a tomorrow. Thank you very much, for caring."

Frank squeezed her hand. "Oh, there's plenty of future out there for both of us. We just got to make it happen."

"But Frank," Karen asked, "what about Sarah? You seem to know so much about my children, how is she getting along? I should do something for Sarah, too, to make it fair."

Frank said, "Now don't you start worryin' your pretty head 'bout Sarah. There's nothing wrong with her."

2.

Sarah wasn't sleeping, though by now it was way late. She was worried, she was fretting: Her pet just wasn't eating, not near enough to keep even a deer mouse alive. Seldom were there seed husks left scattered in the bucket; the little pile of grass seed she left for it each morning was hardly even dented, like by a hungry mouse's nose, when she checked again at night. Sarah stepped out of her bed, tiptoed to the bucket. The deer mouse still had not appeared. She pushed the rug tight against the bottom of the door so she could leave the light on without anybody noticing, sat back on her bed to try to think things through.

* * *

"Blue, what's 'God?'"

"Hoo! li'l girl, when you ask a question, you don' mess around."

"But I really need to know. What do you think He is?"

"You mean, what does He look like?"

"No—really, Blue—how would you know what He looks like. I mean, how does He work? Because Momma says her momma told her everything is in His hands, how we have to answer for each moment we live and everything we think and do, because He knows it all. But then TJ told me all Momma's momma needed was a whack on the head, straighten her right out."

"Hee!—TJ said that? Did TJ say this lately? Like in the last coupla months?"

"No, this was a long time ago. TJ's still not doing so good, if that's what you meant to find out. But, so what do you think, Blue? Could you tell me please?"

"I s'pose I could try. But listen . . . did your momma hear what TJ said?"

"No—sheez! Do you know how angry she'd've been?"

"I can only imagine. So you gotta promise: If I tell you what I think, you gotta not let any of it slip. Deal?"

"Deal."

"An' you got to realize: Ain't nobody knows for certain.

I mean, so what if a person thinks such and such, 'bout God an' all, don't make them right, see? It's all a educated guess."

"But Blue, you aren't educated. Is what you're gonna tell me not true?"

"Huh? heck, no. 'S not what I mean 'tall. I got some real sound ideas, see? But I don't profess to know for certain—I s'pose there's some chance I might be wrong, small chance . . . very small. But that's the risk you take. Do you still want to hear what I got to think?"

"Well, is there anybody else around who might know more?"

"Nope."

"All right then, I'll take the chance."

"Your confidence is overwhelming, li'l girl, okay, le'see, say there's a big storm, out over a lake—"

"What's that got to do with it?—I need to hear about God, not the weather."

"Hang in here with me, you'll see in a bit . . . say there's a storm—"

"There can't be lightning, Blue, not a lightning storm."

"No lightning? That kinda takes the heart out of it, don't you think? Storm ain't much 'thout thunder an'—"

"Make it a drizzle—no lightning, Blue, or else I won't listen."

"Well now, this is some arrangement: Ask me to inform you the truth on so weighty a subject, then you set up all these rules or else you'll go on home."

"No lightning, Blue. I mean it."

"All right—gee whiz!—no lightning. So it sets in to drizzle, out over this here lake. An' you have all them raindrops a fallin'—kerplunk—into the lake water. Now every one's a little different somehow, no two raindrops is alike: None have the same shape nor size nor speed a fallin', nothing is equal, see? Down they come. And when they hit the water they disturb the surface of the lake somethin' awful; make craters an' ripples, foam ever'where, like a rain will. Can you visualize that?"

"I guess so, but—"

"But then after all the fuss they just end up part of the

lake again, no different'n if they'd always been there, which is not surprising 'cause once they was— 'cept in no way can you take back out the original rain, drop for drop, ever again. So you see, all each raindrop was in the first place was jus' part of the lake, only off by itself for a while, sort of a isolated case—"

"But Blue . . . ?"

"What."

"God is water?"

"Well no, doggone it, look: The lake and the storm and the rain and all, they's symbols, see? You know about 'symbols?' They stand for somethin' else, somethin' a whole lot more complexicated. By usin' symbols, we can make a intricate thing be reduced to a size small enough so's we have some chance of graspin' it. We're only tryna get a rough idea here, right? For example, if you had five thousand white sheep, you wouldn't want to count them all each night, true? So, instead, you mix in a handful a black sheep, and hope if any white 'uns stray they take a black sheep along. If then, at night, when you count them black sheep and they's all there, you can go to bed figurin' you got your whole flock. With them black sheep, you got a rough idea—not absolute perfect—but you got a symbol of the total which to get by on. Now that's what I'm a tryna do here: give you some symbols. It's not God Hisself, but it gives you an idea of how He is, savvy?"

"I guess so, Blue, but this seems awful roundabout. I thought a 'black sheep' was somebody who never quite fit in. Isn't that a 'symbol,' too?"

"Like who you got in mind?"

"Well, nobody, really . . . TJ, maybe. I've heard him be called the 'black sheep' sometimes."

"Yes, that's a symbol, true. But that ain't what I'm talkin' 'bout here—I mean, TJ ain't really a sheep, is he? So when folks say, 'He's a black sheep,' they don't mean he's dumb and goes baa. They's just 'symbolizing' him, how he's different somehow."

"But what's this all mean? Is God a black sheep, too?"

"No no no—jus' listen, okay? An' try not to get confused. Where was I? So each and every raindrop is a life. And the lake is the grand total of all life that there is. The sun comes 'round, vacuums up the water, turns it into clouds where it forms into drops, born, kinda-like. When a raindrop lets loose an' falls, that there's a birth. Are you with me? Down the rain comes, wind blowin' it around, flyin' it this way an' that, until it hits the lake. The ripples the raindrop causes are like the waves a life makes in the world, see? Then the ripples fade an' die, and the raindrop becomes only another part a the lake again. So, that there's death: When the ripples disappear and is swallowed up by the lake, raindrop's dead and gone. Follow me, Sarah? See where I'm at?"

"I guess so, but . . ."

"Sure you do, 'cause I'm doing a bang-up job a describin' this here, an' you're a real smart girl. Now each single life moving out of and back into the lake disturbs both the level and the surface of the lake somewhat; makes the currents change and flow a little counter to what you had before, see? Causes droughts to come an' floods to go by, makes the lake a little more or less a what it was original, understand?—this part gets sorta fuzzy. 'Cause if it's a pretty big drop, some giant 'mongst raindrops, it's gonna be missed more from the lake while it's out on its own, make a whole lot bigger splash when it touches back down; 'sa gonna change the flow more, make massiver waves—"

"Like when Caroline died?"

"Ho! I thought so. That's what this is about, ain't it."

"Not really."

"No?—you sure? Well, anyhow—you want me to be perfectly honest here, don't you? I mean, you want to find out the real stuff, good or bad, am I right? Okay then—to the lake, li'l Caroline, or you or me or near 'bouts anybody else, we don't make much splash—wait now, take a deep breath. 'Cause it don't matter, in the end. To the lake, Caroline wasn't a very big raindrop—weren't her fault, she never had a chance to grow up an' be one. 'Sides, most folks don't ever get big enough to cause a wave worth gettin' excited over. You see how big I am? You think I'll make much splash? Shoot, my time won't upset a water bug, mos' likely. They's only a few who can really shake the lake. And often they ain't what you'd call exceptional; it's more because they was in the right place at the right time. Take for example ol' General Grant, or J. T. Snopes, or that pissant Hitler—'cept he musta hissed some when he hit down—them ones can reach out an' rock the lives of more folks than you or me will ever know. Why, their lives 'long side our's or Caroline's would be like tossin' in boulders beside pebbles. See?"

"No, Blue."

"No?—darn it!—why not?"

"I can see the raindrops, and the big rocks and the pebbles. They're more of those 'symbols,' aren't they. But I can't see how one life means more than any other. If we're all a bunch of raindrops, even if I was to study rain 'til I was sick and tired of being wet, I couldn't tell much difference between one drop and the next. How come some get more attention?"

"Okay—le'see . . . take how Caroline died . . . can you talk about that? Take how she was all at once dead and gone. That really rocked us, all us close to her, really shook us up. Here now, Sarah, don' cry. I'm sorry if I hurt you, bringin' it all back. I'll quit, if you want."

"I'm all right."

"You sure?"

"Yes, go ahead and tell me."

"Ah, you're strong girl. Now listen: Right over in the next county they's people don't even know it happened, folks what never heard nothin' 'bout Caroline bein' gone. Didn't read it in the newspaper, never felt the waves. But us bein' closest—you more so—we're the one's what get moved by her goin'. Hurt us real bad . . . tha's all right, go ahead; it don't hurt to cry. But the lake, what's God, remember? He gets moved by every raindrop that falls, each an' every one: It's His in the beginning, and off it goes, and then it's His when it finally comes back home. He's the one what really knows rain; an' He loves every bit of it, because every drop's a part of Him. He gets moved by each bug on th' windshield an' every toad smushed on th' road—

126

big hero or li'l girl, 's all the same to Him, 'cause rain's rain:
Every little drop is another part a His big storm of life."
"How does life get to be there? You know, souls and
stuff?"
"Shoo! . . . you mean like makin' babies?"
"Maybe. Sort of."
"Uh-huh. Well now . . . lis'en, Sarah, le'me ask first:
What can I count on you already knowin', bout this makin'
babies stuff?"
"You mean how a cow and a bull make up a calf?"
"'Zactly!—that's good, you knowin' that much. So
each time you have a baby got up, they's certain stuff you
can count on. It's no big surprise when the li'l feller's got
Momma's eyes or Daddy's color hair, maybe talks like
Gram'pa—"
"Little babies can't talk."
"Or gots Uncle Moe's wart on his butt, stuff like that.
But then, too, they's always things totally unsuspected,
brand new features you'd not thought you'd see. Maybe
this young un's math'matically geniused or can twirl on his
head at the age a three. Or he's got blue eyes in a family's
eyeballs all dark. That there's soul material what God's
pulled outa his supply lake just exactly to fit how this new
one's gonna be, 's what makes everybody different. Then,
too, God's a workin' man, always experimenting with new
raindrops whats never before been seen, so the possibilities
is endless. Point is: Whatever God pulls outa the lake,
that's what makes the new life turn out how it does."
"Owen's got blue eyes."
"Yup, an' your momma's and TJ's is brown. See?"
"How about being stubborn like Owen is? Is that a part
of it, too?"
"Sure."
"And being good?"
"Well . . . good li'l girls? You bet."
"And being bad?"
"Uh (shoo!) . . . I don' know. Seems to me that must
have more to do with makin' choices."
"How about having to die while you're still little?"
"Oh my! Well . . . don't know 'bout that neither. I'm

inclined to think for the most part that might be an entirely different deal. But it's all got to fit in there somewheres—"

"That's the part I want to know about."

"That. And none of the rest of what I done told you?"

"Oh . . . sure, Blue. I learned a lot: raindrops, and the lake, and ripples and all. But I need to know this part, Blue, real bad. Maybe it's got something to do with the place where you threw the rocks in. Maybe you can pick it up from there."

"How so?"

"Can one person change another person's life?"

"Oh, mos' certainly. Jus' think how it is to love somebody. You know, close mushy stuff. There's got to be all sorts a different feelings an' thoughts an' ways a livin' worked out 'fore that can run smooth. Natur'ly, people do some big changin'."

"Yes, but I mean can one someone make another one's life awful?"

"Yes, dearie, happens all a time. Too bad, ain't it."

"Can somebody make somebody else die?"

"You mean jus' out an' out kill them? Heck, yes. Ever' night on the television they's another hard luck story 'bout sombody gettin' conked in th'—"

"No, I don't mean shoot them or run over them or knock them in the head. I mean, can somebody over here do something what will cause somebody over there to end up dead?"

"Well now, been times when one person by what he's done has caused the death a millions."

"But can't we stop it?"

"Don' know . . . I don't think so. You keep an eye out for these ornery characters, hopin' to catch them 'fore they get a good start. But sometimes they escape your attention, 'til it's too late. How you s'posed to recognize them comin'? Could be the person right beside you; how you s'posed to know? Somebody what sets out to do bad ain't agonna jus' tell an' give hisself away, so how you s'posed to find out?"

"I guess you're right, Blue. Thanks a lot."

"'S all you wanted to know?"

"Yes, Blue, that's enough."

"Well . . . okay. But they's a whole lot more . . . ."

"I don't think so, Blue. This is about all I can take."

"Sure, li'l girl, I understand. I been at it lifelong myself. Any time you feel up for the rest, you let me know."

* * *

Sarah tiptoed to the bucket once more, nudged the nest with her fingers, felt it shiver again, as the frightened mouse trembled inside. She spoke to the nest in a furious whisper, "You come out and eat right now!"

But nothing happened—no surprise—Sarah had been sure nothing would. She sighed, switched out the light, and felt her way through the dark to her bottom bunk, where she lay listening to the funny noises her brother made while he slept. After a time, Sarah drifted off, too. And she dreamed.

First, she dreamed a dream of ordinary things, familiar affairs being carried out around the ranch, folks going about their business like nothing could be wrong. Except Sarah's dream was in shades of grey, conveying an awful sense of dread. She dreamed of the dark knowledge that the lives of people everywhere were but one vast sleeping image created in the void of the One God's brain. What He saw inside His dreaming caused everything to be; the whole world kept on spinning, so long as He dozed and dreamed. Sarah realized should God ever wake, the world she knew would vanish.

So she listened: heard those sounds she'd always loved for their clamorous celebration of life; heard them now with fear, and because of that she hated them, for surely the din of such a boisterous world would wake the sleeping God. Cows bawled and crickets sang, coyotes howled and horses screamed; a rooster was crowing and the tomcats were fighting with the dog again—someone was shouting— Lord, who could that be? Sarah realized it was her own voice yelling—she couldn't stop it—not even with both hands clapped over her mouth. The words kept trickling from between her fingers no matter how hard she clamped

her hands; for, she realized, she was a part of this life wanting to make her own noise to mix with the world's uproar—
maybe if she stopped herself, that would be enough. Sarah
went off to find a tiny room where she could lock herself
away.

Inside, the house was dark and gloomy, the rooms all
empty and echoing. On and on and on she went, down
hallways that should not have been there, past doors into
rooms she'd never seen, twists and turns, an endless maze.
Sarah stumbled along, lost and lonely, not daring to call out
for fear of the terrible burden she carried; there sat her
father, downcast, alone, TJ lost, too, inside his terrible grief.
Sarah could see he'd been crying again, his face a mirror of
his agony. He pushed her gently aside and returned to the
business of cleaning his gun. Sarah knew then that TJ could
not help her; she must find someone else who could.

Her mother appeared, Old Tom, too; there was even that
man, Frank, all perched like vultures on the boxes of old
clothing and useless odds and ends piled round the crib in
that tiny room, silent, solemn—frighteningly so. They
unfurled their arms like the spreading of pinions, fingers
pointed at Sarah, shouted, *"You're to blame, Sarah. All
your fault! Look at the results of your godawful thoughts!"*
The tiny figure whose ashen face was pressed white-eyed to
the bars of the crib began to cry, because she was dead and
there was nothing to be done about it. Sarah crept away,
sick with guilt: All . . . her . . . fault.

It was quiet outside, early evening; the last of the sunlight was being stifled by a great storm raising out of the
west: vast, black clouds rolling down from the top like an
enormous wave coming to break on the land, no thunder
yet, no sound. Sarah moved away, conscious of the mis-
eries leaping inside her like a singsong melody of mocking
glee. She plunged through brambles, wicked hawthornes,
which clawed at her clothing and scratched her skin. The
sound of laughter grew louder and stronger until she
crawled out at last on the banks of the spring pond. There
was Blue, chuckling softly, pitching pebbles into the myriad
reflections of faces in the pool. He threw a stone, watched
it strike, giggled merrily. He skipped another, studied the

ripples, slapped his thigh and roared with glee, the gales of his laughter rolling over the fields, bouncing from the hillsides—Sarah tugged at his sleeve: "Blue, please, no! You're laughing too loud!—"

Lightning flashed and thunder boomed, down came the rain. The earth's skin crawled with tiny souls, all crying out feebly, a tumultuous sound. The pond's waters bulged—the surface split—out reached an enormous grasping Hand, flexing Its fingers like a slumbering Man groping His way toward wakefulness, the clutching fingers seeking her. Sarah screamed—

Wednesday,
17th October

1.

Another raw day, same grey sky. There was an icy bite to the blustery north wind running before a cold front sagging down out of Canada, the weather bragging at dawn how things would get worse. Snow drifted in eddies across the hard, dry ground chasing dead leaves crying thin, scratching sounds. Wild flights of geese rode the hard wind in while the riders shoved the cattle off the hills behind the barn. The men leaned back to watch as the gate was closed on the last cow, tipped back their hats and stared up at the geese in the lowering sky, until the cold drove the men inside the barn again, where they took a long moment putting away their horses, before Tom crowded them back out to work.

All through the day then, whenever there was a lull while the veterinarian took longer than usual to search the plumbing of yet another cow to see if he could at least find the tiny embryo of a late-developing calf—he tried hard, the vet did, for the sake of the concern etched on the old rancher's face, what with a third of his herd already tallied out with no calf in them—all day long, when there was time, the men tipped up their faces to stare at a vast pageant assembled over them: great masses of geese circling in confusion, the din of their fluting calls grown in volumn throughout the long, cold afternoon, while more and more flocks sailed in. They wheeled in tiers, some circling a few feet above the treetops, other flocks mere pepper specks against the lifeless sky whose members blew in and out of the belly of the clouds—thousands of birds sandwiched between earth and heaven, all calling down, the lilt of their goose music like cries for help in an alien tongue: Where, from here?

They were still there, with daylight fading, when the veterinarian slung the dung from his gloved and exhausted hand, announced, "Open," for the final time. Tom marked the cow on his tally sheet, grimly began to add up his count, while Frank moved in to watch over his shoulder, shook his head at the high number of unbred cows. He laid a hand of sympathy on Old Tom's shoulder: "Way too many open ones, Tom, I'm sorry."

"What you sorry for?" Tom said without looking up. "Weren't you breedin' them, was it?" Tom took a deep breath. "Let's git on with it, 'fore it's too dark." He led the way again, striding through the gathered gloom back toward the barn.

* * *

Sometimes Owen believed it when he saw his mother weeping, believed her when she called out absently for him to "Look in on the baby, Owen, would you do that . . . oh." Then she would put her hands to her temples, claim she'd forgot: "I'll never get used to it, Caroline's gone," and she'd begin to cry again. Sometimes then she would walk up to him with her arms wide open, biting her lip, and she'd wrap him up and hold him way too tight. He could feel her tears against his own face then; and he would try to hold her like he thought it should be done, pat her back with one hand and say over and over, in a monotone: "There, there, don't cry; there, there, don't cry." Times like those, Owen was pretty sure she really did hurt when she thought about the little dead kid. And Owen understood, because sometimes when he thought how a little kid could just up and die it scared the hell out of him and made him hurt, too.

For a while his mother had made things rough, appearing abruptly, any time of night, the naked bulb in his bedroom all at once blinking on, glaring blindingly bright through the curtain of his sleep straight into his eyeballs. He'd watch her slyly through slitted lids while she looked in on him; then she'd bend down out of sight to tuck Sarah in, murmuring what Owen presumed was the same thing she'd whispered to him: "You take good care of yourself, daughter (son). You be careful, you hear?" He'd wait a little longer, feigning sleep, thinking any second now the damned light would go back out, while she must have stood in the doorway forever it seemed, because he never did hear the fading of her footsteps—until all at once hours later, Owen would wake again, the room black. He'd wonder: Had his mother really been in, or was it just another dream?

Then there was that other time when she'd come in on him in the middle of the night: Owen rousing, squirming, bladder bursting, needing the toilet bad. He'd blundered down from his top bunk, stumbled off along the hallway . . . stood bobbing and listing over the toilet bowl, hadn't even bothered to close the bathroom door. Panic had gripped him—here she was coming! and he'd done it again. Owen reached frantically for the paper roll, trying at the same time to kick shut the yawning door, because hadn't she warned him, repeatedly scolded him? Now here he was, two-thirds asleep, not aiming at all well, and the toilet seat down. Too late—her footsteps were right outside, evidence was splattered everywhere. All he could do was swipe quick with the paper, open his eyes wide and concentrate on the old iron stain where the spring water had dyed the porcelain redder with every flush.

All she'd asked was: "Owen, you all right?" Then she'd patted his head, left him alone, her footsteps retreating back toward her own room while he'd yanked loose fresh paper to clean up the mess which maybe she'd seen, maybe she'd not. Might bring it up tomorrow, catch him unawares, Owen acting it out in his mind how he'd admit he'd forgotten, show how bad he felt by vowing: "If ever

again I'm absentminded, I'll set down in it like you always
told me I should have to 'stead a you"—he must remember
to cross his fingers—"I promise."

Times like those made Owen think maybe there really
was something to all her show of pain. Because she never
thought to mention it, which was totally unlike the old Mom
he'd known.

But there were those other times, like when TJ tried to
talk with her about his side of the story, TJ repeating more
often than he needed to, "I just don't see how come you
think it's my fault," while Owen's mom grew more cold and
withdrawn, until it seemed to Owen his mother just let the
moment come when she could allow herself to break down
and go all to pieces under TJ's constant whining. A time
would arrive when his mother found a hole in TJ's talk and
she would begin to tell how bad she felt, how awful it'd
been for her, how TJ never saw what all this had done to the
mother of the dead child, because what was TJ's only interest? Bothering her with his troubles when she already had
enough of her own. This left TJ broken all to bits, shrunken
smaller if possible than before, because if nothing else he
knew she knew he was guilty of that much; so she'd nailed
him again.

TJ would watch her while she wept, wringing his hands
and looking totally lost . . . until finally he, TJ, pulled up
enough gumption from somewhere inside and tried to hold
her while she let herself come unglued. All the while TJ's
face was becoming more and more hopeless and forlorn, his
voice shading softer and shakier the longer he tried to go on,
until there he was, bawling, too. Those times, Owen
thought maybe his mother might be maneuvering for position—and winning at it, big—by merely allowing TJ to
lose. Because when at last she'd permitted TJ to hold her
and pat her, she'd remain so just long enough for TJ to get
his own crying going good, then off she'd go, flying away,
to a window maybe, where she'd lean, look out, sniff, and
hold herself, leaving TJ over there to finish up alone.

Owen thought, maybe it was true how his mother was
hurt inside from losing something so important as her
youngest child. But sometimes it seemed like his mother

was just playing at being sad; sometimes Owen suspected maybe his mother was finding it harder than anyone trying to figure out just exactly what there was to be torn up about. This made her feel guilty, which caused her to be angry, and willing to put the boots to someone so's she could get it out of her system. And TJ made such a good football.

Owen shifted on the top plank of the fence, working his legs to get fresh blood in them, feeling the pins and needles begin to prickle in his feet. He watched his mother's mare and the palomino stud, the mare squealing like a pig and whirling to kick each time the big stud came near her. TJ's black horse looked on, too, from a corner where the palomino had kept him since early that morning when Frank had told Blue to turn the palomino and the mare out in the corral together, Blue muttering: "Who the hell did Frank think he was nowadays—how many bosses 'sa man gotta put up with anyhow?" Then Blue had smiled, a sly sort of smile like Owen himself might wear while he planned some mischief to play on Sarah, Blue humming a tune while he released TJ's stud and sent the black horse running out to that mare waiting outside. Blue had leaned then for a full five minutes inside the barn, humming that same piece of song over and over again. . . before he moved on at last to yank the halter off Frank's horse, gave the palomino a whack as the horse left the stall.

Owen had been terribly excited at first, knowing full well what was supposed to happen. He'd dreaded the time coming when he must leave for school, prolonged his departure until he'd almost missed the bus again. But that had been the deal: Good grades, no trouble, he'd get himself a horse. Except here, at day's end, homework and chores already done, it looked like those two horses might never get close enough to make him a colt. The mare didn't appear to want any more to do with the palomino now than she had that morning. The only stud she'd let come close was the black one of TJ's, and him only for those precious minutes while Blue had taken his sweet time turning Frank's horse out, the palomino coming charging out of the barn, ears laid back and teeth bared, knocking TJ's smaller horse off the mare and chasing him away to the corner.

Owen thought: Oh it makes me have to do the milking more often, what with the folks always in there, TJ trying to patch things up—mostly the milk cows are my job now. But it ain't so bad as I used to think, gives me some legal reason to get away where Mom can't call after me to find out if I'm dead yet, out here where I could ride the milk cows' calves, at least 'til yesterday, when they went to market with the rest. Just when I was getting good at it.

"Lean back there," Frank had told him, "so's you don't get throwed forward when the calf ducks his head." Still, most times I got throwed in the dirt. So Frank picks me up, dusts me off: "That place on your knee, it's like the crazy bone in your elbow, 'cept bigger—sure brings the tears out, don't it." Owen sighed: I hated to see them milk cow calves go. But Mom's mare and Frank's stud 'sa gonna make me a colt!

Now that was something else, whatever it was between Mom and Frank. Maybe it was fine, maybe not—something just didn't feel right, like maybe somebody was only thinking 'bout doing what ought not be done. Owen was coming to realize that there really was something concrete waiting hidden in the years ahead for him to trip over, answers for these damned deadends his mind and emotions stumbled into each time he tried to fathom any angles possible between Mom and Frank. He just could not get past the hollow-in-the-gut-type feeling that crept over him each time he noticed their recent friendliness. It clashed so with the togetherness Mom and TJ weren't enjoying of late.

But had Owen noticed them alone together, Mom and Frank? If he could catch them at what this mare and Frank's stud ought to be doing, then he'd have something to go on, something solid enough to allow these feelings he kept having make sense, somewhat. But last week wasn't it Mom who'd changed her mind after Old Tom had already arranged so's she could ride with Frank to town? Tom arguing: "Kill two birds—save gas: do your grocery shopping, whatever else, maybe find the undertaker, order that stone; while Frank here loads the cow salt I need, checks on the price of hay." Mom had said back, "There's nothing I need so important it won't wait for a while longer." This after she'd been at TJ all week to drive her in, what with TJ not wanting to go around people ever again, and Mom in her grieved condition not wanting to go alone. So Owen and Sarah had had to brush their teeth with baking soda, wash morning and night with the laundry soap Mom had sent Sarah to borrow from Blue's woman, until Blue's woman finally must have got tired of loaning soap, soup, sugar, breakfast-supper-lunch, told Mom to make a list, get Tom to sign a check and she would be more than happy to motor into town to pick up whatever Mom might need. So yesterday morning it was Blue's woman who'd wheeled off clumsily in the big stock truck with two checks, two lists, and a crumpled note, the one saying what Mom wanted from the store, another written in Tom's scrawling hand: "ton salt, price hay;" and on a stained, frayed, crossed-out piece of paper a description of what to look for in a marker for that last little grave.

How could anything be wrong so long as they weren't ever together? Besides, Frank wasn't the sort to do that anyway, right? so long as one was married to somebody else and both she and the third party knew it; because you don't go around breaking in on things already set and done . . . maybe it was the way they'd both acted that evening, with Tom not back, TJ still gone. Mom had told Frank, "Supper's on the table. You go ahead, I'll wait." And Frank had said, "Aw, come on, Karen, sit down with me. They'll prob'ly be late, you know how they are."

"I don't mind," Mom said, "I'll wait."

"No, you won't. Come over here. Set down an' be like a family again. Wouldn't that be nice?"

"I'd rather wait, Frank."

"Now you wouldn't neither. Come on an'—"

"No!"

Mom had left the room all in a huff, just like she'd acted so often with TJ, and Frank had got up and said, "Better check on the palomino; he's been a little off his feed." Then Owen had watched Frank dust the big horse out all the way to the mailbox and back, not a lick out of sync. It seemed to Owen Frank might be feeling how Owen himself had felt those thousand times he'd asked his mother for a horse and she'd said no, then, too.

So finally, after Owen and his mother had been in the

house alone together last Sunday afternoon, while Owen kept up a running chatter about what he'd hoped was ordinary stuff, he had asked casually, "Seen much of Frank?"

His mother had turned like a dropped cat, said back, "No. Why?"

"Oh, no reason. Just askin', 's all."

"I've seen him as much as you have, coming in, going out. Why are you asking, Owen?"

"No reason, no reason—listen, at school, we're s'posed to have a field trip to town next month, did I tell you? Don't forget, okay?"

"Mark it on the calendar where it will remind me."

"Yeah, sure. I'll do that right now."

And Sarah? She was a big help, lost in something all her own, alone in her bedroom trying to get some reaction out of that stupid mouse; Sarah saying strange stuff, telling Owen: "You know what? God's a big storm," or: "Better be careful, Owen, what you think, because you've no idea what will happen if you're not"—weird foolishness, all of it, making no sense. Sarah dreamed a lot, too, talking out in the dark from her bunk underneath him just about every night, making it creepy. Last night, midnight, while Owen was sound asleep, all at once she'd begun screaming!— brought Owen up in a fright—he'd hit the floor on hands and knees, no idea what was going on; but he was already down there so he'd clamped his hand across Sarah's mouth to shut her up. He heard their mother call: "Owen? You all right?"—heard her coming running down the hallway. Owen had had only time to leap back into his own bunk, not a second more to compose himself, remind himself not to squinch his eyes: a dead giveaway when feigning sleep. But wasn't it better to've been caught not sleeping than down there grabbing Sarah by the mouth? All Owen could do was sit up, eyes squinted already from the sudden light, demand: "Wha'ya got the goddamned—goldurned—light on for?" No, he'd not been yelling; Sarah neither: "Look, she's sleeping—you gotta quit your worryin' all the time, Mom."

* * *

Owen sighed, climbed down off the fence. The men had arrived. He stood watching while the veterinarian set out his tray of tools. It was dark enough now for the doctor to ask that a light be rigged so he could see to work. Owen ran all the way to the shop and back, trailing the trouble-light cord behind him through the snow, hurrying for fear he might miss something, the geese still calling somewhere up there in the night.

"How old's the stud?" the veterinarian was asking.

"The black?" Tom said. "Be three in the spring. Can't think of nothin' but the mares, got to run them in separate pastures. Blue, how come he's loose in there with Karen's horse? Reminds me of TJ, off in the corner like that."

The veterinarian squinted, filled a syringe: "Where is TJ?"

Tom shrugged: "Dunno, he's never around when work needs done."

"But you're sure he wants this horse cut?"

Tom stared: "I want him cut, 's reason enough."

The veterinarian nodded, cleaned a spot on the black stud's neck, while Frank held the halter rope. At the prick of the needle, the horse tried to rear. But Frank held him hard, yanked him cruelly . . . the stud swayed, stumbled, went down.

2.

TJ left the house early, plowing head down out through the cold, grey morning, his mind stiff with the clouds of an alcohol haze. He heard the men yelling the cattle off the hills behind the barn, heard the cows come stampeding in still bawling for yesterday's calves. He tried his best not to notice the new grave by the meadow, but his neck turned his head like he had no say. The road forced him to pass tight by the banks of the dry creek above where bleached bones from decades of dead cows lay scattered in the sand, their bodies rolled over the edge after they'd failed to live long enough to make market. TJ felt all the vast sins of living come crowding in around him. He clenched his teeth in anguish, tightened his grip on the gun; walking, because no one would be there at today's end to bring a horse back from the mountaintop.

Fog lay draped across the mountainside; when TJ stopped, halfway up, he could see neither the summit nor the valley behind him. But he heard the lonely, lovely talk as flocks of bewildered geese kept coming in. There were scattered cedars amongst big boulders; he gathered cedar berries, cupped their fragrance to his nostrils, made him think of a cedarwood fire: Perhaps he could purge himself in the cleansing smoke of that sacred tree before going on. He loitered along, gathering dead twigs, finger-sized branches, tried to whistle a tune in the haunting stillness. But his lips were numb; the emptiness he felt inside sat like a lump of ice.

Wind came to play, knocking snow from the pine boughs. There was a flurry of sleet pellets, rattling down like shrunken hail, blanketing the earth in the moment it lasted; left just the tips of dead leaves ghosting through, tiny black grottos spotting the ground underneath the scrubby cottonwood tree where TJ found a corner for his fire. He knelt, in no hurry, began to sort his twigs for size—*(awful moment, between death and the grave, the dead all boxed for the living to grieve; she'd seemed so fragile . . . skin set like wax)*. TJ became aware of some small sound behind him, swung to see a tiny bird alighted on a limb, a chickadee, with its beady black eyes, short black bib. It offered a thin, lonely song, *dee-zee-zee*, acrobatting like a hungry child upside down along the branch. Whirr of wings, dry, dusty sound; the tiny bird was gone. TJ noticed it had begun to snow again.

The wind had died; TJ watched the big, lazy flakes float out of the fog and feed into his fire, hiss softly out, felt them melt against his face when he turned to look up for the geese he heard winging in somewhere over him. He stood, wiped his eyes, willed his mind away from the memory of his dead daughter. The fire had burned down, so he moved automatically to a scattering of driftwood left by some long-ago torrent come coursing down the mountainside, kicked open the pile and reached with both hands to tear it apart—saw the draping of a shed snakeskin winding through the dead wood—moment of panic! . . . long, slow burn of agonized memory, coming hand in hand with unbelievable heartache. TJ returned to his fire, scooped snow over it and stamped out the smoke tendrils curling up through the mound. He picked up the gun, with its single bullet, climbed on toward the top again.

* * *

There was an acre of granite, slowly tearing itself apart, the summit a victim of its own immense weight, with here and there a fissure tracing through wide enough for a tree to root, deep enough to hide the tree for half a century before the topmost branches reached out to test the real wind. TJ leaned his gun against the tree's twisted trunk, dusted snow from an icy stone. Nothing but dark weather out there before him, snowflakes hurtling in on the brittle north wind. He set the rifle's muzzle underneath his chin, settled in to wait.

* * *

Life's a storm, gathering from the moment you scream your way into the world already wanting for the pain to go away; a blizzard blowing through your heart, cold as the end, with rolling black clouds of lust and greed moved along by ambition's winds until last chance comes calling, the killing frost. Death makes a good knife to shear to the bone.

No—

Prayer becomes heartfelt when the black knight rears up. Death—ugly as sin—no longer lingering out there at arm's length where the mind thought to keep it forever. Hoo! Death has come for y-o-u!

Oho no!

The brain busy-busy, telling itself lies: Now how can I die, vital and alive as I am? Until finally even the mind, with all its powers to circumvent, can find nothing more immediate, more ominously foreboding, than the void opened up at your fingertips. Molds character, you know, peering into the abyss.   The end's here—a mere finger flick—a private matter, none more so.   So choose well, for there is no second chance.

* * *

All through the long, cold afternoon TJ sat hunched while dark clouds swirled about him, and the geese cried out their awful despair of ever finding their way back home. On into the gloom of a miserable evening, while the wind screamed across the mountaintop, driving the bitter nightfall in through his old coat and blasting snow like sand against his bare, blue hand which still held the gun barrel like a prop for his chin, a finger crooked.   Until he'd been there too long for there to be much chance he might live to see another day (some morning soft and warm, the sun shining out of a clear blue sky, birds singing, summertime).   So even after he'd reneged—an act of pure will bent to imagine any reason at all why he should go on living, saw a bed . . . his own . . . his wife waiting in it, solely on her own for the pure sake of wanting him—even after he'd backed out, hoping lying to himself might serve to fill the horrible void he felt inside, the momentum of the day seemed too much to overcome.   When he slowly, carefully, began cracking loose his hand, one cold joint at a time, his numbed finger cramped—twitched—he tried to thrust the barrel away, fully expecting to hear the gun roar then nothing ever again. But the trigger was frozen, snow had melted off his hand and dribbled there, turned back to ice.   His chin fell weakly off its prop, bounced on his chest while his whole being began to tremble violently from how close he'd come.

TJ wept for a long time, stumping around on the mountaintop, trying to work some signs of life back into his frozen self.   He built a small cairn, laid the single cartridge inside, capped it with a stone.   The geese were still calling when he stumbled off into the black night, TJ clinging to a vision: his life, his wife a part of it, because he'd vowed to prove to her that she could believe in him.

Winter
1980

Monday,
17th March

1.

So, it snowed.
All winter long. Guess it'll make grass grow, summer
ever comes.
It's made calving tough. How's your wife?
My wife? Why, she's fine.
You forgot St. Valentine's Day.
Valentine's? Did I? When was it?
Fourteenth February.
. . . I believe that was the day of our first calf. We
weren't supposed to start then; but that first calf came early
. . . lost it. Forgot to get a card. I hope she didn't mind.
That wasn't the last calf you lost. Frank remembered.
Frank? Remembered what?
Valentine's Day.
So? Who's he got—?
Candy for your children, a cute card to your wife.
Frank sent a card? From him to my wife?
*Delivered it in person. It was right after that when Tom
decided to send you with Blue to feed the cows outside,
while he and Frank took on the calving in the corrals.
Remember how the weather turned warm?*
What? . . . yes (Frank, and my wife?), turned warm and
melted, all that snow. Right when calving got going, the
frost went out an' the corrals sunk. Snowed every day, on
two feet of mud. Cows couldn't lay down, so they calved
standing. All you could do was try and catch every one,
because if you didn't—bloop—calf was gone. I seen calves
drown in the mud . . . it's been bad.
*Bad, indeed. Remember the weak cow that went down
underneath the boxelder trees? Tom slit her open, the cow
flat by then and sunk half out of sight, yanked out her calf
hoping it was close enough to term to survive. What did you
think?*
Calf died.
I know the calf died—that's not what I meant. What of

*the ethics, cutting that cow open just to try to save her calf,
knowing full well the operation would kill her.*

Don' know . . . I never give it much thought. Way it had
to be I guess, no choices left.

*Bad business. The day Tom killed that cow was when he
traded with you again, so you would calve the cows in the
corrals, and he and Frank would take care of the pairs
turned out on the meadows. That was when you were losing so many out there, remember? Sick calves dying all up
and down the creek.*

I thought maybe Tom was tired of wading the corrals. I
thought for a moment he in his severe way was asking for
help, taking my end so's he could have the easier part. But
I was wrong. I realized later it was because he didn't trust
me to find all the sick calves, didn't think I'd know how to
save them if I did. I guess he figured I'd do less harm if he
put me in where there weren't so many to kill.

*It was a hard decision, because he knows very well how
twisted a cow's tunnel could get right when it needed to be
all smooth sailing for the calf to come—don't think he never
agonized over turning you loose on it. But when you and
Blue seemed only able to bring home another handful of
dead calves' eartags each time you came in from the meadows, he had no choice—*

Weren't my fault, those calves dying! It was the
scours—they shit themselves to death! Wasn't nothing Tom
or me or anybody else could do to stop it.

*That was two weeks ago, about when the first sore eyes
appeared. That was just about exactly when you found the
first case of pinkeye in the cows. Even Tom couldn't figure
where such a virulent form of eye rot could have come from
this time of the year: no flies. Tom began to think maybe he
wasn't living right: God's wrath on top of everything else.
He wondered if he'd bought it with the hay.*

Actually, I thought of that. Tom jus' never gave me
credit, said at the time it was a dumb idea. But then, later
on, when he'd given it thought, he decided the hay he'd had
trucked in might have been the source. He forgot it was me
first brought it up.

He's had a lot on his mind: calves dying by the dozens,

half his cows so blind they can't hit the ground when they pee. And all the while all the hay he's got left might be the source of half his troubles. Speaking of trouble, you haven't had much time for your wife lately, how can you be certain you're still getting along?

Karen an' me? We got it worked out. She told me what she wants, I see now what needs done—money, our own house—we don't have to talk. But listen, wouldn't any mother want it that way, how we done that sick cow? We were only trying to save her calf. Anyway, it's all Frank's fault. He was supposed to check the hay.

2.

Snowing again, big, puffy flakes, riding gently to earth on the evening's soft wind, filling the area beneath the yard-light, the wind undressing the gravel of the graves—Karen glimpsed a shadow from the corner of her eye, shrank from it! Just the edge of her scarf, lifting in the breeze. She chided herself: being foolish, out here with the dead folk.

She'd imagined coming out to brush the snow off the stones; she'd seen herself doing that while she was struggling into her heavy coat. But the wind had beat her to it. She shrugged, and looked back toward the house.

"I'm gonna take Frank here in and get rid of some junk," Tom had told her, "and I'm gonna git rid of most of it by givin' it to him." Tom nodded grimly, and Karen had stepped aside so Tom could lead the way to the room where Frank slept. She'd waited then for Frank to turn and wink at her. She smiled, life was made up of the little things.

Five graves, what with the old folks. Karen moved amongst them, stopping at the smallest one, which finally had a headstone, a lamb on top, carved out of the marble—not her idea, the lamb—she loathed it: like cheesecake, too sweet. But Tom must have decided mourning could only go so far because when Blue's wife had reported back there was already a stone cached in the undertaker's yard, somebody's change of mind, Tom had pointed out, "Might be months, Karen, 'fore a new one's done. Hell, it might be a year. 'Sides, it sounds pretty much like the one you wanted:

147

right size —it'd save us some money. No, 'course it don't already have a name."

So it goes, Karen thought. She traced along the incised lettering, shivering from the bite the cold stone gave her fingertips—she realized with a start how firmly locked the earth was, frozen hard as a rock, beneath which her daughter slept. Karen felt her chest tighten, her breathing swell against the thought of such a tomb. She moved quickly on:

OWEN JESS BROTHERS

Skull and empty sockets now, where those blue eyes had been. Oh, you were a big help, Jesse, coming home all decked out in your own personal body bag, while she'd created a little turmoil all her own, having suddenly to marry TJ—she was swelled up big as a cow by then, what with the life growing inside her. Ah . . . well.

The wind had dropped off for its evening lull. Heavy clouds shifted to reveal half a moon. The hills were lifted from black silhouette to a soft velvet blue, and the snow began to glitter with moonshine. Karen rested her hand on a stone to watch: beautiful. She could see by vague outlines the horses in the corral, heard their hooves squeak in the snow, felt the cold pinch her nostrils with each breath she took.

Have to admire him, TJ, he gives nothing but respect now, nothing but room. Which left no place for her anger—never seemed a right time for her frustration to show through, no way to wedge it in between the considerations he always was offering. Her monotonous moodiness was wearing a bit thin for want of grounds.

Karen thought grudging: Yes, TJ is being decent. She swung to stare at the light shining from the distant calving shed. But must he spend every moment working?—I need his time, too; surely he knows that. Karen's eyes narrowed, her lips forming a thin line of sullen offense: Maybe TJ meant his time away to be a revenge. Maybe he was getting back at her in some small, mean way by never saying where he was going nor what time he'd return—

Oh come on, after all, he must do his work—don't you

need time for concerns of your own? And does he bother you anymore with any of his troubles? He handles them alone, never says a word. So what right do you have to demand he give you every—?

He's my husband: If any two beings are to understand one another, it must be man and wife—if I can't have him here when I need him, where is the one I can trust to lean on?

Of course you've gone out of your way to establish that trust? Or is it automatically guaranteed, a sacred bond given mutely during that old intimate ritual inside the dubious sanctity of a pickup cab—some boy fool enough to fall in love while all you needed was his last name. Whose own son knows instinctively not to call him father.

Karen unwrapped the violets she'd carried folded in tissue, flowers carefully nursed along inside a sunny south window until there were four blooms set. She left two before the carven lamb, two behind the military stone, where they began wilting the moment she put them down; where the wind would sift snow over them and hide them from sight. She stood, brushed her pants legs, made her way slowly back across the yard toward the light shining from the dead boy's room.

Should she have intervened? Saved some of Jesse's things for Owen? That would have been awkward—should she tell Owen the truth?

Maybe . . . some day

3.

The pictures were stacked in a small wooden box, each written on the back: "To Jesse," "Dear Jesse," so on, each message following the same itinerary: adoration, a hinted offering. Photos of pixie faces with pouting smiles teased onto pretty lips; words written in young girls' swirls, i's dotted with penned teardrops; all stacked on the photo of the young man himself: Jesse was caught by the film in a moment old as Adam, eyes gazing down—not self-conscious—staring hollowly at nothing. The wooden box was beautifully made, the corners dovetailed, horn inlays in the lid, the whole thing with the satin sheen of a hand-rubbed finish.

"He made it for one of them." Tom waved at the photos. "But he liked it so much he never gave it away." Tom lugged a dresser drawer to the bed, upended it. There were letters, more high school memorabilia. Another box, a flat Christmas card box, with the tag still taped to it, saying, "Merry Xmas, From: Mother," contained monogrammed handkerchiefs, still brand new. There was a huge silver buckle—"High School Rodeo, All-Around"—two medals: bronze star, purple heart.

Tom said, "They sent me a letter, some lieutenant commander feller. Got this here letter, sayin' fightin' for his country, blah blah blah. But it never told me nothin', you know, 'bout the circumstances."

On a nail inside the closet was a tooled silver bridle, the leather headstall finely worked, the shanks of the bit curled like a wishbone: to put the whoa to a roping horse. There was a pair of nickle spurs with long, wicked rowels, a nearly new Stetson, unlucky pheasant feather in its band. None of what he'd seen so far was any news to Frank; he'd nosed all through it months ago. Carefully concealed in Frank's own luggage was a gold pocket watch engraved, 'Jesse,' on its back. "Take the hat," Tom said, "wear it, if it fits—shirts, too, if they'll do you any good."

Tom said, "There was a telegram; I still got it somewheres; and a man come by, 'notification officer' he called himself." Tom moved to the window: snowing again. "That's a military stone, I s'pose you noticed—I never even had to buy a coffin. But I did." Tom leaned into the window, hands on the sill. "Government woulda took care of everything, if I'd a let them. Seemed like the government had their little story jotted down, just the names left blank—I even got paid for him . . .'cept I never cashed the check. I ain't sure what I done with it, must be around. Goddamn it, I don' know what it's for!" He swung around. "Wages? Was it wages? Were they payin' me for the time I took feelin' sorry for myself because they killed my son?"

He took a deep breath, stared at his hands. "I guess that's what I want from you, Frank. I never knew much about what went on over there, never took no interest in outside affairs. I just could feel he wasn't satisfied to stay on here, so I took the chance that time away might teach him how good home was."

Tom looked up rivetingly: "Could you tell me, Frank, if what I done . . . by sendin' him off—I don't mean to push, I'm sorry as hell I'm gonna do that—I want you to say, straight out, if what I did, and what I lost, was worth it, to anyone." Tom stared at Frank; and for the first time since they'd met, Frank saw in Tom's eyes the closest to pleading the old man would allow. "Please."

4.

TJ had the evening shift, darkness to midnight, with Blue to take the mornings: two o'clock, and again at four, or five, de-pending on how Blue felt after his first trip through the corrals (hinging more upon the faith Blue put in his own fixed conviction how cows should wait until a decent hour to calve). TJ was sick—not down, not yet—but he should have been, if only he could find the time. He stopped halfway up the hill to vomit . . . hunkered flimsily against the fence and wondered if this was the end.

The weather was cold, wet, snowing hard again on a gusting night wind. There was a new calf born on top of the hill—TJ had feared there would be: tucked away in a corner somewhat out of the weather, birthed by an old range cow who'd never known man to be of much help. She stood over it now, head high, eyes wild, staring into the light wobbling up toward her. TJ peered with his flashlight at the shivering calf, turned, and gazed bleakly back to the distant lights of the shed. He sighed: two trips, one lugging the calf who'd never make it through such a night, another for the cow, who, TJ knew, would refuse to follow meekly along while TJ walked off with her baby, because that stain there was where her water broke, which was precisely where her calf should be.

TJ felt the shivering flu sickness come on again, but he shrugged it off, struggled out of his coat, laid it out on the snow and rolled the wet calf over onto it. Slowly, he began to sled the calf along, dragging his coat by its empty sleeves, the old cow following, bawling her concern, her nose glued to the wet hide of her newborn (as if a piece of the muddy earth had broken loose, was drifting away, carrying her baby with it), the calf flopping off two, three, a dozen times during its voyage to the shed.

There were no pens left, too many calves born day and night, mud way too deep outside for any calf under three days old to stand even a remote chance out in the cold and wet. And with the scours going the rounds, the pens all contaminated by dead calves from days gone by, nearly every calf in there was suffering through some stage of the disease.

TJ lugged one out of a stall, a calf too weak to stand, eyes sunk away, nose dry and peeling, one of those TJ and Blue had kept alive by pouring milk into it through a stomach tube, with no real hope of saving it, singlemindedly doing what they thought best while they waited on it to die. He carried the limp body back to the straw pen, laid it gently down, turned its mother out into the snow. He cleaned the pen, sprinkled the floor with lime to draw the moisture and maybe kill some of the disease, all the while wondering: was he bringing this new calf from a deathbed outside to a more certain one in here? He stumbled along, trying to fight down his stomach, floundering over the stinking piles of old bedding straw—his bowels all at once announced grimly that he had more pressing matters—TJ scrambled for a corner, fumbling for the buttons of his pants.

The wind was beginning to wail when TJ stopped by to gaze down at his sodden coat. He left it laid on the filthy straw while he moved back out again. His tracks from before had been smoothed by new snow, the wind had nearly filled them. He plodded along, bare hands in his pockets, the bobbing light clamped under an arm, plunged blindly into a deep drift, fell flat. . . struggled up and trudged on. He found another calving cow, her water broken, the calf with head and front feet hanging clear, alertly swinging eyes around like it was checking out the weather. TJ hurried past, trying to jog, bouncing his light across the other cattle huddled against the fence—the last thing he wanted

was another calf dropped outside, for he hadn't the strength
left to carry it in, and he'd just about run out of sleds. He
swung and followed the old cow along, the cow hip-bound
and hobbling. Though he was fearful each step that she'd
dump that calf,he forced himself not to rush her. TJ was
working, he sensed, at the far edge of exhaustion, having
had no more than four or five hours sleep a night for more
than a month—none unbroken; sick now, to top it all. And
with no pens left, what to do? He thought: Move the straw,
put it . . . where? He glanced up for the lights, saw them a
hundred yards off, decided he'd not think on his problem
until he was back inside . . . felt the rumblings begin in his
stomach again. But he chose to ignore it, hoping it would
fade; it hit him hard and cramped him over, took him almost
to his knees. And when it was through, leaving him wrung
out and shaking, he found himself leaning against the shed
gate. TJ left it swinging, went stumbling down the alley;
maybe if he rested a moment in the straw pile, a plan would
come to him by osmosis. Behind, the old cow wandered in,
pleased to find such a nice place in out of the wind.

Outside, a flurry, hurled by a strong gust, lifted snow in
plumes off the end of the shed. But the wind outstripped it,
left it to settle, moved on up the creek to rattle bare limbs.
In the chaos of driftwood piled deep against the cottonwoods, two calves had sought shelter from the storm. One
stirred, blinking hollow eyes against the sifting snow . . .
could not quite manage to shake its head. The other was
dead, stiffening already; the wind sniffing past it found little heat to steal. Its body will be frozen when Tom and
Frank discover the pair in daylight. They'll dump one over
the creek bank on top of the old bones, cart the other to the
house in a futile attempt to save it. Tom is averaging thirty
percent losses, his calving half done.

There'd been no break, bad weather constantly, the
calves cold and wet, old cows suffering, too, the earth
walked to a frozen muck wherever there was shelter. All
the calves' energy went to trying to keep warm, until the
scours got them, the bloody flux: bacteria cultured that
caused a calf's bowels to run a steady stream, until the
stomach wall sluffed off, the snow spattered red behind

them. Dry weather was needed to dust things up a bit and encapsulate the bug. But it's snowing hard, here at midnight, the wind blowing a gale. Out in the open, an old cow walks in circles, bawling monotonously for the dead calf in the driftwood pile. She stops to listen, bawls again, swings her head to try to peer into the storm: Nothing out there, she's totally blind, both eyeballs ruptured and leaking from the deep ulcerations of infectious pinkeye.

Tuesday,
18th March

1.

Tom peered at the alarm clock: Old phosphorescent arms glowed minutes after midnight. He eased down, lay rigid on the bed, trying to ride out the vicious ache in his back, hands clasped to his chest where the pain seemed to've spread. He'd not bothered to undress, would be up again in a few hours anyhow. He stared into darkness, his heart laboring, remembering the backbreaking work his father had done.

He built the whole thing; and not from the bottom up, so's he could plan, but from the top back down to somebody else's poor footer, then back up again according to another's busted dream. When Tom's father took over, rotted shingles lay scattered away from the barn revealing precisely the pattern of the stiff prevailing winds. There was no foundation under it, except for decayed logs laid on dirt, the dirt floor gone, too, buried beneath half a decade's manure, Tom's father's horses leaving more each night all through the first summer; until it reached the point where his horses could no longer back out of the holes they'd tromped in the dung, he'd had to tear out the stalls so his horses could turn to see what they were lunging up out of so he could lead them to water and then on to their picket pins each dawn. If he'd not yet found time to rebuild the flat fences where was the free week necessary just to shovel out the barn?

The clapboard house, which had never known paint, had

the same curling shingles that sailed down in the easiest breeze; inside, leak-stained plaster dangled on the strands of horsehair that was used initially to fortify the mortar. There was a filthy outdoor john, reeking, wasp-nested, caving in—too close to the well to dare drink the water. (No sign yet of the joy supposed to come from wresting a living from this, your very own land.)

But the cattle he'd bought were hardy enough stock, culled thoroughly by the hard winters before, except they began calving in August while he was still fighting the fences, continued on through next July, the calves trickling out four or five a week. For he'd bought it all, cows, land, machinery too, all coming complete with failure inbred. The owner before him had found out at last that the only true and worthwhile pastime was to sit on the back porch with a water glass full of mash and swat at the flies as they buzzed through the torn screen, while the house and the fences fell down around him, his wife beginning to harp seriously: "If you plan to keep it, fix it so's it'll work somewhat, if you're not a gonna, fix it enough so's maybe it'll sell." By then the bulls had spent the winter with the cows, so—what the hell—he left them in all summer, too, ensuring that next year's calving would take a whole year. Tom's father had had no choice but to climb down off the crumbling machinery pulled behind two swaybacked old workhorses and pack the newborn calves just far enough aside so he could go ahead and mow, using haying equipment that constantly broke down and finally collapsed in a rusted heap. Tom's father was forced then to borrow more money, not to buy something new or at least worth using, but to purchase another set of worn-out stuff exactly like what he owned: to strip for cheap parts.

He'd got the horses though, not just the broken-down nags he tried to work, but a herd he'd never seen rumored to be somewhere in that big pasture south. He'd planned to hold ends together with the help of a hired hand or two willing to work hard, cheap: help him break the colts out of those mustangs turned out long ago and simply left to breed. That owner before, though, had forgotten to mention how he'd had similar plans until he'd tried to tame the first one, busted a leg instead. It was either shoot them then or turn them loose, so that first owner's wife had opened the gate while the mister lay in the wagon bed waiting impatiently for her to come bump him across the twenty miles to town, that first owner somehow neglecting to point out that the colts out of those mares had never even seen a man beyond a quick glimpse over their shoulders as they followed the black stud away into the canyons.

Lord, how'd he do it? Where'd he find the strength, the spirit to keep on? And *why?* Why, that first year he reroofed the buildings, built a new john, cleaned the spring, dunged out the barn. Got up what hay there was, scraped out the ditches, plowed a new one in for the garden (yes, a garden, out front where Mother wanted it, in the sun away from the worn-out soil behind the house where it'd always been). He tore down the fences, built them back with new pitch-pine posts he cut and packed by hand up the steep hills, pushed his cows off the meadows, turned his horses out. He screened the porch, patched the ceilings, picked rock (blew up the big ones, the ones ruining his machinery; cracked them with black powder and dug them out). He built a breaking corral in the mouth of the canyon, hired two men—

With borrowed money he hired two men, like on borrowed money he did everything, piling up debt until it resembled the barn floor—

I remember the crack of the rifle aimed to kill the black stud, the horse lunging at the shot, scattering the men like barnyard chickens—the bullet burning along the stallion's cheek when it should have buried itself in the brain. Though I could not see the shot, of course, I saw blood leap out all along the jaw line; and after that first screaming, thrashing roll down the slope, I saw the other wound, a splash of red high and far back on the horse's flank where the slug had plowed on in, the useless hind legs following half a turn late and out of cadence. I watched the stud quit its screaming, the broken walk, hindquarters trailing foreignly through the sand, face around and gaze back into the clouds of dust, searching for the one who'd ruined him. Then he collapsed like a bludgeoned cow, slammed nose-first into the sand, flanks no longer heaving, quivering now, as the second crash from the rifle drifted by. My father strolled out of the dust, drifting through the haze to cautiously tap the stallion's forehead with the loaded gun barrel, drifting back again, unchambering the unnecessary load . . . I was trembling: Was it over, the killing? or was it only beginning?

So what's its worth, old man, this ancient memory, except to bring to mind something you should have taken care of half a century ago and, never did, except to hide beneath blankets trying to escape the bad dreams, huddled in the scratchy dark; little bursts of lightning playing in the recesses of the wool: "God, make that bloody black horse please leave me alone, amen"—until finally morning did arrive again. From down the hallway came the rattle of the stove's lid as the first fire was being built by the very man you'd once believed you could take even your worst dreams to, but never again. What's it worth now, reliving a memory no more relevant than any of a thousand other childhood cataclysms? For even if you'd found the pluck necessary to speak to your father about the tough time you'd had because he'd shot that black horse—how come—his answer—spoken all too brusquely, either because he had not, or else did not wish to take, the time necessary to explain—would have been: "Good God, boy, if you can't take on bad dreams, how you ever gonna be a man?" Would you have done it so different?—could you both kill a symbol and then explain why to your son, you, Tom, who has the one son left, and named after you to boot? Of course this one son left already knows better than question anything you do—

It was too much for him to do alone, I know that now; no time for him to show me how, I knew that, even then. My father hadn't time for anything but all that work. I tried my best to keep up with him, so's I could at least have that much, a moment or two beside him at whatever he decided was next to do. But all he did was work, never took time to stop and talk. He did his thinking working: I remember watching him, seeing him stop—not to rest, he never rested, he fell like a dead man into bed at night—paused, in the midst of whatever forkload or shovelful needed moving then, the tool arrested, midthrow. And when the thought had run its course, he picked up right where he'd left off and finished out the arc; and the next throw was made like nothing had happened other than time had stuck for a moment and now it was greased and ticking on again. God knows I was too little help for him. But even then it was too soon for a boy to be learning there was no more to life than his own ability to work himself to death.

Why?

It's inherited, I think, under as much your control as the color of your eyes, man's work. I grew up knowing I could no more turn my back on this place than I could cut off my nose to spite my father's face—he never asked, never inquired whether I would go or stay; I don't think he took it for granted, I believe he never thought on it either way. The land is an entity, see? I've an investment here . . . my father's bones; my wife married into it, bore me two sons.

* * *

That time vivid, like brassy sunlight shining from a vacant sky—no clouds—no shadows, no relief . . . reality having once and for all blown the mind clean, when my wife, mother Mary, lay down to die. Taking on herself the never ending tide of well-wishers, she reached out, offering sympathy, as if the pain they suffered for her was her own fault, it was up to her to relieve them of it, make it right. Here, in this room, in this very bed, her thinning grey hair spattered like dirty cobwebs against the pillows swallowing her emaciated face, she accepted the long slide toward the ever-end so gracefully, a living model of how to die right.

She liked best then the shallow folk, who had no grasp on the concept of death. Oh, some day it would take their husbands; they'd begun rehearsing for it, widowhood. No doubt it surprised them when their husbands kept showing up each evening after work. They read her obituary, clucked over it: such a brief highlight, all there'd been to her life. They'd never know how Tom agonized writing it out the day after Mary died. Those shallow folks required no more from her than for her to ask them easy questions, the answers they would use to fill up their lives, as if life was no larger than a neighbor's poor choice of drapes.

Her last days were passed that way, so unlike the rest of her time, while she slid down the path her doctors told Tom she'd take: "She will become, ah, weaker, certain bodily functions will—um—fail: control over her bowels, an unavoidable inconvenience. She could die of heart arrest, uh, from the strain the tumor places on her other systems. But I think not, her heart is strong from working hard; her will is still sound. She'll most likely survive until the tumor spreads, and—ah—she is unable to take its stress. Perhaps a blood vessel will burst, that would be nice. Tell Mary this pickle relish is fabulous."

Mary would beam up from her death bed: "He liked it, really? He's been so kind. But then . . . did he leave? He did, I see. No, no, don't try—he's done so much for me. It's just that . . . I thought that . . . maybe he could explain what's going to happen. Its nothing, really—you go ahead, Tom, do your work.

"But Tom? Is it time? If it's time, I'd take another."

So Tom would break open another ampule, fill a syringe, and slip the thin needle through her dry skin into the muscle of her arm, or, when the muscle there was gone, into the flesh of her leg, leave her to float inside morphine dreams. Dreams, which became . . . rough: She talked out while she slept, and the revelations she offered loudly might have been on anything, foolishness; until their nonsense became so commonplace we were guilty of not listening, when even then we were preparing for last words. She'd wake from the dreaming, know she'd been carrying on, be embarrassed by it. She'd become so much thinner, lost most of her hair . . . came not to recognize her face: "That's me?—oh, my!" Something slipped: She announced she was tired of all the visitors, the last hangers-on, who'd come again, one last time, to appraise how she'd withered, never failing when they left to remind her to get well soon. She looked right through them with bright, beady eyes: Recover? *Hee!* Don't make me cry.

It was shocking then to hear Mother curse. Tom would

arrive and find a total stranger occupying his bed, who whined at him in a thin, shrill, bitching voice, laced with profanity he'd not been aware she even knew. Still, she kept coming round, the visitors sent away: "She's sleeping, tough night. Thanks for coming, we'll tell her you stopped by." Right then, just as the folks were turning to go, Mary might choose to shriek out a string of the most scalding oaths: pitying glances, perhaps an awkward embrace, silent strength offered for what was to come.

For late on, I asked if it bothered her, worrying how we'd get by, afterwards. She stared up at me, said finally, calmly: "Why hell no, Tom, what are you thinking of? You miserable cocksucker, you'll still be alive!" Then she floated back like a wisp of fluff down into her swallowing pillows.

Then one night she sat up again, her will able to lift her after her strength was long gone, to curse me in a tone she'd once used to scold the dog, "You son of a bitch, Tom, I never asked for much, but somehow you managed to give me less. You decided, on your own, what we'd do with our lives, then you never even bothered to say thanks." Then she spat, both boys watching: little, wrinkled bag of bone-filled skin, her eyes like marbles set way back in a shining skull. Watched her sitting, staring, spittle on her chin, until TJ moved, then Jesse, too, to push her back down so she could go ahead and die. All the while she never quit staring, while first one son and then the other told her, "Now mother, here now," her eyes locked to mine, until I had to break away. She was muttering, "No . . . no," until the word became her death rattle, a gurgle in her throat. She died like that, just before sunrise. I realized I could no longer hear her breathing; and when I switched on the overhead light (which she never used, because the ceiling was so cracked and ugly, made her downhearted), I was in time to watch the pulse dwindle in her throat. I waked the boys.

Jesse yawned, "So she finally kicked the bucket. Whata we do, close her eyes?"

But TJ couldn't take it, I remember. I heard him go out—

* * *

160

Damn! Tom thought, I was gonna get over there, take a look around the shed. I hope to hell TJ hasn't screwed things up again. I sure wish Jesse—
Tom thought: Frank, now, he wasn't much help. But I s'pose it's true how head injuries, like the one Frank says he got, can cause you to forget. I was counting on him though, I thought Frank would come through.

2.

Frank rolled up, switched on the light, rummaged through his suitcase: After three in the morning, by his new pocket watch. He'd heard nothing from the kitchen for some time now, no memory of the wheezing bawls from the dying calf for an hour or so. He had no guilt for the relief he felt knowing the calf had finally died—it'd been too hard trying not to listen, wondering how godawful long its dying would take. He carefully worked open the window he'd loosened months ago from the grip of old paint, lit the last of his cache of marijuana sticks; watched the smoke drift out into the night.
Like you did, Frank, that midnight when you had to take off.
Yeah, well, what else could I do? He lived alone, his lights were off—anybody would've thought the doctor wasn't home. Black bag full of goodies had to be around. I smelled his pipe, that's what turned me, saw him standing in a doorway.
Must have been quite a shock—
I thought to scare him, so I could duck by and run. But when I lifted that ashtray, he never even blinked: "Frank, I smacked your butt, the day you were born, I'd do it again, if I thought it would help." He said: "You're an embarrassment to your parents and a nuisance to the town. It's time we did something about that."
He called the police, informed my folks. But if I should happen to join the service he'd not bring any charges: My fingerprints were all over inside his house. He said that for the sake of expedience he and the county attorney would give me a lift tomorrow to the recruiting office—would bright and early be all right?

So you really were in the armed forces?

The closest I've come to soldiering is hearing the story told to me by a long-haired man that first night in this town, about the death of a woman, how he'd had such a bad time over there he'd vowed never again to hold a gun. Because I wasn't home early next morning, and they haven't seen me since—I don't even know if they're still looking for me; which ends me up working like a dog in a hole like this.

* * *

They, Tom and Frank, no longer felt it necessary to greet each other, mornings, for it no longer seemed like a night had come and gone, no longer felt as if the work had been broken off for the cure sleep was supposed to bring. Their labor began each day way before dawn, when Tom switched the light back on out in the barn. After the two men had done hours of chores out there they moved up the creek about first light to pause to catch two dozen or more calves sick enough to be run down, doctored half that many pinkeyed cows lured blindly in to the sound of a motor on the feed ground. They chased sick calves through snow and mud too deep for a horse, wrestled down big cows until they were either out of penicillin or else too exhausted to go on. They took time then to fix the tangle of wires and broken posts that used to be a hay pen, before the hungry cattle tested it and found it wanting: One whole side of it laid out across the meadow, half the stack torn down and ruined. They changed a flat tire, down in the mud, the heavily loaded feed truck teetering on the sinking jack, while the famished cows piled in so thick even a good dog couldn't keep them off, the cattle dragging down the hay and trompling it in the mud so fast there wasn't much left to salvage by the time the men beat the cattle back.

Walking out the bottom, they slogged through waist deep drifts, discovering other blind cows and the bodies of more sick calves—one was a teensy bit alive, the calf passing a bloody gruel that smelled so distinctly of death. They mother to the calf not quite dead yet, Tom cursing TJ because the barn corral was still full of cow-calf pairs Tom himself had ordered be left there until he, Tom, had had a chance to look them over before they were let out—finally threw up his hands and opened the gate, because daylight was gone and they couldn't see anyway.

Still, there was no end in sight, all those mother cows bawling at the barn door wanting to be let in and paired with calves too sick to bawl back let alone stand. But first they had to tail up most every cow, for inside the barn was the only dry spot the cattle had seen for months. The lead cows lay down as soon as their feet hit the plank floor, the others couldn't be driven past until the men waded through and whacked the cows back to their feet, shoved them into pens with calves they hoped were right.

Karen came by, lugging a bucketful of tricks: pillguns and boluses, syringes full of antibiotics, and powders to be mixed with milk, all of which had failed to work. Owen wandered in, too, to lend a hand, after he'd finished with his own cowbarn chores: tried to hold a cow mesmerized with a stick in her face, while Tom or Frank urged a sick calf to its feet, sneaked it up, and tried to finger a teat into its mouth, the cows walking incessantly inside those tiny pens, the men crooning, through clenched teeth: "Whoa there, whoa now," while the cows walked right on over their weak calves, knocking them sprawling time and again—until a man's patience broke, marked by the tattoo of a stick on cow hide, a furious voice beating cadence to the blows: *"I. . . said . . . whoa!"*

They turned the cows out to spend the night in the mud for fear they'd lay down inside the tiny pens on their own sick calves. They fed in the corral, hauling each bale by hand back under the trees where the mud didn't seem so deep. Frank swung round, halfway to the house, to return for the calf both he and Tom had forgotten, the sick little calf losing a handful of belly hair to the frozen puddle on the floorboards of the pickup truck.

Owen was blunt (half past eleven by the kitchen clock) when he told Tom, "Three," because Tom had asked the same question each night for a week: How many calves were on the milkcows in the other end of the barn? Owen felt certain Tom hoped maybe one of those calves had died, leaving room for another to make a little less work in the horsebarn morning and night. "I'm takin' too damn good a care for any of them to kick the bucket, so's they's gonna be three on each cow 'til we sell'm next fall."

Tom nodded, while Frank dumped the sick calf on a rug spread in the corner by the stove beneath a heat lamp, told Owen: "You're through in here, get to bed. School again tomorrow."

"I just come in!" Owen protested. "I ain't had time to eat!"

"Don't talk back," Frank warned. So Owen swung and went off down the hallway, while Frank set a bottle in a pan of water on the stove to warm the milk again. Both men slouched at the table, too tired to eat; while Karen leaned in the hallway entrance, watching the mud melt off the men's boots and puddle on the floor, smelling her kitchen fill with the stench from the dying calf, while the food she'd kept warm for hours grew cold. She turned, and followed Owen.

It was Frank, finally, who took a breath, stood to test the milk on the inside of his wrist—cursed, and swiped his arm across his shirt to wipe away the scalding pain, ran cold tap water across the bottle to cool it down again. The two men rolled the frail calf up, mouth cold as ice, eyes glazed, nose blue. Tom felt for a heartbeat: yes, but very faint. They worked a tube down the limp calf's throat, listening for sounds of stomach fluids indicating they'd not entered a lung. They forced the calf to eat, who, warmed some by the milk, gagged and kicked feebly, tearing loose the tube. Frank stared, stupid with fatigue, while the milk gurgled out on the floor. He glanced at Tom; but the old man said softly: "Gets kinda tired out, don't it son."

They toweled up the floor, missing spots here and there for Karen to find to kick off her morning. They gazed for a moment at the cold supper set out for them . . . stumbled wearily off to bed.

* * *

164

Frank stubbed out his smoke, studied what was left. It was all he had, he must get to town, look up that long-haired man—he needed time off, deserved it, too, slaving day and night, month after month—he'd been worked like a dog!—trying to save this old man's cattle about which Frank had a hard time working up even a hired man's passing interest. And wasn't this boss man coming to count on him like family? When all Frank had needed was a place to hide—when all he'd wanted after he'd first seen the woman was a piece of her action, out here in the country knowing she wasn't going anywhere else. But all Frank had got so far was to play uncle to her kid. Made Frank sick!

. . . Now there was a thought.

3.

Blue stumbled, hurrying, still more than half asleep. He was late, he knew it—the alarm had waked him, true, half past two, right on time. But lordy it was hard crawling out of bed then. Snowing still, six inches of new stuff on top of yesterday's old. He knocked apart a knot of cows huddled against the fence, shoved them into the open so he could take a better look. Blue followed one with his light: big, wild-eyed cow that walked away nervously, back humped, tail all in a kink. Suspect, he thought, shied her toward the open gate, watched her dash through into the dark.

But Blue could find no sign of TJ's midnight tracks, not those going nor any coming back. This surprised Blue, worried him, too. TJ had been so efficient of late Blue had begun a month ago to warn him he couldn't keep up the pace. Blue puffed along, thought: Maybe ol' TJ's finally collapsed, slept the whole night through in there cuddled with his cute wife where he ought've been all along. Blue turned aside, waded through a deep drift to poke at a wad of cows tucked in a corner. He pushed them apart so he could study each one, heard the tinkle of icicles clinging to their hair singing like crystal chimes. He hustled on . . . found a tiny heifer standing all alone, hunched and spraddled, confused and forlorn, staring woefully into the beam of light. Blue groaned when he saw her, hurried on past.

There was an old cow in the alley, new calf beside her already tongued clean, unsteady on its feet but nursing noisily. There was another cow in the first pen, her calf scrubbed, too, and struggling to stand. Blue found TJ huddled amongst the straw bales—no coat—shivering in his sleep. Blue shook him gently: "Son?"

TJ woke with a start, stared around—gaped at his watch and bounced to his feet, nearly falling on bloodless legs. He hobbled along until he could see the old cow in the alley, called to Blue: "You pull this calf?—why'nt you wake me?"

Blue said: "TJ—hey!—hold up there, son. You worry too much. She's big ol' cow, could calve baby el'phants. You're gonna spoil the whole bunch, word gets around—they'll be lined up at the shed gate, waitin' to see Doctor TJ. I jus' come over, but I s'pose you been here all night."

TJ nodded. "I got the flu."

"Then you ought to be in bed, dumb fool kid—you go on now, see your wife. I'll watch 'til sunup. I got it under control."

"Did you check them other cows? I ain't checked them for hours—I'll go take a look."

"Already done it," Blue said; then lied, "There ain't nothin' gonna happen. You run along. An' don't use your light, 'cause them cows outside is bedded, I don' want them stirred up."

"Well then," TJ swung around, "we need to put this big cow somewheres, look in on the sick calves." TJ pointed; Blue turned, saw stiff legs sticking out of the straw pile beside where TJ had been sleeping. TJ explained: "That one didn't make it."

"An' what you been doin', TJ? Sleepin' with it?"

TJ nodded. "I thought maybe I could keep him warm, give him a chance. But he went ahead and died."

Blue patted TJ's back: "You can't save them all. Look here, you're makin' me feel bad, like you don't think I can manage. You go on, leave me a turn."

But TJ loitered, wandering from pen to pen, moving in

to check a sick calf. Blue yelled at him: "TJ—goddamn it—get on home!"

"Right," TJ said, face ashen, eyes hollow. Still, he hung around, got down the fork and began to clean wet straw from the pen up front, until Blue snatched the tool away, glared at him fiercely. "Right," TJ said again, went stumbling out the door.

Blue sighed, turned and hurried down the alley to begin moving straw bales. It would give him an extra pen; but he needed more: one for that heifer outside, another for the wild cow—he heard TJ yell, from somewhere mid-distant: "Blue? Hey, Blu-u-ue!" Blue dropped a bale: TJ, sheezus! He already knew what TJ had found.

"Looka here," TJ was saying when Blue came puffing up, "look what you missed: Heifer's gonna calf. We can't go messin' round, Blue. Gotta find ever' one—"

"Oh hush, TJ!" Blue was blowing hard. "I already knowed she was here . . .'cause I already seen her. An' they's . . . another somewhere's . . . so if you notice her on your way out, don' be astounded. Now git!"

"But I can't go now." TJ stood weaving. "I gotta see if these two can calve."

"You're makin' me feel bad, boy," Blue said. "You're sick, give it up! Go get well so's you can lend a hand when I break down." Blue pleaded, "TJ, please, go on home."

But TJ was already staggering off toward the shed, calling back, "Bring the little cow, I'll get th' gate. Then we'll find the other . . . ." TJ's voice trailed away.

Blue grabbed a handful of snow, flung it after him. "Hee-yah!" he yelled in the heifer's face—she sprang back, astonished. Blue stopped then to have a talk with himself, forced himself calm. The young cow stood shaking, crippled by the pain of her first birthing, staring at Blue with big, dismayed eyes. Blue pushed her gently toward the fidgeting figure waiting in the light at the open shed gate . . . watched TJ hunch over to vomit in the snow.

* * *

They stole two panels off the watergap fence, took them inside to fashion a makeshift pen, Blue doing the carrying, while TJ sort of floated along behind, weaving, stumbling, trying his best to guide his end. Blue built the pen, while TJ huddled in a corner where Blue had sent him, Blue warning: "If I look, you better be there. I'll tie you down with balin' wire, TJ, I swear." Blue said, "This is selfish of you, 'cause where'll it leave me if you up an' die? Can't calve all these damned cows all by myself, so what you thinkin'—?"

TJ nodded, sinking, began to retch. Blue moved over to pat the boy's back until the sickness passed.

They closeted the two pairs inside the new pens, TJ arguing feebly how he'd had to stay put only while Blue built that new stall. They turned the snow-covered heifer into that last pen, moved outside again for the wild cow.

She was going to calve, no question about that—broke her water, third time she got past, TJ yelling, screaming, trying to make a stand—diving aside just in time, the wild cow thundering across his tracks. She outran the flashlight TJ hurled after her, while Blue, following with his own light, was certain that he'd seen the hind feet of her unborn calf. TJ said, "All right, here's wha' we do: Wait 'til she calves, carry it in."

"Calf's breech, TJ," Blue announced. "Calf's backwards, I'm sure."

TJ stared at him . . . said slowly, with dawning wonder: "Why, yes, 'course it would be. No cow so pig-headed would have it any other way."

"You should know," Blue said. "By nature, you an' her is twins."

They won out at last by running her down, plaguing her, until she'd tried everything else; she dived into the shed as a last retreat. Blue rushed to slam the gate as TJ staggered up, deathly pale.

"P'monia," Blue wheezed; "I see your gravestone now . . . TJ died a p'monia . . .'cause he was too dumb t' go home."

TJ fumbled out a cigarette. . . could not get it lit. He held it up for close inspection, found it drooping, soaking wet.

* * *

The little heifer seemed about ready by then: exhausted from straining, too small, it seemed, to deliver on her own. While the wild cow claimed the distant end of the shed, head high, eyes wild, pawing at the alley's litter, Blue rolled down in the wet straw behind the small cow, told TJ, "You stay put, son, this won't take long—li'l girl's too tiny for more than one to work anyhow. Prob'ly vanish completely, soon as I get this calf out."

But the little cow had big problems: no fluids, no sac; when Blue tried to check her, his hand ran into a tight dead end. "She's tortured," he announced. "We got to call the vet."

Tortured? TJ thought, crouched in the corner. "You mean she's torsioned, Blue?"

"Tortured, torsioned, same damned thing: got to call the vet." Blue dried his hands on a filthy rag as he headed for the gate. "TJ? You comin'? Where the hell you gone to now?" Blue wandered back; found TJ down on hands and knees inside the pen, checking the little cow for himself.

"Blue?" TJ said. "How'd you used to fix complications like this back before there were vets?"

"Shee whiz, TJ," Blue said, "I ain't that old. But le'me tell you, 's funny thing. They used to—oho no!—TJ, why you askin'? We ain't a gonna try nothin' like that. We ain't even gonna think 'bout nothin' like that. TJ, you un'erstand?"

* * *

The little cow lay trussed like a turkey for roasting, legs lashed tight to her belly by a saddle rope wrapped round and round her. Blue was begging, "TJ, please, this here's a old farmer's tale. I ain't never seen it done, I only heard it was attempted—"

"We ready then?" TJ said. "Let's give it a try."

"Christ sakes, boy," Blue muttered, "you ain't heard a word I said." But he moved up beside TJ to take hold of the rope. Slowly, they bumped the cow over, two tired men sweating and cursing, unwinding her across the width of the shed, her head twisting round, eyes rolling desperately as she tried somehow to keep the world upright. When the rope came loose, spilling the men in the filthy straw, Blue shook his head, "Ain't no good, TJ. Got to call th'—"

"Once more," TJ wheezed.

"You go ahead," Blue said, "I'm not gonna help." He vowed: "I won't, TJ, this time I mean it."

"Okay," TJ nodded, and he began struggling to rewrap the cow by himself. Blue closed his eyes for a moment, like in silent prayer—angrily yanked the rope from TJ's hands.

Twice more they rolled her, two more mean trips across the shed—two more spills full-length in the spoiled straw. Blue lay sprawled, proclaiming loudly: "All right, that's it. All's we gonna do is break th' cord, drown that calf. An' I won't be a party to it."

"Don't have to," TJ said, his voice muffled from behind the little cow. "It worked."

"I'm serious, TJ, I will not . . . whataya mean it worked?" Blue struggled up, moved to look, saw for himself the feet of the unborn calf, the little heifer gaining, straining for all she was worth. "Well, I'll be damned," Blue whispered reverently. "I never heard that it ever worked."

They helped the little cow deliver, each tugging on a leg—TJ pounced on the newborn calf and began furiously pumping it to life; until Blue laid a hand on his shoulder: "You're gonna kill a perfectly good calf, son, if you don't stop." They turned more cows out into the snow, whose calves seemed to be the strongest (eyes still bright, noses not so fever-burned); put those calves together in a corner fenced by straw bales, and moved the new little mother into a freshly vacated pen. Blue guided her along while he lugged her wet calf, with TJ following, grilling him:

"What we gonna do, Blue? Still got that wild cow. Pretty soon she'll try the gate; then she'll be gone. What we do to get that backwards calf?"

Blue grunted, trying to think, while he waded over the piles of old bedding, the calf in his arms like a bag of wet sand. He stumbled, tried to catch himself—stepped down on an old afterbirth hidden beneath the spoiled straw (like putting a foot on a yard-long banana peel). Down he went—so fast—TJ faced a vacant space when he looked up again.

"Blue?" TJ called. "Blue, where'd you go?" Blue had vanished like he'd never been there. TJ felt prickles run up his backbone. He moved a cautious step forward . . . found Blue spilled in the valley between two mounds of rotting straw. TJ hunkered down: "What we gonna do, 'bout that ol' wild cow?"

"Don' know yet," Blue wheezed. "Workin' on it. Drag this calf off me, would ya, so's I can get my breath."

They brought the wild cow up the alley, TJ flying, skimming over the piles of straw, his legs working like pistons, the cow right behind him blowing in his hip pocket—TJ soared: up and over the far wall of the pen as the wild cow crashed into the boards underneath him—she whirled for the gate, but Blue slammed it in her face. TJ lay curled on the floor, and Blue patted his arm.

They waited her out then, biding their time, until she turned at last and faced the chute so they could rush her like they'd decided: Blue with his bulk supposed to hit her from behind while TJ came off the fence to crank on her tail. She flung TJ off like a centrifuged fly, took Blue in a rush back over the gate, Blue landing on his paunch in the alley. Blue summed it up: "Need . . .'nother plan."

So they roped her, head and hind feet, stretched her out thin across the pen. But she was thrashing around so they still couldn't get the calf puller lined out; until at last she choked down. "You hold off there, son," Blue said to TJ, who was hovering over the shivering rope with his pocket knife.

"She's gonna suffocate, Blue—I can't get no slack!"

"I don' care!" Blue said. "You wait, 'til I get hold a this calf." Blue hooked up the puller and pried down hard on the shaft, hoping the pressure would keep the wild cow flat. He uttered a prayer, told TJ to let her loose. But when he'd freed the rope, TJ decided on whim to throw himself on the big cow's head to try to hold her down: She piled him in the corner, TJ's face ghastly white. Blue was left all alone to crank on the puller for all he was worth, his own face blood red, breath coming in gasps. The puller shaft was quaking as the wild cow came around—Blue felt the calf's hips pop through the pelvis just before the puller was snatched from his grasp.

TJ had found his legs again, wobbly and trembling; he was straightening up, when the heavy head on the puller shaft came whistling around, caught him in the wind and hurled him back against the fence. Blue watched the cow try to take the gate, saw her smash down halfway over. She hung there bellering, battering the wood with her hooves, her half-born calf thrashing, drowning.

The chain jingling cheerfully in the midst of flying splinters that kept Blue pinned down like by rifle fire. He glanced at TJ, saw him piled like rags. Blue stood, and gathered the slack rope from the litter of straw, leaned in above those murderous hooves and threaded it through the rattling chain still hooked around the calf's hind legs. Then another board gave, spilling the cow into the alley—Blue found the nearest post and managed two dallies, closed his eyes, and hung all his weight on the end of the rope. He heard a beat of hooves, the rigid pounding of a running cow—Blue wondered, did he have on his gloves? His eyes flew open, flickered with despair. Nope, both hands were bare.

4.

Karen stirred, reached out for TJ . . . found nothing but an empty pillow. Where was he?—why was he gone? She was so tired of waiting—would he never come home?

5.

One door turned slowly, creaking in on its hinges; the two-by-four that had barred it lay shattered on the ground. The other door hung sprung, dug into the snow; and beyond, just visible by the light streaming through the opening, the top rail of the fence was gone.

Blue was badly hurt, he knew without looking. He held his hands gently cradled, not yet ready to peek, blew delicately into his cupped palms. The soft warmth of his breath brought the pain straight to the top. Oh my!" he whispered, and opened them up.

The rope had gone sizzling—he'd not have been able to hold it had not the knots come along, sucked both fists tight against the fence post. He'd have lost them both then, had not God in good spirits caused the calf to come. Blue spread his fingers, and held both palms out for fearful scrutiny, peered in upon vast expanses of glossy meat, lily-white fish-flesh, recovering just enough to begin leaking pinpoints of blood. Blue stared in horror while the blood came oozing back, popping out at a hundred different points. He gritted his teeth, sat waiting for the real pain—

Behind him, there was a soft moan. Blue swung to see TJ trying to sit up, his face an awful shade of grey. TJ's lips were moving like he was nursing a teat, his cheeks sunken, his mouth caved in. Blue heard a vast sucking sound, air returning in a rush to fill TJ's lungs.

"I got that calf pulled, TJ," Blue said, "whilst you was layin' 'bout." Blue watched TJ tip forward, fall face first in the straw.

The calf was still alive, blowing bubbles out its nose, and flopping its droopy wet ears, still trying to figure how best to use this foreign air. It swung clumsily to watch the two strange figures come hobbling down the alley, TJ doubled over, gasping for breath, whispering in an amazed voice: "Blue . . . wha' this? How . . . calf . . . ge' 'ere? Goo' lor'. . . Blue, wha' . . .'appened?"

"Long story, son." Blue crouched down. The rear legs of the calf were stripped of skin from ankle to hock, the loose hide bunched like sagging socks around the base of each hind hoof. Blue gently removed the chain, tenderly flexed a foot: "Aw hell, ain' so bad, nothin' broke that I can see." He patted the wet back—winced: "We'll jus' pull them socks back up an' sew them on, be good as new."

TJ said, "Bu' where's . . . th' cow?"

"Tell you in a bit, son, you jus' foller along for now. See, that ol' cow left in a hurry, took out the back door, cre-

173

ated a awful draft: whisked this poor calf halfway down the alley an' sucked most the skin off my hands." Blue gave his gloves to TJ. "Hold these open for me, so I can put them on." Blue gingerly crawled into them, gritting his teeth, stopped to study TJ closer: "You all right?"

"Oh . . . sure." TJ was doubled over, breath coming in quick gulps, while he tried not to breathe at all. Blue squinted at him, then gently moved TJ's hands aside and lifted the boy's shirt. He whistled.

"Well now, maybe it's you oughta go see the vet. Got some busted ribs there, 's my guess—bad bent ones, sure as hell. But anyhow, how's breakfast sound? No? Well, 'peals to me. You can set, watch me eat. Here, son, I'll get th' gate . . .'cept maybe you'd best help me with it. Here's my plan: We'll not bring that wild cow back in—not even think about her no more, like she's vanished from the earth. We'll sew her calf back together, put him on that other cow whose calf died in the straw pen, you follow me, son? Can you wade this snow? Here, lean on me. We still could shoot that ol' bitch I guess, stick her in a ditch, say tha's how we found her—hell, I'll think a somethin', I always do, TJ—hey, you, TJ! Get back here! Don't you even think 'bout lookin' at them cows. I mean, what can we do? You can't hardly walk, an' I can't carry you. Turn off your flashlight, TJ, you're wastin' the batt'ries. 'S near 'bouts daylight, you notice that? Anyhow, cows don't never calve in the daytime, only way late at night."

6.

Sarah squinched her eyes, concentrating, the tip of her tongue stuck out to help. She carefully finished shaping the wooden plug, studied it to see if it was right . . . Sarah was becoming quite adept at the repair by now. What a battle, morning and night, between Sarah and the mouse.

Early in the winter TJ had made Sarah's mouse a wooden cage with a glass top. Sarah had scattered it with grass and bits of bark—whatever she could find to make a deer mouse feel at home. Leaves and twigs, cow hair for its nest; there was even a little pile of cedar berries, stacked like a tiny mound of cannonballs, which TJ had brought back from off the mountain, hinting how they might be magic, maybe just the thing to coax her mouse to eat. Sarah remembered that first night after she had moved the deer mouse into its new home.

* * *

Midnight, her mouse at last had stuck its head out of its ragged nest, wiggling its nose, testing the air, gazing about with those depthless dark eyes. There were lots of new odors outside the nest tonight or maybe they were old smells, which the mouse had not smelled for such a long time. The deer mouse scampered out onto a musty piece of cottonwood bark and quivered with excitement: Bits of grass and leaves and sticks were strewn everywhere; and over it all came the pungent smell of juniper. The mouse leaped down and began to skitter its way cautiously across the floor toward where the juniper scent seemed strongest. There, in a corner, was the careful mound of cedar berries. The mouse leaned way out from a rough piece of wood, poked its nose at the pile and was off and running instantly when the corner of the heap gave way and all those hard, round berries came tumbling down. The deer mouse streaked around in half a circle and sat up to look back.

There was a thick chunk of wood leaned up against the far wall. Sarah had thought it would make a nice ramp, mouse-sized, for her pet to climb. The deer mouse vanished, reappeared halfway up the stick, braked there for a look around, then dashed on to the top in a blurred rush of speed—bumped its head hard against the glass lid of the cage. The mouse nosed against the strange, imperceptible roof, leaning way out as far as its legs would allow. Everywhere it tried to go the invisible ceiling stopped it. Suddenly—again with no warning—it stuck its nose out through one of the airholes TJ had drilled in a neat row along the top of the wooden wall, the hole nearly too small for even a deer mouse nose, its whiskers bent back and crumpled.

Sarah was jubilant—the nose of her deer mouse was

inches from her face! She watched it curl and wriggle—discovered how the mouse could actually bend its nose this way and that like a tactile member, the mouse testing the odors beyond the wall. Sarah saw the tiny nostrils flair and pinch, the rich pink color inside, and the fine, white skin in through the dark fur. She wanted so much to reach out and touch it, but she dared not move. It was more important tonight to see if the mouse would eat. A moment more, then the deer mouse was gone—materialized again down on the floor, sat cleaning its face vigorously using its two front paws exactly like tiny hands. Sarah watched the creature sit bolt upright. She held her breath as the mouse reached out and snatched up a berry, cradling it like an apple and inspecting it closely. Then the mouse began to eat.

Sarah was overjoyed—TJ was right—the berries truly were magical! She sat perfectly still, scarcely daring to breathe, while the mouse shelled the meat off the seed faster than Sarah's mom could peel an apple. The deer mouse hunkered down, eyes closed to slits, its thin, nimble fingers spinning the berry like a top. But when Sarah shifted, just a little bit, to ease a cramp beginning in her leg, the mouse was down on all fours and set to run, the seed rolling forgotten across the cage. Sarah froze, not daring to blink . . . until at last the mouse fluffed its coat, scratched vigorously at its belly fur, snatched up another seed, and began again to eat. Sarah watched while it finished the meat and shelled the tough nut to eat the embryo inside; watched while the deer mouse ate three more exactly the same way, while Sarah's legs cramped dreadfully and faded at last to numbness.

Then all at once the mouse was off and running again, bolting in a mad dash all around the cage, zipping along the length of sticks, flying over the floor with a great scattering of leaves and a flood of tiny scritching sounds to reappear suddenly at the top of the wooden ramp. The mouse stuck its nose out through the airhole again, twitching its nostrils this way and that, then it set to work gnawing at the edges of the hole with those keen front teeth that had made shelling the hard stones of the cedar berries no task at all.

"Hey!" Sarah cried, "You're trying to get away!" Sarah

was astounded—she'd not imagined such a thing could happen. But she was no more amazed than was the mouse: a thunderous voice, coming all at once from out of nowhere, freezing the deer mouse to the stick like a furry brown lump. Then the deer mouse was gone; the thistledown nest skidded sideways and bumped up against the far wall, sat quivering like a tiny heart thumping with fear. Sarah paid it no mind: She was examining the hole closely where the mouse had been at work. Though the wooden walls were thick, she could see already the results where the deer mouse had been gnawing. Sarah lifted the glass and knocked down the ramp. Shee whiz! she thought. Now what do I do?

* * *

Sarah heard the kitchen door open, close, knew it wasn't Tom, for she'd heard her grandfather go out way before first light, and he rarely came back in again once he'd stepped outside. She crept down the hallway and looked in on the kitchen. TJ was slumped in a chair, coat off, shirttail pulled up, painfully trying to twist around to see the big, bloody bruise spread across his ribs.

"TJ!" Sarah cried. "What happened to you?"

TJ jumped—gasped—tugged down his shirt. "Nothin'," he said, sat up stiff and straight. "Di'nt do nothin'." Sarah watched him stand and cautiously limp off to rummage in the cupboard. He sat back down and tried to nibble a soda cracker. Sarah said:

"Where you been, TJ? You been working all night?" TJ merely grunted, so Sarah reached out for his shirt. When he flinched away, she asked again: "What happened to you there?"

"Nothin', I tol' you—don' ask no more." TJ shaved bits off the cracker with his teeth, swallowed them and sat trying to keep it down, while Sarah watched him. She wanted his advice, needed his thoughts badly. She started to speak, stopped herself . . . decided at last she would:

"TJ? You know my mouse—?"

"Sarah!" TJ snapped. "I got no time for your damned mouse! Either kill it or let it go, I don't care which, but leave me alone about it, 'cause I don't want a hear."

Sarah turned abruptly and went back down the hallway. She'd begun to cry, didn't want TJ to see. Her father had too much to think about already; he didn't need to start worrying about her.

* * *

TJ sat, no longer trying to eat—he'd felt the tiny weight of what he'd swallowed hit his stomach like a stone. He sighed, and eased himself to his feet . . . tried his best to hang up his coat, but it was just too heavy, soaked and muddy; he couldn't bear to lift the weight of it high enough to reach the hook. He stood for a moment, trying to think it through, finally left the filthy thing slumped soggily against the wall. TJ paused outside the bathroom door wondering if his stomach would allow him to pass by . . . limped on to his own room, turned to stare in at an empty bed. He was deeply disappointed, wanting so to see his wife—where could she have gone, so early? He never bothered to undress, eased himself down, searching for a position where his ribs wouldn't hurt him, decided at last there was no such place. He told himself it didn't matter; he could only rest for a minute or two . . . must get back out . . .

7.

Tom sent no one, came himself, asking clipped questions of his grandchildren at the breakfast table. "He's in there," Owen informed him, "asleep." Tom found TJ's coat slumped in the corner, shook his head grimly as he hung it up.

"Hey you! Git outa bed—whataya think this is?" Tom shook his son, poked his ribs. (Had he heard TJ gasp with pain? Tom guessed he must have scared the boy—now wasn't that just like this fainthearted son.) He stared as TJ tumbled off the bed.

"What the hell's wrong with you? Can't you even stand? How come you're here sleepin'? Ever'body else out workin' like they should be—includin' your own wife."

"Don' feel so good." TJ tried to roll over.

"Well, by god, you don't look so good, neither. You been out late?" Tom squinted at him: "You drinkin' again, TJ? So help me—don't matter—you gotta come. I got one man off his feed already, 's all I can afford. You an' Blue will help me today, 'cause Frank's real sick." Tom nudged TJ with a boot. "Tell Karen she's to drive Frank to town—no, I'll tell her myself, save time. You find Blue, meet me at the truck. Need two men just to replace Frank. Now git!"

* * *

The snow had ceased falling when TJ knocked at the bunkhouse door; the clouds were thinning out, sun coming up. TJ could see it would be a very bright day, thought wearily: Sunburn some cows' teats, 'fore nightfall. Blue answered the door stripped to his long underwear, hands done up in bandages. "TJ," he said, "lis'en: We done our best, so you turn 'round, go on home. I been back already, sewed up that calf. You go to bed now, get some—"

"Tom says we're to help him today, 'cause Frank's sick."

Blue stared at TJ, then looked to the floor, said, "Is that so."

* * *

By seven-thirty, they'd nearly finished cleaning up the last of the hay from one of the few remaining stacks, the bales all loaded on the pickup truck, Blue suffering terribly, his hands a torment, while he hoisted the bales up by their strings to TJ who rolled them into place on the truck as best he could, his teeth clenched, too, against the raw agony in his ribcage. Tom was walking out the bottom, came back driving a lank and stumbling cow: "You two clowns know what I got here?"

TJ blinked, squinted into the brilliant sunlight. "A cow?" he offered, looked to Blue for help.

Blue shrugged, "Sure looks like a cow, don' know what else it could be. Tom, why'nt you tell us, save some more time."

Tom was livid, turned away to get a grip, fists clenched, jaw working . . . came slowly back. "This cow's the best I got. She first calved as a two-year-old, all by herself, an' every year since then, she's brought in the biggest steer calf we market each fall. But she's aged real bad—I should a sold her last weanin' time. 'Cept I had too many open cows an' the market was awful. So I decided to keep her, see if she'd give me a heifer calf. Which she did, first one she ever had, either of you recall that? 'Course not, like you forgot to remember to check her good when you left her in the barn corral for me to turn out yesterday. Now look at her: plumb full of infection because she never cleaned right— one shot of penicillin, 's all she needed. Just look at her now!"

Tom scowled as both men hung their heads, said: "All right, goddamn it, who's gonna drive?"

Both men jumped—TJ wheezing, clutching at his ribcage, trying to find some way to climb down off the load—both talking at once, babbling, each concerned only for the other's welfare:

"You drive, Blue."

"Oh no, TJ, you."

"Yeah, and what about your hands?"

"Well, what of your ribs? I s'pose you're gonna tell me they feel jus' fine."

Both them went wrangling on, while Tom stared, dumbfounded, ordered at last: "Blue—Jesus Christ!—git in the cab!" So TJ, who'd finally managed to slide off the hay, had to crawl back on again, while Blue moved down past him, Blue offering TJ a forlorn look as he passed by.

* * *

Blue drove along glumly. Tom had bested them again. Now Tom was up there, cutting TJ to bits. Blue squinched

into the dazzling morning—first sun he'd seen for days—
felt the light come echoing off the snow, blinding him,
another agony. He stared out the window at the bony cows,
sickly calves; nothing new, all misery. Blue began to feel
severely down. Sun'll burn them cows' tits, calf slobbers'll
chap them; wind'll come along an' make them crack. None
of those cows is gonna want for a calf to suck; that much
more on top of ever'thing else. He sighed.

Off to the side he could see Tom's shadow gliding along
over the snow, saw the thinner shade TJ cast as the boy
hacked the strings and fed the hay off to the hungry cattle.
Blue watched Tom's silhouette stride back and forth, heard
Tom's voice chewing at TJ like a dog on a bone.

Up ahead there was a thin, dim line, faint blue shadow
in the snow, suggestion of a ditch. Blue slowed reflexively
. . . cocked his head and began to grin: Now that wasn't a
nice thought, too bad he didn't have the balls for it. . . Blue's
grin turned wolfish as he pressed down on the gas pedal.

Tom was really rolling now, shadow waving, hopping
about. Blue could hear him getting all wound up, picking
out the finer points of every stupid thing TJ had ever done,
Tom striding across the bales as if he walked on solid earth,
yelling back to where TJ worked mutely at the rear of the
load, while Blue came roaring down on the ditch.

And never, not ever, if he lived a hundred years and his
brain turned to stone, would Blue forget the look on Tom's
face when the old man came flying headfirst down across
the windshield, slithered over the hood and vanished
beyond the grill. Blue sat, foot still clomped down on the
brake pedal, stomach convulsing, hands over his mouth,
trying his best to stifle his laughter: Hoo, lordy! That was
fine! But wait! Got to get holt of myself, get on up there
and see if the old fart's still alive.

He set the brake and leaped from the truck, giving TJ a
conspiratorial wink—TJ's eyes grew wider, his lips forming
the incredulous word: "You?" Blue hurried on ahead, bent
down to look at Old Tom.

"Tom?—Christ sakes!—you all right?" He hauled the
old man roughly to his feet. "I never even seen that ditch,
never noticed it, 'til there I was, right on top—I knew if I

didn't stop I'd tip off half the load." Blue acted out his great disgust: "Them goddamned brakes! Gotta get them brakes fixed, I tol' you so—you sure I never mentioned it? Well, you know now. You okay, Tom?" Blue slapped some snow off Old Tom's coat, managing to dust most of it down Tom's neck; Tom winced: "Hurt your shoulder? Your back, too?"

Blue ducked away, scurrying beyond reach, as Tom's hand came scything around like to lop off Blue's head. He watched the old man hobble to the rear, shrugged to TJ, and climbed in behind the wheel again, Blue thinking: Now what's come over you? Tha's risky business—lose your job some day over somethin' that silly.

But it sure shut Ol' Tom up, didn't it?—hee!

Tom made TJ follow the sick cow home, waved at her rigidly as Blue drove back by; and TJ obediently slid off and limped along behind her all the way to the corrals. Tom left orders: "Take care of things," and TJ nodded, leaning vacantly over the fence. He watched as the truck drove away . . . banged his chin on the top plank, dozing off.

He was halfway through the corrals, trailing the wobbling cow, holding her tail like a blind man, when he heard Frank and his wife come back home. Frank was talking loudly; TJ heard them both laugh. He left the sick cow there, moved on past, returned from the shed with a needle and syringe to give her a dose where she stood. He wondered then if she might appreciate a drink, so he pushed her over the muddy bank, left her wobbling at the edge of the rising creek. He'd return for her after she'd drank her fill. TJ slowly skinned the cold hide off the body in the straw pile, cut leg holes in it, and dressed it over the calf he'd named Sox. He checked Blue's stitching, nodded approval, and carried the calf in its new coat in to the grieving mother whose baby had died.

The mother cow was ecstatic! . . the old range cow leery; the cow as a whole was completely confused, for while the tail of this calf smelled like her own, the ears and nose smelled all wrong. TJ buried the strange scent of the calf's head deep in the cow's flank, fingered a teat into the hungry calf's mouth. He sat back and watched it nurse greedily while the old cow nosed at her own calf's hide. At last, the cow began cleaning the new calf's dirty coat, convinced that things were right.

TJ grinned. His ribs ached dreadfully and he was deathly tired, but now the world was roses. He eased himself carefully to his feet, and headed for the straw pen. He would allow himself a short break, rest for a bit curled up in the afternoon sun streaming in through the shed's broken back door.

8.

Tom dropped Blue off just at dark, sent him to the house with another sick calf, and turned the pickup up the snowy road toward those upper meadows where he wintered the bulls, for no one had found time to feed them yesterday nor the day before. Tom rummaged on the floorboards while he drove along, searching for a hammer and a handful of nails. He assumed by now the bulls had broken into the haystack and had fed themselves.

The wind that had come up hard in the afternoon, and had dropped off grudgingly for an evening lull, was gusting again now: Snow snakes and streamers ran across the headlights—no tracks, except those of a drifting coyote, whose trail wandered briefly along the right-of-way, the tracks filling quickly, just about gone. Tom drove absently, trying to plan.

* * *

So in the end a man is willing not only to chase his father's dream, dedicate his life to its pursuit, but he's not satisfied until he's committed the lives of his family, their families, and countless hired men to chasing it, too. Why? Why work twenty hours a day for sixty years with no break other than funerals, no end either other than your own, watching the dream come no closer—the truth is, the banker informs you, it's grown more remote—until all reason to continue has dimmed to an afterglow like the head of a used match. The only fact certain, other than knowing there no longer are those sixty years ahead like once there'd been, is that you'd need even more time, plus inconceivable luck, to ever even come close. The only light at the tunnel's end—this not some new plan—hinges upon your own ability to persuade young muscles to follow the same path chasing your father's dreams—

Now wait—goddamn it—look at those buildings, house, barn, shed, those corrals. Look at the meadows, where once there was sage. Tell me, straight stuff, has a man slaved in vain? Look at those heaps of stone picked by hand from fields by men whose backs used to ache only in the evenings. Do you believe I wasted my time? Maybe it's not right to treat cows like cattle, maybe it's wrong to work like a dog. I've looked at it hard, and I see no other choices . . . it's a little late now for second-guessing anyhow. May be all that matters is to raise up a family, make sure your blood passes on down the line. But it seems to me that's not quite right: seems a lifetime should arrive someplace.

* * *

They'd fed themselves, as Tom had feared. He sat slumped over the steering wheel, watching the bulls in the headlights, just their rumps showing, head and shoulders deep in the hay pen's ruined slabs. He studied them at work, admiring their technique: hook a horn into a crevice, tear loose a board using only a small fraction of their tremendous strength. Tom climbed out, spoke to the bulls, slapped some butts, moving them ponderously out of the way. There was a broken horn tip left like a lost pry bar, the snow dyed all around by spurting blood.

He tried not to rush, working tediously to nail the corral back up; he felt strangely fragile, clumsy and light, unearthly shadows too often catching his eye, making his heart leap. His hand did not seem his own, out there at arm's end, his mind trying to guide the hammer, too often missing the nail. The night wind hissed—he stared wildly around, chest tight, neck hair prickling! But it was only a bull, strolling across before the truck, its bulk for a moment

184

blocking the lights. Tom returned to his work, ashamed of himself. He tried to think on what still needed to be done, but his mind wouldn't focus, went wandering off. He gave up on planning, worked awkwardly until he'd repaired the fence as best he could, poorly done, he knew, but he could not bring himself to care.

He struggled wearily to the top of the stack, stood breathing hard . . . realized then that he'd not backed the pickup in so he could load the hay. He tried to convince himself he must climb back down, do it right. If he simply rolled the bales off into the snow the younger bulls would not get their share. But it seemed too much bother; he began battling the top bales, trying to break them loose from their mortar of ice and snow, struggling despairingly—how come everything's so hard! Tom sat down abruptly, hand to his chest; his heart was racing like the valves in a motor wound way too tight. His arms felt numb, strange shooting pains running into his chest. Fear arced through him. Was he about to die?

But if this was the end, Tom was too tired to care. He fumbled for his pocketknife, hacked at the strings, rolled the bales off a slice at a time. Tom drove hunched over the steering wheel, not wanting to think, yet knowing he must decide.

And soon.

Yes, soon as I can find time—it's more complex than anyone could ever know. He's my son, after all—

He's inept.

The problem then is not with deciding. The problem is with knowing, whatever I choose, it's not what I'd have picked, had I any choice.

Decide!

If TJ can't do the job, I'll find someone who can.

There now, you're getting somewhere. But what if there's no time left?

What's that s'posed to mean?

You're an old man, with chest pains—might not be the time necessary to go off searching. If TJ can't do the job, no use in looking outside for someone who can.

Karen's a woman, Owen's too young. Nobody else . . . maybe TJ will come around.

9.

Dark, no moon, clouds riding in again. Blue woke TJ and queried him gently about the status of things. TJ grinned back sleepily, brushing off straw, informed Blue that everything was fine. TJ tried the old flashlight kept on the shelf between the scour pills and teat grease; it flickered dim and yellow, the batteries weak. He slapped it against his palm, trying to knock some life back into the old cells, wobbled outside to check on the cows.

Freezing again; TJ shivered, but he hummed a tune while he teetered along, his feet plunging through the frozen crust formed on the mud like trying to wade a deep berry pie. He held his ribs; but he didn't care now how much it hurt him. Things were coming together, life was looking up. TJ searched through the first corral, pushing the weak light ahead of him like a short stick . . . noticed a cow standing at the watergap gate, ears pricked, head held high. TJ spooked her aside, shined his light down toward the creek: dim gleam off rising waters, something else? TJ couldn't make it out, but his heart all at once was hammering. Something was down there—big black lump. He hurried forward, shoving his light out before him, saw the body of a cow, obviously dead, water running in a dark swirl over her head.

* * *

"Blue, please!"

"But she's done for, TJ, surely you can tell. Her head's under water, we can't help her now—"

"I know she's dead—gotta turn her out. Drag her off some'eres—listen to me: mos' important calf ever born! Christ sakes, Blue, can'tcha see!"

"Yeah, I can see real good that you're talkin' crazy— she's dead, son. We can't turn out no dead cow, 's impossible; she can't no longer walk. 'Sides, Tom'll find her outside, see she died after all, figure we let her out again—oh. 'Course. How stupid a me. But we can't move her nohow. She must weigh half a ton, 'fore she got soakin' wet. What

186

you got in mind? Throw her on your shoulder an' tote her up that bank?"

"Hey, we could! No, we can't—we'll bring over the tractor, yank her out, load her on the wagon, straw on top— say we cleaned the shed—needed cleanin' bad."

"TJ, remember why we ain't cleaned the shed before? It's because we can't get nothin' through the mud to haul it out. You recall that fact, TJ?"

"We'll use boards, build a slab road all the way to the shed—he can't find her dead, Blue, worst thing could ever happen."

"Can't be done, son."

"Aw, Blue, please!"

* * *

TJ told Tom, you must give him that. Stood blinking in the headlights while Tom drove up, owned up to all of it, though Blue tried his best to weasel in on the blame, saying: "Now that there was my fault, Tom. I shoulda knowed better'n leave the cow on water. I shoulda knowed she'd never get back up the bank."

TJ smiled sadly, grateful for Blue's fierce loyalty, reminded him: "You wasn't home, Blue, when I drowned that cow."

Blue said: "You know what's your problem, boy? You never understood somebody wantin' to help you, 'cause you never could see how you was worth the bother."

They watched him drive away, all except Tom, who kept on walking toward the barn where the shutters were swung open so the faces in there could try to see what the fuss was about, TJ steering his way out to the county road, pointing the lights of his old truck toward town, Blue yelling after him, across the yard: "You take the morning shift, TJ, I'll cover for you tonight." Blue turned then to hurry after Tom, grabbed the old man and swung him around. "He's got busted ribs, you know that, Tom? 'Course not, you ol' dog—he's sick, too, ain't slept a night through in who knows how long. Why, he's been goin' at it harder'n you have, Tom, ain't that somethin'? He's a good boy, doin' the

187

best he can; an' he's doin' it for your sake, you know that?—you sonofabitch, Tom, you list'nin'?"

10.

Sarah heard a motor start, ran to her window to see. TJ's truck was leaving, headed out the lane. Sarah sighed, she supposed things were not going well. She folded her pocketknife and peered in through the glass to the bottom of the cage. The deer mouse was still there, tiny hands folded, sitting looking up at her with big, black eyes.

"Go 'way!" Sarah whispered fiercely. "Stop staring at me!" Though the mouse trembled some, it never ran, but sat gazing patiently, like it was waiting for her to finish.

Sarah knelt down, and began working the plug she'd just carved into the mouse-gnawed hole. There were dark circles underneath Sarah's eyes now, and her cheeks were hollow from lack of sleep, from getting up way early, staying up too late, wondering what on earth to do.

* * *

If only I could put them all together someplace and force them to stay there, maybe then they'd work out their differences. But the most I can do is keep this poor mouse penned up, and all he wants is to get away, too—

Isn't anything free—we're all only waiting to see what He does next. I bet they don't know it, I bet they don't even think how they can't stop God from doing exactly what He wants: He points His finger—bang—everything's changed; and all we can do is put up with it, wondering when it will end.

If I had a cage big enough to put them in, maybe after a while they'd see how accepting each other isn't so bad. When they'd learned that, I'd let them go.

But you haven't let the deer mouse go—

Such a pretty thing, just like a baby. I know it's not right, still keeping it now—I only meant to keep it until it was well. But each time I think of letting it go I feel like I can't breathe—I couldn't stand not knowing whether it was all right. I guess I'll have to guard it for the rest of its life, because there are an awful lot of dangers out there: barn cats, coyotes—rattlesnakes—no way else could I know it's safe, unless I take the responsibility for shutting it up. I'll let it loose, I promise, when it gets smart enough to care for itself.

But how will you know? How will you be able to judge when it's ready for the world?

It will figure some way to escape.

* * *

Sarah sat on the edge of her bed, rolling the old gnawed plug between her fingertips. It had been chewed nearly through; the mouse had almost got away today. Just a little longer—

There came again the scritching sound, tiny feet, the deer mouse was about. She tiptoed to the cage, watched it climb nimbly up the wall and saw it set to work gnawing at the new plug she'd just finished. A great anger welled up inside her—she threw the old, scarred piece of wood as hard as she could, bounced it off the glass and sent the mouse scrambling for cover back inside its shabby nest. Sarah gritted her teeth, and retrieved the ruined plug, meaning to throw it away like she'd done with all the rest.

Instead she stood for a long time staring into the glass-topped box, until the deer mouse grew bold enough to creep back out. She watched it sit up and stretch its nose out toward her, front paws folded as if in prayer. It trembled, but it never ran when Sarah raised her arm like she meant to hurl the scrap of wood again. Suddenly Sarah twisted loose the new plug she'd just whittled and replaced it with the ruined one she still held in her hand. She opened the window, the tiniest crack, no wider than a deer mouse would need to squeeze through into the night. Then Sarah went to bed, pulled the covers over her head and shut her eyes tight.

Wednesday,
19th March

1.

A freezing fog lay along the river for folks to inch
through as they crossed over the bridge; mist rising off the
channel of black water left to thread its way between the ice
floes backed up behind the pilings and pushed out onto the
frozen banks. Here, now, at midnight, the fog had crawled
into town, huddled round the buildings, and crept along the
streets, dragging the few cars out almost to a stop, the street-
lights nebulous, wasting their energy on a few feet of night.

Inside a narrow two-story brick building—cafe on one
hand, a sadly graveled alley crowding the other side, with
its cheap apartments all rented overhead though the sounds
of drinking went on throughout the night—cigarette smoke
hung in a thick, murky haze beneath a ceiling still showing
bullet wounds from the early days, an historic place, now
nearly a dive. There were two women in the room, an
ancient crone, who came in alone each night to stand and
talk to herself and drink, and a girl from New York on her
way through in a derelict car that had made it here before
falling in a heap, the girl drawing men like flies to dead
meat, who bought her all she'd ever wished to drink and
more, until everything they said was funny. She laughed,
loud and often, staggering some as she sashayed away from
all the clutching hands.

TJ had set out to drink himself to death, had failed at
that too, left his vomit splashed on the restroom floor for the
old woman up front to discover when the bartender handed
her a bucket and a mop at closing time. TJ was still drinking, but slower now, feeling as empty as the night. He wondered if anyone cared whether he lived or died? He wondered if he should phone home to find out?

The door bounced wide on a gust of wind, the fresh air
smelling odd mixed in with the smoke and stale bodies; it
set the old woman to cursing, a monotonous, slobbering
sound. TJ swung, head bobbing, saw—no one he knew—

some long-haired man in a drab trenchcoat, a woman following, who was caught for a moment staring the length of
the bar straight into TJ's eyes. TJ grabbed for his hat—
Ma'am—but the woman had turned away, and TJ found his
tipped hat fielded instead by the long-haired man, who
smiled back automatically. TJ swung away quick, sat
hunched, peering in the mirror in back of the bar for the
couple to move past behind him, hoping maybe the woman
might hang back a step and return his smile. She didn't, but
TJ saw again the lovely profile; he wondered if the bartender might know her name?

"Now how the hell would I?—she jus' came in,
can'tcha see?" The barman rolled away with more of TJ's
money: "Stupid drunks—cowboys the worst. Set all day on
their lazy butts, watchin' cows git fat, while people like me
gotta work." TJ wondered what he'd said had made the bartender turn so surly?

The couple had been led aside by one of the crowd gathered in the space between booths and the bar. There was an
urgent, whispered conversation, while TJ watched blearily,
saw something come out of a pocket of the trenchcoat and
be passed to the other who bent to sniff. There was a transfer of money, while TJ waited patiently for the pretty
woman maybe to glance back his way. The crowd, jostling,
noisy—hormonal—dueling for position near the New York
woman, abruptly quieted; and she, who'd grown used to all
their attention, had suddenly lost it, the crowd shifted laterally to form a new nucleus. They glanced sidelong at the
barkeep, their backs shielding their doings, walling the
woman out.

She stood stunned for a moment at the fringe of the
crowd—came fighting back, ducking beneath arms, stepping on toes, reaching again for that coveted center,
shouted: "Hey, what's this? What's goin' on?" The men
hushed her at once, peering at the big barkeeper, who still
remained oblivious, grubby, unshaven, rereading yesterday's paper. Then even TJ could smell it, the cloying,
burnt-weed odor of marijuana smoke. He had no idea what
it was, but he fumbled for a smoke of his own—

"Wha'sat you got?" the bartender growled, TJ trapped

already in his awful grip. He twisted TJ's hand up to look, grunted, and dropped TJ's arm—plop—on the bar. "Hey, you!" his voice pierced straight into the group. "Yeah, you—bring that here, now!" The big man leaned scarred hands on top of the bar like he meant to catapult over. "Wha'ya think this is? Goddamn drug store? Bring that shit here or I'm comin' across, break some heads—I'll call the cops, see if I don't."

Instantly, the butts of all those magic cigarettes found the floor—the crowd thinned out like smoke, in hopes the barkeep would let it go. The New York woman, who, given her late start, still had come by more than her fair share, inquired distantly, "Will he . . . like . . . really?"

"Naw," some man told her, arm around her shoulder. "He don't want the heat in here more'n anybody else. They're lookin' at his license already for the trouble there's been." He led her away, explaining why: "He'll forget faster if we keep out of sight." TJ motioned to the barkeep and laid more money down.

Never had the bartender inquired of a customer, don't you think you've drunk enough? Because he didn't much care—money was money—he kept a list on the wall scrawled with the names of those he'd had to deal with, once and once only. In a corner by the coffee pot leaned a four-foot piece of pitchfork handle. TJ smiled moronically and, balancing his drink, went wavering off toward the click of balls coming from the pool tables around the corner.

The girl from New York was just peaking out, and reeling off an unbroken winning string of games of pool. There was a short line of quarters on the rail ahead of the one TJ laid down for no other reason than it gave him an excuse for staying in the same room where the pretty woman sat, alone now. TJ flopped in a chair beside her . . . found nothing to say . . . while New York took the next three games (each for a dollar and a drink, the one she stuck in her tight jean's pocket, the other she sucked down through a swizzle straw). "Next!" she sang out to the men no longer clustered near her, no longer laughing with her either: They slouched, staring sullenly at the floor.

So TJ had to stand again, managed it with some difficulty, gallantly offered the pretty woman: "Game's fer you." He swaggered off, listing slightly, never noticed the woman shake her head, shrugged when New York yelled at him from three feet away like he was stone deaf, "Dolla'? an' drink?" TJ watched her sink three stripes on the break, heard her wild whinnying laughter. She burped loudly, then she ran out the table, never gave TJ his chance to try. "Gin sour," she blared, "dollar on th' side, ha!" TJ stopped by the pretty woman: "I lost, so le's you'n me go somewhere's else."

He gripped her arm, tried to haul her to her feet, heard her breath catch and thought he'd hurt her so he released her at once, stood faltering out an apology. He noticed then that she was looking past him, staring at someone coming up behind. TJ swung and saw the long-haired man coming back across the floor, smiling innocently: "Hey man, what's going on?"

So TJ hit him as hard as he could, with all his weight behind it, right on the chin button—knew he'd tagged the man a good one, felt the blow jolt up his arm. TJ stood weaving, peering over the woman's shoulder, while she held the man's head in her lap. She said to TJ—neither in outrage, nor fear—but in a maddeningly normal voice: "What did you do that for?"

But TJ had turned away, smug, self-satisfied, feeling confident and strong for the very first time; strutting, swaggering, he headed for the door . . . there came a sound like a soft wind shushing, the whisper of rain on aspen leaves. TJ ran into something so solid and concentrated, it seemed a spot of air had turned to stone before him—swack! He hit the floor flat on his back, while the bartender leaned across the bar and nudged him in the ribs with the knob end of his hickory stick: "Giddap, cowboy, you ain't hurt. Giddap, an' git out." He poked him again, but TJ was gone.

It was the pain in his ribs though that brought him back, a searing agony like a fire in his side, the ache there worse than the new one radiating from the shiny big goose egg above his eye. He heard the bartender talking, somewhere far off, heard him say again how TJ wasn't hurt, heard a strident voice call out, "Hey, don' le'm get 'way! Owes me dolla still." TJ heard her coming, trailing her stick across the floor: "Say now, 'shere hat looks 'bout dollar worth."

But he couldn't move, not even his tongue. He was dragged outside, left flopped on the concrete, the bartender going back in to scrawl on his list, "Skinny Cowboy," for want of any more particular name. TJ was still there, trying somehow to get something to work, when the long-haired man and the woman came outside. TJ cowered, arms over his head, as the long-haired man crouched beside him.

"Hey buddy, you all right? Better get off of the street before the police come by. You think you can make it? Here, take my hand." The man and the woman got TJ to his feet, limped him along to his pickup truck, TJ crying some about how sorry he was, the man saying it was all right and wishing him luck. The woman made him promise to drive safely home.

2.

Karen couldn't sleep, didn't try, her thoughts scrolling by like the replay of an old movie, her brain a screen for her soul to view: promises made to her long ago by springtime, whose vows summer must surely keep.

She should have known better, for it started out wrong, way back in November, he being the wrong one leaning against her locker door, not allowing her to open it until he'd wrangled a commitment, which, even then, late for class, she'd refused to give. Instead she kept on ending up in his company while he'd sit like a bump too shy to speak in front of her friends; then when they were alone together her mere presence made him so anxious he couldn't shut up until almost out of desperation she'd plugged his mouth with her own. His only attraction from then on was how awfully bad he wanted her like a dog needed petting after the first time it was stroked. So she'd let him keep at it because it was winter: He was something at least to make a little difference between one day it snowed and the next two the wind blew.

That night was coming as surely as the days grew longer, making the moments seem more urgent between when it finally grew dark enough for him to decently park his pickup truck and her ten-o'clock deadline, school nights. Karen was only practicing—not willing it, not waiting either—lying half naked on the pickup seat working on things whose contours had neither walls nor ceiling except for the limits of her ability to imagine him someone else. She couldn't yet let herself define what she was waiting on, beyond making TJ's face a blank while it hovered over hers; still, she knew this was a rehearsal for the big play coming whose opening date wasn't yet set, the leading man not cast.

It was during the springtime, with its mists of green leaves, its guarantee that winter really was going to end, when the blank face above her began to take on shape— TJ's fault, partly, because when he spoke of his brother, in bits and pieces like TJ talked about everything, his resentment rang of envy. Then there was the news of that jungle war that had captured the headlines all through her high school years, running like solemn music in the background behind homework and girlfriends and telephone calls. When TJ mentioned, early that spring, that Jesse had been drafted, it had seemed almost a family thing for her to take time out to watch the evening news and see for herself what he was headed into. She saw soldiers in her mind then before she slept at night, in that far-off Asian country with its jungles and its war; she saw him going into battle, doing gallant deeds. TJ was a little boy, compared to what she dreamed.

It would be hot and sticky, steamy like a jungle, with thunder and lightning, and lifegiving rain!

But the lightning that night was way off east—did she hear it thunder?—she'd felt the whole thing as a quick tearing pain down there inside her. And when she'd opened her eyes finally back at again all she saw was a smear of her own blood mixed with what TJ's brother had left behind; the only thing fertile was her own naive willingness and the organic mystery of her egg-laden womb.

Karen sighed. Tom was right. TJ is still useless. Too bad he was TJ, not somebody else.

Frank, today, rambling on, while she'd fought the icy road bringing him home—too fast, she knew, but she'd not slowed down (though Frank never had seemed the least bit ill). She saw the magpie shearing sidelong, skidding, trying to turn, then diving for more speed, pumping hard to cross before her . . . dull, dry thud, the truck's tires sliding on the hard packed snow. When at last she'd regained control and found time to look back, there were long black tail feathers swirling in the mirror.

But Frank had never left off, plodding on and on, voice dull, dry as feathers, the same as when Karen had picked him up. Frank had already been talking then, too, slouched against a brick-walled building on old First Street, visiting with some long-haired man and an attractive woman who were shifting, edging off like they wished to get away. "Who was that?" Karen had wrinkled her nose. And Frank had said, "Oh, he's a wheeler-dealer, I git a kick outa him." Frank smelled of burnt tumbleweeds? eyes glazed and red, from the flu, Karen had thought. Frank was still talking when Karen ran over that poor bird, his voice showing neither shock nor concern, only a moment's hesitation—thump!—and then the listless sound of him going on again picking up right where he'd left off.

Then they were over the hill. Karen could no longer see the bottom where the dead bird lay—it had happened so fast . . . Frank was asleep, chin rocked forward onto his chest. Karen wondered, Had there really been a bird? Or was it all some sort of weird daydream?

* * *

She stared out the window, the night wind was up, scudding clouds past the moon at a terrific pace, tearing them to pieces and flinging them away. She thought of her mother, who'd lived for the dreary business of caring for a family on a clerk's meager salary and told Karen so with a sigh when Karen had brought home the news of a pending grandbaby. Because the dreary business itself was not the ultimate cause for pain, the unspoken rule all along having been, I'll take care of you, child, but when you grow up then it's your turn to take care of me. I'm not concerned that you foot the bill for my stay 'til I die in some old folks' home.

Rather, it's up to you to bear responsibility not only for your own peace of mind but for mine, too. You must do for me all the things I wanted to do—dreamed I would . . . never got around to. The pain was no longer sharp, worn smooth from handling, one generation to the next, until there comes a time when someone must get selfish enough. Who's gonna take that step?

Maybe Karen had used TJ some, in the beginning—hadn't he got back his share that summer and fall, after Jesse was gone? Karen stepped from her bed. It was growing light, a rooster was crowing; she heard a gate creak, Blue coming or going, making the rounds to the shed. She heard a motor turn off the county road, but she never faltered: walked down the hallway on bare feet, never knocked, went right on in, dropped her robe to the floor—never even bothered to kick shut the door.

3.

TJ staggered, grinning, blinded by the morning light, his head a torment, both from drink and the big blue knot formed just at his hairline. He blinked, squinted, got more or less lined out, stopped to urinate on the gravel mound behind the military stone, patted his mother's marker like a friendly dog. He wandered off, wondering what his face must look like from having been dragged across the tiled floor out onto the cement walk, made his way as quiet as he could down the hallway past the room whose door had been kept closed for eleven years, weaving, shuffling, bouncing off the walls, his mind focused on the bathroom mirror where he would study what he saw, make plans from there.

So he almost missed it, nearly passed by, had not something in there caught his eye . . . registered belatedly inside his brain: Now what would Karen's robe have to do with that hired man? TJ backed up carefully, turned at the door and gazed in:

He saw his wife looking back at him, that man Frank in the bed behind her, neither of them obviously with more than a bed sheet on. TJ said stupidly, "Karen? What you doin'?"

He heard his wife sigh. "Go away, TJ. And don't come back."

But of course he never went, no, not quite yet. TJ stood staring, drawn by the wonder of it, not breathing—no reason to—not thinking either, except to feel bad, because here he was, intruding somehow, third wheel in the midst of things most private. He saw Karen close her eyes, squirm back against that man, back arched, neck offered (Frank all the time watching him, seeming not to have to blink). TJ noticed then how Karen was ready, if he wouldn't leave, she'd just do it anyway, saw her lift her knee for Frank behind her, hand moving beneath the sheet to reach between them—saw her twist and urge, mouth open, eyes smoky, the sheet falling away—

TJ felt his stomach roll—sent him careening toward the bathroom door. But the cramps caught him and jackknifed him down—he tried his best to crawl on across the floor. . . heard his wife cry out that hired man's name.

4.

Tom couldn't raise anyone by shouting from the back step, so he went on in, found his son sprawled in the bathroom. Tom checked for a pulse, then stood for a long time looking: his only son, sleeping it off in his vomit underneath the sink. Tom made no effort to stop the sounds of young footsteps coming down the hall. Owen stood at the door for a long moment looking, too, before he stepped over TJ's form to use the toilet bowl, Owen wrinkling his nose:

"Phew! What's wrong with him?"

"Drunk," Tom said, and moved aside so Owen could go out again, Owen calling from the kitchen: "Dead calf out here." But Tom already knew; he'd seen it the first time he'd trudged to the shed, beating Blue that trip by an hour.

Tom went back out, slogging through the corrals, found a calf, just born, by a cow he'd missed somehow when he'd come by half an hour ago: My son! . . . only one . . . well, I got to decide. He lifted the calf, and carried it as far as he could before his arms gave out, tromped a place in the snow so he could put it down. He turned and followed the path of mud oozing through the watergap gate, stood on the creek bank gazing down at the body: best cow he'd ever owned. Tom slid off the bank, waded through the muddy water flowing near the tops of his overboots, reached to yank her eartag, sat down abruptly on the cold, wet carcas. *His son*—each time he'd decided, his mind brought that up again, tangled things around. Tom waded out, slopped back past the calf. He'd tell Blue—no, ask Frank: Would Frank mind going over, take the calf and its mother on to the shed? Frank would get it done, trust to that, good to know.

Karen was at the barn, already had let the cows in. They were jumbled up, bawling for their calves; Karen was try-ing to get them straightened out, having no success. Tom nodded, "Morning," and she smiled to him. They both stopped to listen while Owen worked in the cowbarn, Owen trying to get the cows to behave in there, too. There was a string of profanity—a milk bucket collided with flesh—rat-tle of hooves . . . silence. Karen rolled her eyes.

Tom dragged a bale down from the loft, one of the last ones up there, he noted. He scattered it in wafers in all the pens, trying to get the cows to settle down . . . watched them tromp the hay under, too, along with their calves. Maybe he could fashion some feed bunks, get TJ to help—Tom shook his head.

He felt moved to say something. Perhaps he should tell Karen his thoughts, warn her somehow, because if he ditched TJ, he lost a good girl.

"Karen, I know I don't say it often enough, all's we've gone through, what a help you've been."

Karen smiled again, a bit thinly this time. "You've never mentioned it, Tom. But I understand."

Tom gripped her shoulder, one quick squeeze, started for the house, then changed his mind in the middle of the yard. But where was there anyone to send to find Frank? He went himself through the corrals again, drove the new mother in, dropped her wet calf in the alley for lack of pens. Frank was waiting when Tom came back, Frank grinning, looking fit, leaning against the pickup truck. Tom didn't bother to ask where he'd been; he was just glad to see a happy face for a change.

* * *

They drove along the bottoms, checking on the cows, watching for full bags, looking for bad eyes, Frank lazing in the seat, saying little, waiting each time for Tom to decide who would get out to check on some miserable calf Tom had spotted huddled back in the snow. Tom set Frank out where the willows were thickest, told Frank he would circle, come back from the other end; they'd meet in the middle someplace.

Frank sighed, stood wasting time, playing with his rope, for longer than he knew it would take Tom to go around. But Frank no longer cared—he'd got what he'd wanted. Had it been worth the bother? Probably not, but not half bad. But it was time now to be moving on. Frank waded on in, he guessed he'd better go tell Tom that he was leaving.

Halfway through the tangle, Frank spotted a calf, undoubtedly dead: laid out flat, with frosted eyes, protruding blue tongue, frozen bubbles of saliva collected at its mouth. He flipped it over, not stiff yet, flopping like a rag doll, left a shadow melted in the snow like a homicide's silhouette. Frank slipped a loop on a dead hind leg, leaned to haul the body away—heard Tom shout somewhere behind him, but Frank merely grunted, finished dragging the calf to the meadow's edge, dropped the rope, and turned back.

Tom was circling in front of a big cow, trying to hold her in a tiny opening. "She's got sunburned tits," he called, "blind in one eye. Where's your rope?" Frank gestured with a careless thumb; and Tom frowned. "You forgot it? Well, bring her past. I'll try to snag her, dally 'round this tree." Frank shrugged, whooped, brought the cow in a rush.

The willows were thick—no chance at her heels—Tom dabbed a quick loop on her neck, afraid if he missed her first shot she'd get by, get wild, force him to spend all morning trying to rope one cow. She never slowed down, dragged him badly—big, powerful lady, thin old man—took him through the willows, across the creek rocks, and out the other side, where he held her for a moment: caught half a turn round a scrawny sapling at the meadow's edge.

But she hit the end hard, burning him seriously while he tried to hang on—stripped him around the sapling and took him along for a few more steps, Tom running hard, trying to keep up—left him sprawled in the meadow snow, stole his rope and went pounding on. Tom lay twisted, gasping for air, holding his shoulder and trying to calm his hammering heart.

Frank leaned waiting, chewing on a twig, wondering absently what had happened. He'd heard some crashing as the cow went out, had not seen Tom rope her, figured she'd got away. Frank was slowly, obliquely, letting his thoughts run down the road: no future here, time to look somewhere else. He hummed a tune as he strolled across the creek, discovered Tom at the meadow's edge.

Tom was in a bad way, blood everywhere, streaming from raw wounds in his hands and arms, thin lashes where the willows had cut his face, Tom hunched and pale, gritting his teeth. Frank hustled up to him, shocked by his appearance, Tom insisting that he was all right; but he looked like death. Frank walked him to the pickup truck, hovering over him with grave concern. "I'm fine," Tom said. "Don't start thinkin' 'bout takin' me in."

But Tom sagged in the corner of the cab, breathing hard, face grey, waiting on Frank to finish up outside. Frank's rope was a tangle, the calf a sodden mess, so he never bothered in his hurry to load either one, merely hitched the rope to the bumper of the truck, thinking the weight of the body would straighten it while he towed the calf to the dump. Frank took time then to carefully roll back Tom's shirt-sleeves, shuddered when he saw the peeled palms, the shredded places on the wrists and forearms. He gently picked a few bark fragments out of the wounds, told Tom, "Don't you think we oughta at least stop by, wash you up a bit?"

"Later," Tom said. "You got business to finish here?"

"No, Tom," Frank said gently. "I found another dead calf. I'll kick him off in the pit on our way past." Frank looked to Tom, and Tom nodded finally, mouth set tight against the pain: All right, take me on in. Frank glanced in the mirror as he spun away. The little body was following, tumbling, throwing out a spray of snow.

"You stay put," Frank told Tom when he skidded to a stop at the bank of the creek; "I'll only be a minute." The old man nodded, seemed to accept that; but Tom was out before Frank could untie the rope, Frank chiding him, "Now Tom, I can do this. You ought to've stayed inside, shouldn't be on your feet."

But Tom was gazing past him, staring at something back of Frank, Tom's face so anguished Frank jerked around to see. Frank gasped—couldn't help it—watched in horror as the little body he'd dragged all that way kicked its feet feebly and gave out a strangled bawl.

"Tom!" Frank said. "I didn't know—I looked at it, seemed dead an' froze. I thought—"

Tom laid a good arm round Frank's neck, hugged him over and whispered, "Will you stay with me, Frank? Will you stay on, son?"

5.

TJ rolled over . . . could not quite manage to sit up, fumbled for a cigarette, but they were gone, too. He teetered, wondered maybe he was dreaming—hey, maybe he'd died?—choked on bile, leaned and gagged: No, not quite dead yet. TJ remembered then about his wife, hung his head and wept.

Someone had cleaned up the mess on the floor, wiped at it some; he could see the swirls. TJ knew it had been Sarah, shook his head in grief. He would miss that little girl, this being a school day, he'd not see her again. He pulled down a towel, tried to finish the cleaning, could not see a reason why, and gave it up. He stood weaving, staring down the hallway toward his brother's room. It was over then. He would tie up some loose ends, visit the mountaintop, one last trip. TJ slumped, weeping, slid down in a heap.

That was where Sarah found him. She came from her room with two full paper bags, squatted beside him and touched his arm. "Sarah?" TJ said. "What you doin' here? Why ain't you gone to school?"

Sarah shrugged. "Not time yet. And anyhow, I told them I was sick. I used some of yours, from here off the floor. It worked real good, made me almost throw up my own self while I was spreading it on my rug."

TJ blinked, trying hard to follow—he felt he should know what she was talking about, but damned if he could figure it out? "What'd you do that for? I thought you liked school. This ain't like you, tellin' folks stuff like that. Why'd you go an' lie? An' where is ever'body? They leave you home sick alone?"

Sarah reminded him. "Calving time, TJ. Everybody's out." She stared at him with level eyes. "Mom stayed with that hired man, didn't she, last night."

TJ blinked at her . . . hung his head.

Sarah nodded. "I thought that's what happened when I saw her coming out this morning, putting on her robe. Don't worry about it, TJ; you didn't have much together anyhow."

"Did she seem . . . happy?"

"How should I know, I'm a little kid. But don't worry, I'm gonna take care of you, make sure you don't do anything stupid."

Sarah got him to his feet, made him wash, while she tried to clean up the rest of his mess, until TJ stopped her, told her to leave it: something they could have to remember him by. Sarah sent him out with the bags full of her clothes—he made several trips for her things, one for his own, TJ stammering, trying to explain, "Sarah, now, I don' think you un'erstand. I *got* to go, I mean, for good. I ain't sick, you know, 'least not *sick* sick—I had the flu yesterday, but this here is different. Thing is . . . well . . . today—"

Sarah nodded, "I know, today you're drunk, Owen told me: 'drunk as a skunk.' You wouldn't last a week without somebody to look out for you." Sarah checked to see if her father had forgotten anything. Underwear, socks?— "Where's your hat, TJ? Well, never mind, take this one of Frank's, with the feather, see if it fits."

She sent TJ to the shop to find a wrench, told him to take the ball off Frank's pickup truck, use it to steal Frank's horse trailer, because if TJ intended to take along the black horse, it sure couldn't ride in the cab. TJ was still trying his best to be a good father, peering down the road and seeing only bad weather:

"Sarah, honey, be sensible. I got no money, I got no job, no potential—no place to go." He warned her, "I might end up someplace where there ain't no school, you can't never tell—"

"Oh, hush, TJ." Sarah was disgusted. "It's not like we're going to the moon." Sarah rummaged through the cupboard, loading a box full of canned goods, while TJ sat slumped at the table. Sarah turned on him slyly, "You wouldn't know where Old Tom kept some money, you know, just layin' about?"

"Sarah! That ain't right!"

"Okay, only an idea—forget I brought it up. Let's go load your horse."

But TJ wandered off through the house, looking around, touching things . . . took down a picture of his wife and all three children, worked the ring off his finger and left it hanging on the nail. TJ swung suddenly. "Sarah, where's your mouse?"

Sarah blinked, and tried to say lightly: "Oh, didn't I tell you? He got away—don't matter, just a dumb ol' deer mouse." Sarah wiped fiercely at her eyes. "Let's get out of here, TJ. We got to go now."

They sneaked the black gelding out of the corral, TJ skulking along, trying to hide, the black horse towering over him, nickering loudly. They tried to load him quietly into Frank's trailer, the horse shying back, banging around. Sarah slammed the door of TJ's truck. "Start the motor, TJ, and drive."

But TJ had seen Owen, watched the boy hurry by with two full pails of milk, Owen stopping in midstride to stare at them. Then he turned to rush on, late, as usual, for the school bus. Sarah shook her head: "Owen's so weird. What the heck was that about?"

But TJ was remembering a time long ago, on this very spot, when Blue had lost that little finger while he'd rammed home the sickle bar through the guards of the mower. No one had thought in the rush that followed to

204

send the shorn finger along to see if the doctor could sew it back on. They left TJ home, Jesse then, too, to chase down the chicken and recover the stub. The two boys had buried the poor severed thing in a box at the graveyard. But a week or so later they'd dug it back up, the finger a mess by then, stinking fiercely, rotted and black. But they'd had to look, one last time.

"I s'pose I understand what Owen was doing. Sometimes all you get is to see things end." TJ turned the key, nursed the motor to life.

6.

So there you have it, full circle, dear mouse: Tomorrow's the first day of spring. The future's set, same as done—no hope left, nothing to count on. All this snow and the rains of summer will bring good grass, a fine crop of hay. But the cows will breed back poorly after the hard winter, calf prices will be down again, worse than last year. In the interest of economy, Frank will convince Tom they can get along fine without shiftless old Blue. Owen is growing, he'll soon fill Blue's shoes: In the spring, Frank has Owen out picking rocks, and then stacking bales by himself under the scorching summer sun. Frank will send Owen off alone into a thunderstorm to find the pregnant mare when she doesn't come in (Owen scared out of his wits, out there in the lightning, crying—screaming—by the time he comes home). Karen curses them all, Frank, Owen—Tom, too— while they spend the night in the barn, watching by flash- light because the storm has knocked the power out, waiting for the mare to foal. It has frightened Karen so, fear of los- ing her last remaining child—though Frank has worked hard to change all that, her monthly by now is months late— all at once the time has come for Owen to have a horse, wild, unbroken, and—wouldn't you know it—a stud colt, black as the night. Frank wonders, "Now how in hell can the colt be that color?" and Tom will answer, "Damned if I know. Sure looks like TJ's gelding though."

Tom finds an envelope, written "Check for Jesse," in a bold, feminine hand, presumes without thinking Mary must

*have labeled it (Mary of course dead and buried by then);
Tom not actually finding it—not gone searching for it,
tracking it down. There it is all at once in his dresser
drawer alongside his clean socks; inside, payment in full for
one dead son. All Tom has to do is strike a match or else
run out of reasons for needing to know why. He sends it,
endorsed, to town with Frank, tells him to put it on the note
at the bank. Frank cashes the check and runs.*

No—

*Tom will die—too bad; but then don't we all. In the fall,
one evening, his back causing him so much pain Tom goes
straight to bed, the cramps spreading up his arms and into
his chest. He never wakes, his heart . . . you understand.
Karen will have him buried out there with the rest. The
bank gets the ranch; Karen moves to town. Owen must sell
his horse, not enough room in his grandmother's back
yard—*

No, by God, there's got to be hope! I know, somehow,
there's still room for—you—get out there and find me some
hope!

* * *

They drove slowly along the snowy road, neither of
them talking, just looking around, one set for adventure, a
brave new start, the other headed down this road for the last
time. TJ at last broke the silence, asking, "Why you s'pose
folks want it in the first place, all this land?"

Sarah said, "Oh, probably it's like having your own
national park, where you start out believing you can do
what you want. But then you work all the time trying to
take care of it, kind of like having a baby."

But TJ wasn't listening (never expected an answer anyhow). "I sure made a mess of things, didn't I, Sarah."

Sarah sighed. "Don't you ever get tired of being the
cause for all the world's troubles? This is just the way it is,
TJ, nothing you can do about it."

"Yeah, I know, but it's all my fault. I screwed up
ever'thing. I don't know how I can make it up to you.

Where we gonna go? What we gonna do? I don't know anything else. How will we get by?"

"We'll go west, TJ." Sarah's eyes were shining. "It's the only place left for folks like us. The further the better—maybe clear to the ocean. Must be plenty of room for us out there."

"I sure am sorry, li'l girl, for all I've put you through."

"I forgive you, TJ."

"Yeah, an' what good does that do? How's it gonna help, you forgivin' me? I guess I don't understand how forgiveness works, when it don't change a thing."

"It lets you begin brand new, that's what forgiveness is for. Lets you put the past behind and have hope again so you can start all over."

They rode along quietly again then, while TJ's heart began to swell, and heal, from all the love he felt for this little girl. She trusted him, had faith in him. He swore he'd make it right for her, if he had to die trying. TJ glanced at Sarah as he steered along, and then again . . . until Sarah burst out, "TJ, what! Why you keep looking at me?"

"Sarah, lis'en, maybe . . . well . . . you s'pose you might could start callin' me, 'Dad'?"

"Shee!" Sarah said. "I don't know, TJ—that's a pretty funny word, 'dad.' Just say it one time, sounds stupid to me." Sarah sighed. "Okay, I'll try. But I don't make any promises, see? I doubt seriously if it'll work out."

After a bit, TJ asked her, "Well, how 'bout 'Pop' then? Does that make a better sound?"